ADVANCE PRAISE FOR
SOME THERE ARE FEARLESS

"In *Some There Are Fearless*, Becca Babcock explores the fear, tension, and complex emotions of motherhood, as well as the joy. With tender subtlety, she digs deep into the terror of loving, while wanting to protect the ones we love, the guilt and grief of our own powerlessness, and the ways in which childhood scars stifle our best intentions as we desperately try not to recreate the past."
–CHARLENE CARR, author of *Hold My Girl*

"When we love, we want to protect. And when we can't protect, what then? A Cold War novel—and a novel about cold wars—*Some There Are Fearless* takes us to the radioactive dangers and careful hope of the human need to love and be loved."
–MICHELLE BUTLER HALLETT, Thomas Raddall Award–winning author of *Constant Nobody*

"A touching, quietly suspenseful novel that beautifully captures the complexity of human connection and the anxiety of growing up under threat of disaster. Babcock brings her characters to vivid life on the page, skillfully weaving a narrative that leaps through space and time to consider the unpredictability of life itself."
–RENÉE BELLIVEAU, ReLit–nominated author of *The Sound of Fire*

"*Some There Are Fearless* is an absorptive read rooted in the post-Chernobyl era that follows a woman's trepidatious journey through family and career tensions against a backdrop of lurking peril, and had me rooting for her to triumph."
–ALISON DELORY, Kobo Prize–shortlisted author of *Making It Home*

PRAISE FOR BECCA BABCOCK

"If you grew up in a rural area, you knew about the Bogeyman. There were always people who were outcasts—who were strange or insular and didn't fit. Sometimes they were just ordinary people but, occasionally, they turned out to be something else. This is the underlying conflict in this terrific debut novel by Becca Babcock, based loosely on the real-life case of the Nova Scotia Goler family."

—THE GLOBE AND MAIL

"A strong, confident debut novel about a complicated homecoming, peopled with characters you will remember and even almost recognize. Brimming with compassion, *One Who Has Been Here Before* explores family in all its forms, those we're born to and those we build, those we lose and those we find again."

—REBECCA SILVER SLAYTER, author of *The Second History*

"Rebecca Babcock has done what most good writers do: taken an old story and made it new again. *One Who Has Been Here Before* is wonderfully written, evoking thought, questions, and ponderings long after the last page is read. First novel? I'm betting it won't be her last!"

—DONNA MORRISSEY, award-winning author of *The Fortunate Brother*

"A contemplative and compelling novel about a young woman's fascination with a notorious Nova Scotia family. *One Who Has Been Here Before* is an artfully braided book about the power of storytelling, history, and, ultimately, belonging."

—HARRIET ALIDA LYE, author of *Let it Destroy You* and *The Honey Farm*

"Rebecca Babcock's debut novel takes us beyond the whispers of scandal, humanizing a story of shame with fully-drawn characters, keen attention to detail and superb pacing. It's a heartbreaking story of a shattered family rooted in Nova Scotia's not-so-distant past."

—NICOLA DAVISON, award-winning author of *In the Wake*

SOME THERE ARE FEARLESS

SOME THERE ARE FEARLESS

BECCA BABCOCK

Vagrant Press is an imprint of
Nimbus Publishing Limited
3660 Strawberry Hill St, Halifax, NS, B3K 5A9
(902) 455-4286 nimbus.ca

Editor: Whitney Moran
Design: Heather Bryan
NB1641

Printed and bound in Canada

"Some There Are Fearless" by P. K. Page reprinted from *The Hidden Room* (in two volumes) by P. K. Page by permission of the Porcupine's Quill. Copyright © the Estate of P. K. Page, 1997.

This is a work of fiction. While certain characters are inspired by real persons, and certain events by events which may have happened, the story is a work of the imagination not to be taken as a literal or documentary representation of its subject.

Library and Archives Canada Cataloguing in Publication

Title: Some there are fearless / Becca Babcock.
Names: Babcock, Becca, 1978- author.
Identifiers: Canadiana (print) 20220455821 | Canadiana (ebook) 2022045583X | ISBN 9781774711545 (softcover)
ISBN 9781774711552 (EPUB)
Classification: LCC PS8603.A255 S66 2023 | DDC C813/.6—dc23

Nimbus Publishing acknowledges the financial support for its publishing activities from the Government of Canada, the Canada Council for the Arts, and from the Province of Nova Scotia. We are pleased to work in partnership with the Province of Nova Scotia to develop and promote our creative industries for the benefit of all Nova Scotians.

In streets where pleasure grins
and the bowing waiter
turns double summersaults to the table for two
and the music of the violin is a splinter
pricking the poultice of flesh; where glinting glass
shakes with falsetto laughter,
Fear, the habitué, ignores the menu
and plays with the finger bowl at his permanent table.

Tune in the ear; in tub, in tube, in cloister,
he is the villain; underneath the bed,
bare-shanked and shaking; drunken in pubs; or teaching
geography to half a world of children.

In times like these, in streets like these, in alleys,
he is the master and they run for shelter
like ants to ant hills when he lifts his rattle.
While dreaming wishful dreams that will be real,
some there are fearless, touching a distant thing:

the ferreting sun, the enveloping shade, the attaining spring
and the wonderful soil, nameless beneath their feet.

– P. K. Page, "Some There Are Fearless"

"We had a childish image of the world; we were living life as depicted in children's stories. It wasn't just us; the whole of mankind wised up after Chernobyl. We all grew up...."

– Svetlana Alexievich, *Chernobyl Prayer*

Radiation is energy released by an unstable nucleus—the atomic core of an unstable isotope emitting ionizing radiation. Fissioned isotopes in a nuclear power plant are also radioactive, though this type of energy is not the same as the spontaneous radiation emitted from these unstable particles. In nuclear fission, atoms are forced apart in order to harvest the energy that they were using to hold themselves together.

The nucleus of an atom—which is blasted apart in nuclear fission—is made up of protons and neutrons. On their own, neutrons are unstable. They decay, transforming into a proton and an electron. But within the nucleus of an atom, snuggled up against a number of protons, they can achieve stability. Sometimes.

Different numbers of neutrons within atoms with the same number of protons are called isotopes. These are the same elements as other atoms with the same number of protons and electrons. The difference in neutrons, however, results in different nuclear masses. The nucleus of a stable isotope does not decay. But in a radioactive isotope, the nucleus will spontaneously decay, emitting radiation as it forms new isotopes. The original, unstable isotope is called the *parent*, and the resulting isotope is called the *daughter*. Sometimes, the daughter is a stable isotope. But often, it is not. This pair is said to reach equilibrium when the rate of formation of the radioactive element and its rate of decay are equal. In secular equilibrium, the half-life of the daughter is significantly shorter than the half-life of the parent. The element approaches a state of equilibrium, but never reaches it. But in transient equilibrium—transient because it only lasts a tiny moment—the rate of formation and the rate of decay are balanced. Precariously and ephemerally, but balanced.

Uranium passes through many decay species—daughters and daughters of daughters within the decay chain—before finally becoming lead.

ONE

For about a hundred Euros, you can book a tour out of Kyiv and visit Pripyat, the abandoned Ukrainian city near Chernobyl. Scientists say it won't be safe to live in Pripyat for another twenty thousand years, but you can tour the city for an afternoon without absorbing dangerous levels of radiation. On your tour, you'll visit the Dytyatky checkpoint at the entrance to the exclusion zone, you'll see the town hall and the hospital, abandoned schools and homes, farms and apartment buildings. You'll visit the swimming pool and the Ferris wheel in the amusement park that was scheduled to open just a few days after nuclear reactor Number Four exploded.

That's the authorized tour. The legal, sanctioned tour. But if you talk to the right people in Kyiv, or Korosten or Chernihiv, or across the Belarusian border in Mazyr, you can book an unsanctioned visit to Pripyat. If you want, you can camp for days, even weeks, in Pripyat's abandoned buildings. These apartment towers and hotels and schools and farms and houses are now home to a small number of illegal tenants. Some are long-term residents, like the mostly elderly women who returned to their family farms after the evacuation, or who hid, refusing to leave the only homes they've known. The only homes their parents or grandparents or great-grandparents ever knew. Others are thrill-seekers like you, paying as many Euros as it takes to experience life in a post-apocalyptic city.

The amount of radiation exposure varies widely within the town, but you'll be exposed to around 3 microsieverts per hour during most of your visit—up to 22 microsieverts an hour if you visit the Pripyat cemetery. If you're sensible, you'll camp out in one of the abandoned residential neighbourhoods where the radiation registers at under 1 microsievert an hour. You can expect that during your illegal vacation, you'll be exposed to 72 microsieverts per day, more than twelve times the average daily natural dose. In most places on the planet, you'll be exposed to between 2 and 4 millisieverts of radiation per year. One year in Pripyat will give you about 26.28 millisieverts of ionizing radiation.

In September 1986, the world had known about the disaster at the nuclear power plant in Ukraine for over four months. Animals as far away as Sweden were being culled, their radioactive corpses entombed in concrete. As the fallout cloud drifted over northern California, land bird populations plummeted suddenly. In the area surrounding the Point Reyes Bird Observatory in Petaluma, California, it seemed that no young birds were born at all that summer and the surviving adult birds stopped singing, their silence washing over the landscape. Cattle across Ukraine and Belarus absorbed radionuclides and began producing milk with dangerous levels of radiation; over the decades to come, this would result in thousands of cases of thyroid disease among the children who drank it, who ate ice cream and cheese and yogurt. In Ukraine, by the fall of 1986, well over one hundred thousand people had been relocated. Although the Soviet Union listed the official human death toll from the disaster at only thirty-one, over four thousand people likely died after being exposed to the radiation.

In September 1986, I was over seven thousand kilometres away, starting grade three at École Medley. Medley was the name of the community that had been constructed to house the residents of CFB Cold Lake. The school had been erected thirty years earlier to educate the children of military personnel. For the past three years, the air force base had been the testing ground for the American military's Tomahawk missiles. As we sat in our classrooms inside the modular building, fighter jets roared overhead. Inside them, pilots were trained to protect us from the Soviet war machine that menaced us from just over the North Pole. The Soviets would have to fly over Santa Claus to get to us. We students

4

and the teachers all got used to punctuating our lessons and conversations with long pauses as the jet engines bellowed. Then when silence fell again, our voices would resume, undisturbed.

My teacher that year was Madame Lefebvre. She was a round-faced, round-bodied, perennially smiling woman. Her dark hair was cheerfully permed, and on the first day of school we pointed to each other in gleeful recognition—we had *almost* the same glasses: blue plastic above the eyes, pink plastic below. I had chosen them because the optometrist had said, as she placed them on my face, "Stylish! Like blue eyeshadow and pink blush." I imagined that if someone wasn't looking too closely at me they might, for a moment, think I was wearing makeup. I was wrong. And so I had hated those glasses until that spark of connection between me and Mme. Lefebvre.

Right up until the end of summer, I had thought I would be in Mademoiselle Thornton's class, and it was well known that Mlle. Thornton was a *mean* teacher. She shouted. She gave detention. She gave a *lot* of homework. But a week before school began, my friend Nicole told me that there would be a new grade-three teacher that year. We were sitting facing each other on the top of the monkey bars. My mom and Nicole's dad were inside the school, getting their classrooms ready for the new school year. My mom taught grade one (though, thankfully, they'd put me in Monsieur Reynolds's grade one class instead) and Nicole's dad was the vice principal. Nicole and I had been friends since we were babies because of all the days our parents had carted us to school with them, dumping us off at the playground or the gym while they worked away at their desks—my mom in her classroom, and Nicole's dad in the main office. I suppose we were best friends, but we never really called each other that. I don't even think we liked each other all that much. A few years later, by the time we finished elementary school, we would be unacknowledged enemies, telling secrets and talking behind each other's backs. Of course, none of that had started yet. For now, it was nice to have someone to play with while my mom was busy. Somewhere on the school grounds, my older brother Kyle was skulking with his basketball, but there was no way he'd ever let me play with him.

Nicole braced her ankles against the crossbars. She lifted her hands and pulled the mauve scrunchee out of her hair and smoothed it back into a ponytail. "She's really nice. Dad brought me in yesterday to meet her. She let me pick out a sticker, and she has, like, the puffy ones."

I tilted my head, examining a black scuff mark along the white edge of my sneaker sole. "Maybe she was just pretending," I said, rubbing at the mark with my thumb. It wouldn't come off. "Maybe she just wanted your dad to *think* she was nice."

Nicole shook her head quickly, her long ponytail swishing side to side. "No way. I would know. I can tell when someone is pretending." She clasped her hands to the bars next to her hips and swung around upside down, her feet making a three-quarter rotation before landing on the dusty ground. Without looking back at me, she sauntered toward the school.

"At least we won't have Mlle. Thorton," I said. I dropped awkwardly between the bars, my feet landing straight down beneath me. I followed her inside, hoping we'd be allowed to play with the badminton rackets and birdies in the gym.

"At least," Nicole called over her shoulder.

Not that the prospect of a *mean* teacher really frightened me. In fact, I suspected that I would probably get on well with a mean teacher. My other teachers had been nice. They'd been nice to other students; they'd been nice to me. But it was not the same between me and them as it was between them and the other girls in my class. There was a shade, a difference—a stiffening in their smiles when they turned to me, a tightness to their voices when they praised me that I didn't hear when they told the other girls they'd done something well.

Last year, Mlle. Fillion had been nice. She was younger than most of the other teachers, and we all admired her for her beauty. Her blond curls plumed around her face like the feathers of a tropical bird, their bright yellow tips fading to a soft brown at her scalp. She carried a pink lipstick in her bag, fishing it out at the end of class and reapplying the soft colour to her mouth.

At recess, the other girls, especially Estelle, Stephanie, and Nicole, would swarm around her, and Mlle. Fillion would sing popular songs with them, "Ma blonde m'aime" and "Tes yeux noirs." And, if no other teachers were around to hear, she'd sing "Footloose" or "Say, Say, Say" with them, all four of them holding invisible microphones, gesturing to an invisible crowd. We weren't allowed to speak English on school grounds, and English music was expressly forbidden. To be allowed to sing the songs at school that we heard every day on the radio was a treat.

But Mlle. Fillion never sang songs, English or French, with me. Or perhaps I never sang with her. I'd sidle up to the group, wanting to join in, wishing I could grasp my own imaginary microphone, but I felt the chill I brought with me. Mlle. Fillion would smile and say, "Bonjour, Jess. Tu t'amuses bien?" Her smile was soft, her eyes clear, but there was a hood, a veil there. Estelle, Stephanie, and Nicole would sulk, chins tucked into their chests, until I left. I did not have their power to draw the music from her. Or from myself.

In class, however, I could always be sure to have the teacher's absolute approval. Up to a point, anyway. I'd raise my hand for almost every question. When no one's hand went into the air, or when another student offered an incorrect answer, the teacher would turn to me, and I always got it right. I would wait, electricity charging through my chest, for assignments to be returned. "Bravo, Jessica," Mlle. Fillion would say, her warm smile lighting on me and only me.

But if a mark on a test surprised me, if I discovered a mistake I hadn't noticed early enough, that electrical buzz turned into a cold fire, choking off the air passage in my throat, squelching tears out of my eyes. And when that happened, the warm smile would fossilize and Mlle. Fillion's voice would compress and flatten. "C'est pas ci grave que ça, quand même." And when she said it like that, gently but with a flinty edge, I'd feel the world rush back in and I'd see my classmates, their smirks, their eye rolls. I'd press the tears back and sit up as straight as I could in my chair, my eyes locked on the blackboard.

Nice teachers had their limits. They'd soften if a student cried in class because they'd lost a toy on the way to school, or they'd slipped on the ice and bruised a cheekbone on the edge of the slide, or even if they'd gotten a C- on a math test and were afraid to show their parents.

But there was no softness left for a student who was disgusted at an A- when she'd been expecting an A+.

So I pretended to be relieved when Nicole told me we had a new teacher, a *nice* teacher. But I felt a sinking unease in my chest as I followed her in toward the school gym. I had wondered whether a mean teacher might not be more prepared to understand what I expected of myself.

I observed Mme. Lefebvre the first days of class. She made jokes that the girls pretended to laugh at and that the boys, led by Benoît and Sébastien, met with bold, feigned guffaws, a barely concealed derision. Soon, whenever Mme. Lefebvre told a joke, Estelle and Stephanie would snicker—not at the joke, but at the boys' increasingly bold mockery. Nicole still laughed at the teacher's joke, but I did not laugh at all; I was afraid Mme. Lefebvre would think I was laughing along with Estelle. I did not want the teacher to think I was a party to that.

I made sure that Mme. Lefebvre knew I was the smartest girl in class (even though Nicole sometimes got higher marks in math and art). My hand shot up at every opportunity. I was always the first to pass in my assignments (except for the times that Sébastien wrote his name on the top of the paper and handed it in without a single answer completed).

"Bravo, Jessica," Mme. Lefebvre said as she handed back our math homework at the end of the first week: 8/10. My gaze snapped to Nicole. "Bravo, Nicole." Mme. Lefebvre tapped her shoulder lightly as she set the page down on her desk. Nicole held it up: 9/10. I felt my throat tighten. I looked at the two errors on my page. Pressed my fingernails into the palm of my hand. Felt my chest harden and squeeze.

Mme. Lefebvre turned to give David his homework in the seat behind me. Her gaze fell on my face. She paused. "Tu vas bien, Jessica?"

"Oui, Madame," I whispered, determined not to let any tears out. I could hear my pulse in my ears—not a hammering, but a continuous rushing, like gusts of wind.

She flashed me a soft, quick smile and finished handing back the assignment. As soon as her back was turned, the tears escaped. I wiped them away before anyone could see.

At recess, I followed Estelle and Stephanie outside. Nicole ran to catch up as we reached the hallway. I could feel her thoughts as she bounced on her heels, her rush of pleasure at getting the highest mark on the first homework assignment of the year.

We made our way toward the monkey bars, but there were already three fifth-grade girls sitting at the top, so we followed Estelle as she swung back toward the pavement by the door. Someone had marked hopscotch squares in white paint. My mom had told me that she'd played hopscotch when she was little. She'd thrown a broken chain necklace into the square that you had to skip over as you hopped your way to the big *10* under the yellow half-sun at the end. I watched now as Estelle hopped idly from one square to the next. She was wearing a ruffled knee-length denim skirt, and she pressed her hands to the sides of her thighs to keep it from bouncing too high as she jumped. I could see a soft pink spot just below her knee where a summer scab had healed and peeled away. Estelle had short blond hair, cut so it curled over her forehead. Today, she wore one side pulled back with a rainbow barrette that matched her T-shirt. Tomorrow or the next day, I knew Stephanie would come to school with a rainbow barrette, too.

"Do you like her?" Nicole asked.

"Who?" Estelle turned to hop back down toward the *1*.

"Madame."

"She's nice," Stephanie offered.

"She's not as pretty as Mlle. Fillion," Estelle said, hopping back up the painted squares without giving anyone else a turn.

"No," Stephanie agreed.

"I like her," I said. And I did. I thought about the look she'd given me in class. It was a soft look, not tight and cool like Mlle. Fillion was sometimes. She *was* nice.

The door next to us opened and Mme. Lefebvre stepped outside. She looked over at us and smiled, her soft round cheeks pushing up her glasses. Reflexively, I jabbed my own up onto the bridge of my nose.

"Allô, les filles," she said.

"Bonjour, Madame," Estelle and Stephanie sang together. Estelle kept hopping idly from square to square without glancing up. When she reached the end, just behind Madame, she turned and made a face at Stephanie, puffing her cheeks out grotesquely. A fat face. Stephanie, whose own cheeks were naturally fleshy, turned red, but she nodded theatrically at Madame and she and Estelle stifled a giggle. Nicole watched them with a frown. She didn't laugh, and neither did I. Then Estelle gestured toward the swing set. She and Stephanie took off. Nicole hesitated for a moment, then moved to the chipped white 1 of the hopscotch board, taking Estelle's place. She hopped like Estelle did: slowly, unenthusiastically, as though she were afraid someone might think she was actually having fun.

Madame moved to leave us, but before she did, she pulled me into a quick, loose hug. I could feel her soft belly against my shoulder blades. Her hands passed in front of my face, and I smelled the drugstore scent of her hand lotion. It was a quick movement, a surge of warmth. Instinctively, I pulled away, surprised and repelled by the sudden affection. She gave me another smile before she strolled off towards a game of soccer that some older kids had started across the playground.

I watched her, bewildered. I could still feel the pressure of her arms on my shoulders. I shrugged, as though I could brush the lingering feeling away. A teacher had never hugged me before. Even my mom kept her hugs to herself when we were on the school grounds. The thought of the embrace left me with a squishy feeling in my stomach.

Nicole looked at me, her eyebrows raised, as she turned and hopped her way back down toward the 1.

That night, Mom called for me as soon as she came in the door. "Jess? I need to talk to you." She said the words before she'd even finished easing her shoes off.

I came out of my bedroom and stood, waiting for her to hang up her coat.

"Madame Lefebvre came to talk to me in the staffroom after school."

I looked down at my socks, my chest tightening. An 8/10 was still pretty good, wasn't it? You didn't get in trouble for 8/10.

"You know it's not worth crying about, right?" Mom strode past me into the kitchen. I followed her slowly, watching as she took a glass out of the cupboard. She turned the cold tap on, running the water over her finger until it was cold enough to drink. "If you want to do better, you'll just have to work harder."

"I know," I said.

She looked at me and sighed. "You're too sensitive, Jessica. You're going to have to learn to toughen up."

"Okay." I waited in case there was something more. There wasn't.

She took a sip of water then started looking through the freezer for something to make for dinner. I slipped back to my bedroom and pulled my math homework out of my bag.

THAT WAS THE YEAR NICOLE DEFINITIVELY SURPASSED ME IN MATH. I held onto the top marks in every other class (except art and gym, but those classes didn't really count), but Nicole was always just ahead of me in Math.

The second week, I got my homework assignment back with a 10/10. I glanced at Nicole. She was holding her homework up as though to read it, but I could tell it was so that she could see the mark: 10. The week after that, I got 9, and she got 10 again.

When Madame handed back that homework, her hand lingered on my desk a moment. I looked up, and she locked eyes with me. Her eyes were soft, wide open. Something about her stare made me look to Nicole's desk. I saw her mark. My throat burned, but I didn't cry. I didn't even have to press back the tears—not with Madame looking at me, the threat of another hug lurking in her gaze. Even after she moved on, handing back homework down the next aisle, I could smell the drugstore scent of her hand lotion, feel the full softness of her forearms and her belly. The tears didn't come. They didn't come again. Not at school, anyway.

Not that I cried much at home—not about schoolwork. That December, when I brought home my first report card of the year, my mother barely glanced at it.

"At least I never have to worry about Jessica," she said. She glared across the counter at Kyle, who was separating the tiny cubes of carrot from the rest of the vegetable medley on his plate.

"I passed," he mumbled, shrugging as though there were something pressing on his shoulder.

Mom sighed. "It's different when you're a teacher's son," she said.

"People expect different things," Kyle said along with Mom.

She glared hard at him, but he didn't look up. "Well, they do," she snapped. "*Especially* from a single mom."

Kyle speared two peas on the end of his fork and slipped them through his barely open lips. He chewed them slowly. "There are way worse kids in my class," he said at last. It came out almost a whisper.

"So that's the standard now?" Mom stood up, sliding her stool back from the kitchen counter. She snatched up her plate and pushed it into the back row of the dishwasher. I could see that she'd gotten some barbecue sauce from the chicken strips on the sleeve of her blouse, but she hadn't noticed yet.

"Can I be excused?" Kyle mumbled at his plate.

"Finish your carrots," Mom snapped. She grabbed the cookie sheet with its leftover bits of chicken breading and shoved it in the sink, turning the hot water on all the way.

Kyle glanced at Mom's back, then slid the plate across the counter. He pushed the carrots from his plate onto mine. I looked up at him. He locked eyes with me and jutted out his chin, defiant. I just kept staring at him until he swiped his empty plate and dumped it into the dishwasher.

I pushed my plate back and opened the tan cover of my report card. Science, Social Studies, English, French, Music: A+. Gym: B. Art: B+. Math: A-. I turned it slowly on the counter so that the marks faced my mom, who was still standing at the sink, watching it fill with sudsy water. When the soap bubbles reached the top, she shut off the water and left the cookie sheet to soak.

"Don't forget to put your plate in the dishwasher," she said. She left the kitchen without looking back at me.

I closed my report card and slid it back into its brown envelope.

THAT YEAR, LAURA CLAYTON BECAME MY NEW BEST FRIEND.
She lived a few blocks away from me. Her family had moved in the
previous spring, but Laura didn't go to my school. She went to the low
stucco building with its wide grassy fields just across the street from her
own house. Grand Centre Elementary. Laura walked to school every
morning, and she walked home every afternoon. If her mom wasn't
working the daytime shift as a cashier at the IGA downtown, Laura
also walked home for lunch.

I would have walked to school, too, if I went to Grand Centre
Elementary. Instead, I walked to the empty lot half a block away from my
house to wait for the yellow school bus that took me to École Medley.
The other students on that bus were all from military families—their
parents (mostly their fathers) were enlisted in the air force, but instead
of living in the narrow PMQ homes in Medley, they'd bought houses in
Grand Centre, or else in Cold Lake just down the highway. And every
morning, the school buses scooped up all the military kids from the
towns to drive them to the school on the base.

All the military kids, and me and Kyle.

École Medley was supposed to be just for military families, but it
was also the closest French school in the area. There were a few kids who
took the long ride to Bonnyville, where there was a non-military French
school, but they rode the bus an hour every morning and another hour
every afternoon.

Kyle, Nicole, and I got to go to the French school on the base
instead because our parents taught there. I suppose we could have
gone into school with Mom instead of taking the bus. After all, she
drove there every day. But she went in early—even before Kyle and I
had to walk to the bus, leaving us to pour our own cereal and eat it in
a glum silence before we locked up and trudged to the bus stop—and
she stayed late.

Before Laura moved into my neighbourhood, I hadn't thought
all that much about the difference between the two schools. And even

though it was only a few blocks from my house, I'd never been inside Grand Centre Elementary.

But the summer before grade three, I walked past that building almost every day on my way to play at Laura's house. And I started to notice its tall windows. The wide grassy field that surrounded it instead of a concrete-paved yard. There was no fence. And it had two—two!—sets of playground equipment: one at the end for the little kids, and one out back for the big kids.

Laura and I spent the summer playing on that playground. The one for big kids, naturally.

I had met Laura because one afternoon, not too long before the last day of grade two, I wasn't allowed to stay home with Kyle while my mom went grocery shopping.

"How come Kyle gets to stay home?" I asked, kicking at the back tire of our dark red K-car while Mom dug for the keys in her purse.

"Kyle's eleven," Mom snapped, yanking the back door open. I considered making a play for the front seat, but the tightness around Mom's mouth made me decide against it. I climbed into the back and slumped against the door.

Mom parked in the little lot in front of the IGA and the Field's Store on Main Street. I followed her as she grabbed a cart and chugged up and down the aisles. She let me pick out the cereal—Sugar Crisp instead of the Frosted Flakes Kyle liked—and the granola bars for our lunches. As we lined up at the cashier, I glanced at the magazines that lined the rows. On one cover, a woman in an orange bathing suit glowered at us with dark-rimmed eyes. I wondered whether that makeup would feel sticky if it got wet. Wouldn't it just run down her cheeks? What was the point of wearing makeup with a bathing suit?

I didn't recognize the cashier. That wasn't all that unusual where I grew up—military families transferred in and out all the time, and the women often got jobs behind the counters in the stores on Main Street, or as waitresses in the hotel restaurants that lined the road on the way out toward Cold Lake. But this woman had dark eye makeup all around her eyes, a bit like the bathing-suit woman. I peered at her closely, wondering whether she could feel that much stuff on her skin and her eyelashes.

She caught my gaze and smiled at me. "What's your name, kiddo?"

I glanced at my mom. She was loading the groceries onto the big disk that slowly spun them into the cashier's reach. "Jessica," I said. I looked at the cashier's name tag. It said *Nadine*. Under her name, there was a sticker that said *Trainee*.

She glided the groceries over the scanner, making them beep. "How old are you, Jessica?"

"Eight."

Mom kept loading the groceries, but I could tell she was listening.

Nadine the cashier pumped her fists next to her face, a kind of little cheer. "I thought so! That's almost exactly how old my little girl is! Maybe you go to school with her? Her name's Laura."

I thought about it. "I think there's a Laura in grade four," I said.

Nadine shook her head. "My Laura's in grade two."

"Grand Centre Elementary?"

"That's right!"

"I go to school on base."

"That's too bad," Nadine said, ringing through my Sugar Crisp. "You seem like a nice girl. We just moved here, and my Laura hasn't made very many friends yet."

"You're not military?" my mom asked. She'd finished putting the groceries up on the counter and was standing at the cash register, wallet in hand.

Nadine shook her head. "My husband's an engineer with the oil field."

My mom gave a slow nod. I saw her survey Nadine: her dark eye makeup, her shining hair pulled neatly back, the little gold studs in her ears, and the fine gold chain that glinted at the collar of her uniform. "Maybe we could get the girls together to play sometime."

Nadine's face broke into a wide grin. "I'd *love* that. I know Laura would love it, too! Would you like that, Jessica?"

I nodded. I wondered whether Laura really *would* like to play with me. I wondered whether we'd play at my house or hers. I took a mental tally of my toys, logged the scuffs on the My Little Ponies, the tangles in their manes. The pogo ball contraption my grandparents had sent for Christmas that I'd put in the front porch, waiting for the spring, then forgotten about until now. Or maybe we'd go to her house. Would Laura be the kind of kid who wanted to bring out all her toys to show them off, but not let me touch any of them? That's what Estelle had done at her last birthday party, lining up each of her Barbies, then all of their outfits, before finally picking out only one for Stephanie to play with, one for me, one for Nicole, and one for Erica, who was in the other grade two class, before sliding the rest out of our reach.

Nadine wrote her phone number on the back of our receipt. My mom tucked it carefully into her purse and loaded the groceries into the cart.

As we drove home, I caught Mom looking at me in the rear-view mirror. Mom wore makeup, too, but never dark rings that made the whites of her eyes stand out like Nadine's. My mom only ever wore a soft smudge of pink or green across her eyelids and a sweep of pink across her cheeks.

"Engineer," she said, catching my eye. "That's a very impressive career. If you work hard, you might be able to get a job like that someday."

"What do engineers do?" I asked.

Mom flicked her eyes back on the road. "All kinds of things," she said. "Ask Laura's dad when you meet him."

As we turned down the road toward our house, Kyle buzzed past us on his bike. He pretended not to see us, even though he passed so close to the car he could have reached out and punched my window. I saw Mom staring at him in the rear-view mirror, watching him pedal madly away standing up, the bike jerking back and forth under him as he sped down the street.

TWO

Freya is asleep, finally. She keeps making little sounds like a frightened puppy, but whenever I crack open her door her eyes are closed, dreams rolling them back and forth against her lids. Her skin looks so delicate, white and translucent like soaked rice paper. I want to kiss her forehead but I'm afraid of waking her up, so I close the door as quietly as I can and come back out to the living room.

I've poured myself a glass of wine. I could use a second, or even a third, but I'm afraid if something happens I won't be sharp enough. What if I need to drive her back to the hospital? Or even just call the health line to find out if I *should*? What if I have to talk to Adam, and he hears the viscousness in my voice?

On the table next to me, my phone buzzes. I know it's probably Adam again, or else Yash telling me I should call Adam, or maybe even my brother. Whoever it is, they won't stop, and eventually they'll call, but I can't deal with that right now. The light glowing around the screen of my phone, face-down on the table, knots my stomach. I can't.

I sit down on the couch, make myself lean back into the cushions, but more mewling comes from Freya's room, so I bolt up. I put my hand on her doorknob, listen, stop breathing. Nothing. I don't open the door again, afraid to disturb her. I make my way back to the couch and take a measured sip of wine.

There's a stuffed dog on the living room floor. Freya named it— Geraldine—but it's not one of her favourites. Last I saw, she was playing some kind of football game with it, kicking it across the room. I shouted at her that she was going to knock something over and if she didn't give it a rest I'd take away her favourite T-shirt. It has a picture of a unicorn wearing '80s-style neon-green sunglasses on it. Ever since Freya was a toddler, clothes have been her prized possessions. No use in taking away toys or screen privileges. Take away her favourite clothing item, though, and it was instant, tearful contrition.

I pick up the stuffed dog and set it on the couch next to me. It slumps over, resting against my bare feet. I pull the blanket over both of us.

If I fall asleep, I'll hear Freya. If she calls out or cries, or starts coughing, I'll hear her. Her bedroom door is only a few feet away and it's cracked partway open. I won't sleep through any crisis. She won't be left awake, alone, scared, in pain.

Sometime between tomorrow afternoon and the next morning, I'm supposed to change her bandages. That's a twelve-hour window. How will I know when it's the right time? Is it better to leave the bandages on longer, or check the incision sooner? I don't know. They never explained. I should have asked. Or Adam should have.

We need to wash the incision with soap and water to prevent infection. We need to check for excessive bleeding, redness, pain, or swelling—though, again, I don't know what *excessive* means.

Medicine is a science. Doctors are therefore scientists. Science should be precise.

Engineers would not use a term like *excessive*. We would use firm metrics, a clear range, units of measurement. A nuclear power plant has defined safe parameters: there are defined limits for the temperature, the pressure, and the reactor power level. If anything causes the reactor to exceed these levels, the control system triggers a shutdown. The shutoff rods drop, the poison system injects neutron absorber into the core to stop the reaction. These protocols are automatically triggered when operational limits are exceeded. Control systems eliminate the margin of human error. It's simply a matter of observation and control.

Why couldn't hospitals design a portable control system for post-operative care? Let the system monitor the wound for cleanliness, test for infection, and assess the levels of seepage instead of waiting for the patient or their caregiver to notice something is wrong. A portable monitoring device could alert the hospital as soon as an event that exceeds acceptable healing parameters is detected.

My phone buzzes again. I turn on the TV and find the crime show I've been streaming. I turn the volume way down so I'll hear Freya if she cries or calls me, no matter how quietly, but I can't make out what anyone's saying, so I turn on the closed captioning and turn the volume almost all the way off. I take another sip of wine. Halfway through the episode, I drift off to sleep.

THE YEAR FREYA WAS BORN, EYJAFJALLAJÖKULL ERUPTED IN ICELAND. In the middle of April, the volcano spewed a massive cloud of ash into the atmosphere. Between April 15 and 23, flight paths across Northern Europe were closed, grounding planes around the world. As Eyjafjallajökull coughed volcanic ash into the path of thousands of flights, it was feared that the engines of airplanes flying through the massive cloud could be damaged, causing them to crash to the ground or into the ocean. Airspaces were shut down intermittently across Europe for weeks. Although Canadian airspace was never closed, there was an estimated 30 percent chance of volcanic ash reaching St. John's, Newfoundland. So, on April 19, flights leaving that province were grounded.

On April 19, 2010, I was thirty-six weeks pregnant. I had no plans to travel, and even if I had, I would have had to book a ticket on an American carrier because Canadian airlines do not let pregnant passengers fly within four weeks of their due date. Adam couldn't understand why I was obsessively following the flight ban.

"You got vacation plans I don't know about?" he teased.

"It's not about that," I replied. I was standing in the kitchen, using the door jamb to stretch my shoulder and chest. A couple of weeks earlier, my left elbow had gone numb. My obstetrician guessed that a nerve somewhere in my shoulder was blocked.

"Will the feeling come back?" I'd asked. It was strange, not being able to feel it when I leaned on the table. My feet had swelled up, and I felt them tingling all the time, like a sensory alarm constantly ringing, and the baby inside me seemed always to be scratching at my innards. I felt so much all the time, and yet it seemed that somehow, this one part of me, my left elbow, had become detached, no longer registering on my sensory scale. Something had to go, I guess.

"It might," she replied. "Go in for a massage after the baby comes. They might be able to get things working then."

"Might."

She gave me a little smile. "Some things go back to the way they were. Some don't."

On the way home from the doctor's, Adam squeezed my hand. "I can give you a shoulder rub? That might help."

"You know how to release a blocked nerve?"

"Could help you relax."

I turned to look at him. He was wearing his sunglasses, the sleeves of his shirt rolled up to his elbows. He'd cracked the window, and the breeze was swishing through his hair. I shifted in my seat, trying to ease the tight, pinching feeling at the base of my back. "Don't tell me to relax."

"I wasn't—"

"Just don't."

I'd had what you could call an *easy pregnancy*. I knew that. My friend Esmé had been sick the first four months, hardly able to keep anything down. Then at seven months, she developed a separated pelvis and could hardly walk. Me, I hadn't really been sick. At about six weeks, I'd suddenly hated meat—the taste, the smell, the look of it gave me the spits. The first time it hit me, Adam was making us BLTs for lunch one Saturday. I walked into the kitchen, and the smell of the sizzling bacon made me turn and walk right out the front door. I stood on the step, shivering without my coat, breathing the thin, early fall air in through my nostrils and trying to force down the mounting nausea. I ended up having to sit down on the step, cradling my head in my arms, as the nausea turned to dizziness.

Adam poked his head outside.

"Close the door," I begged as the rancid smell wafted out.

"What's wrong?" He leaned down and rubbed my shoulder awkwardly.

"Close the door!" I snapped, fighting to keep down my coffee, the one cup I was allowed. "The smell, get rid of it, please."

He pulled his hand back. "I was just trying to make you lunch," he muttered as he closed the door.

I waited outside until I was shivering, then I took a deep breath and headed back in. Adam sat at the counter, a plate of sandwiches in front of him, midway between his spot and mine. I grabbed an apple from the bowl on the counter and darted up to our bedroom, shutting the door behind me.

I hated meat, I was sleepy all the time, and I couldn't have a drink or more than one coffee a day. When I poured my eight-ounce cup in the morning, I felt Adam's gaze on me.

Of course, right after meat, I lost the taste for coffee and tea, too. I didn't tell Adam. Sometimes, I'd pour myself a half-cup in the morning, letting it cool before finally pouring it down the sink when he wasn't watching.

The second trimester was better. I never really got the taste for meat back, but one morning at around five months, I woke up craving a latte. I didn't fall asleep at eight o'clock every night. I didn't have to leave the house if Adam wanted to fry up a steak. And I wasn't showing much yet. I could still wear most of my winter dresses, or my shirts over the stretchy-waisted maternity pants. No one knew I was pregnant unless I told them.

I made Adam wait to tell our families until almost five months. "What if something happens?" I said. "I don't want to have to go around un-telling everyone, repeating bad news over and over."

"Nothing's going to happen," he replied, rubbing my neck. "You're young and healthy. What did the doctor say—a 98 percent chance of carrying to term at this point?"

I shrugged his hand off. "That's not a guarantee."

He sighed. "Okay. But *if* something did happen, wouldn't you *want* our families to be there for us?"

21

I immediately thought of Kyle, tried to imagine him offering his condolences. I just kept picturing him shrugging, his hands shoved as deep in his pockets as they could go.

"No."

"All right, then."

But at twenty weeks, I couldn't find any more reasons to put it off. We'd had the ultrasound. We knew we were having a girl. We knew her name, Freya. And, in case ours was one of the 10 percent of cases in which the gender is inaccurately determined, Linden for a boy. I was thirty-two, I'd started taking folic acid months before Adam and I had even started trying, so the most common birth and genetic defects—Down syndrome, spina bifida, anencephaly, and other neural tube defects—were unlikely, and the probability of a miscarriage (though it would be considered a stillbirth now) had plummeted to under 1 percent.

We drove out to Wolfville to tell Adam's parents first. They were always asking us to come to Sunday dinner. It was easier to put them off in the winter—bad weather, bad roads. But we'd had a dry January so far, and they'd been on us to come out for a visit.

Gayle, Adam's mom, had made a roast. I was glad I wouldn't have to make excuses about not eating it anymore. We agreed to tell them as soon as we sat down to dinner.

"So you're getting married, then?" Those were Gayle's first words.

"No," I replied, certain.

Adam looked back and forth between me and his mom. "No, not married," he said. "Just a baby."

Adam's dad, Gary, stood up from his spot and reached over to give me a kiss on the cheek and a one-arm half-hug. "Boy or a girl?"

"Girl," Adam said.

"Have you picked a name?" Gary asked.

"We have," I said, taking a sip of water.

"We're keeping it a surprise," Adam added.

"Well, congratulations," Gayle said, recovering herself at last. "What wonderful news! Our third grandchild."

"First granddaughter," Gary added with a wide smile. And he leaned over and gave me one more half-hug. Gayle passed him the roast.

AT SIX MONTHS, I FINALLY HAD TO START WEARING ACTUAL MATERNITY clothes. I opted mostly for empire-waisted dresses and blouses for work, nothing that hugged my belly. I had to go to St. John's for work, and Adam made me promise to call him as soon as the plane landed.

"It's not like this is my first time flying," I said.

"Can you just call me?" he asked.

"Okay," I said, letting him kiss me on the cheek.

As I boarded the plane, the man behind me insisted on lifting my carry-on suitcase into the overhead bin.

"It's fine," I said. "I've got this."

"Please, let me." He hoisted the little bag over his shoulder with a grunt. His belly strained against the buttons of his shirt, and I could see the sweat beading on his neck as he tried to jam my suitcase through someone else's bag.

"It just needs to go to the side," I said, reaching for it.

The flight attendant rushed over. "Let me help you with that," she said. "You just sit down, ma'am."

The flight attendant wedged my suitcase into the compartment and the man tapped my headrest, smiling through his moustache. He jutted his chin toward my belly. "Precious cargo," he said as he trudged toward his own seat.

When I got to the office in St. John's, the site manager tried to help me set up my laptop. "I remember how to work my own computer," I snapped as I plugged the cable in. He wheeled in an office chair for me to sit in during my presentation.

My spine, just above my tailbone, had started catching if I stood too long, a sharp hook of pain. If that happened, I wouldn't be able to walk for the rest of the day without limping.

Plus, I'd be able to hide my belly under the board table.

"Nothing wrong with my legs," I said to him, parking the chair farther down the table. I stood through the presentation somehow without

23

my spine hitching. Afterward, I crouched down and reached under the table to unplug my own laptop.

AT MY NEXT DOCTOR'S APPOINTMENT, I ASKED ABOUT HAVING A GLASS of wine. "My friend's doctor said she could have a few glasses a week in her third trimester."

The edge of her lip curled up a touch. "Is your friend in England?"

"Scotland." Esmé had worked with me a few years earlier as a summer student before returning home to Glasgow. We'd kept in touch over social media, mainly to talk about our pregnancies.

She nodded. "The official stance of the Canadian Society of Obstetricians is that no amount of alcohol during pregnancy is safe. But I might not get angry with you if I found out that you had a couple of glasses of wine a week."

"Got it."

"And no more than one a day."

"Understood."

That evening, I pulled a bottle we'd brought home from our trip to France out of the cold room. I remembered tucking the bottles into our suitcases the year before. We'd wrapped them in layers of socks to keep them from knocking together during their transcontinental journey, nestling each puffy, bottle-shaped gym sock into a Ziploc bag in case it broke, and then fitting them neatly into the centre of the suitcase. The packing system had been Adam's idea, and it worked—we got all six bottles home safely, not a single casualty. Now, Adam stared at me as I poured two glasses.

"What?" I said. "I'm drinking for two now." I handed Adam a glass and took a sip from mine. God, it was good. The tingling alcohol feeling filled my mouth, making me think of fireflies. I felt as though my taste buds were tipsy from the first drops.

"I trust you," he said, taking a small sip.

"Good."

He glanced at me again and took another careful sip. Then he set the glass down on the counter and didn't touch it again.

Like I said, it was an easy pregnancy. Nothing like some of the stories I'd heard—no hyperemesis gravidarum (severe nausea and vomiting), no diastasis symphysis pubis (separated pelvis), no gestational diabetes mellitus. Considering everything that could have happened, I had nothing to complain about. At seven months I got sleepy again, but it wasn't so hard to deal with now that the idea of food no longer turned my stomach. We'd settle in on the couch and Adam would watch his shows, trying to rub the puffiness out of my feet as I dozed next to him. Gemini, our cat, liked to curl up with me, her paws gently kneading the mound of my belly, her claws retracted as though she knew she had to be gentle. It was a peaceful time, really.

It was odd, feeling the baby move and press inside me, but it didn't hurt. It just felt as though my innards were being probed by rough hands.

And throughout all of this, I waited. I waited to feel the rush of motherly love toward my baby. That feeling didn't come. Weren't pregnant women supposed to become mothers the moment they realized they were pregnant? I was sure I'd heard people say so, and I kept waiting for the swell of love, the attachment to the small being I was gestating. It didn't come. Instead, I felt the burden of her—the toll that growing her took on my body and the weight that being a mother would press onto my life. That, and the guilt at not loving her the way I was supposed to. What if I never did? Could I pretend, for her sake? Pretend to love her for her entire life, the whole time carrying around this nothingness when I looked at her, held her, kissed her tender cheek? And if I did pretend, would she know? Would she feel the chill from me, and would it warp her and crush her? Who would she be if she knew her mother couldn't love her?

I wondered whether there might be something clinically wrong with me, something that blocked my feelings of love. Sometimes, when she was still within me, not moving or bumping, I'd have to push away the thought that maybe it wasn't me; maybe it was *her*. Maybe she was wrong, poisoned, and I could sense it. Maybe that was why I couldn't love her yet.

To quiet the thought, I turned to research, clicking between websites published by obstetric organizations and big hospitals and peer-reviewed articles.

"More than one in ten women get postpartum depression," I'd said to Adam. I was about seven or eight months pregnant at the time. We were having Saturday breakfast together, coffee and pastries.

"I'm sure you'll be fine," he said. "You're strong." He took a long sip of his coffee and gave me a smile that was meant to be reassuring. I felt the irritation curdle in me like lava.

"*Strong* has nothing to do with it. It's a medical condition. And if it happens to me, you're going to have to step up."

"Step up?" He set his coffee down sharply. "What does that mean?"

"It means you're going to have to take an active role in parenting our child."

"Which I was planning to do, either way."

"I would hope so," I replied. I knew what he wanted me to say—that he was a great partner, that I knew he'd be a great father. But that would just sidetrack the conversation. I needed him to walk through the contingencies with me *now*, not fish for meaningless reassurances. "But if I'm incapacitated—"

He laughed a little. "A bit dramatic, don't you think?"

I clenched my jaw, willing back the rage that threatened to erupt. "I *think* you need to take this seriously," I replied. And in my voice, I could hear it: my mother, her cold rage. I could feel the corners of my mouth pulling tight, and I knew who I'd see if I looked into a mirror right then. The idea was repugnant. I opened my mouth, trying to ease the muscles in my jaw, my face.

Adam stood up. He swept up my empty coffee cup and his, both of our empty plates. "So I think maybe we need to take a beat, don't you?" He stalked to the kitchen, set the plates next to the sink, then disappeared out the front door.

I leaned back in my chair, watching him through the kitchen window as he snapped on his bike helmet and pedalled off down the street.

I rubbed my taut belly, still trying to coax the muscles around my mouth into standing down.

I'D STARTLE UP AROUND 5 IN THE MORNING, AN HOUR BEFORE EITHER of our alarms went off. The baby in my belly slept on, not bumping and shifting like she was sure to do just before breakfast. I'd lie in bed, my hands on the taut skin of my abdomen, wondering what it would be like to hold her, my baby, outside my body. I made myself consider what I might have to endure before that would happen. My mind raced through all of the possibilities. I learned the differences in procedure between scheduled and emergency Caesarean sections. I looked up the recovery process after an episiotomy. I researched the rate of long-term neurological effects of an epidural. It felt simpler to consider these medical possibilities, rather than the more indistinct circumstances of motherhood.

What would I feel when she cried, when she smiled? And later, when she misbehaved, how would I react? I thought of my mother, of the hardness that would suddenly flash over her eyes, of the steeliness in her limbs as she gazed at Kyle or me when she was angry. I'd feel all the love drain out of her then, and sometimes it would take days for it to come back, a slow trickle. Was it genetic, that cold anger? Would I hate my daughter, too, when she made me angry? And I'd press my hands against my belly, feeling for a bump that might be a knee or a heel or a head, and try to will myself to love this little invader, this stranger I was growing in my body.

"It's fine," I thought to myself as I got up to pee one night in May. "I've got a couple more weeks. The mommy hormones should kick in by then." Then, to brush away the gnawing doubt just under my ribcage, I said it out loud: "It'll be fine."

The next morning, as I made my way to the bathroom, I felt a seeping dampness in my pants.

I went to Adam, who lay dozing in bed. "I think my water just broke."

His eyes snapped open and he swung his feet onto the floor. "Oh, shit."

"It could be hours before I go into labour," I reminded him. I was trying to keep my brain from calculating how many days remained until my due date. If I knew exactly how many, I wasn't sure I'd be able to resist searching that number online to identify risk factors and rates of complications. A baby born at 37 weeks is full term, I knew. Had I reached the 37-week mark yet, or was I still 36 weeks and change? A baby born at 36 weeks was considered premature. What were the risks? How much difference would that week make?

"Right," he said. "What do you want to do?"

I started downstairs. "I'd better get some breakfast."

The contractions started just before noon. They didn't hurt much at first, and I had trouble timing them. When did I start the timer—at the beginning of a contraction, or the end? Adam wanted to go to the hospital shortly after lunchtime, but I resisted. What would I tell them when they asked how far apart my contractions were? Were these even contractions I was feeling? In the first hour, I was able to comfort myself with the knowledge that it could be a full day between the time my water broke and the time my contractions started, and then a day or more until the baby was actually born. She could have a couple of extra days, even more, to develop. That would be better, wouldn't it? But soon, I couldn't deny what I was feeling.

By mid-afternoon, Adam had become insistent. By then, the contractions had me stopping in place, counting slowly in my head until the gripping pain released. I gave in and made my way to the car.

"Should I call Mom and Dad?" Adam asked as he drove.

"No way," I replied. "I can't deal with that right now."

Our daughter was born just before seven that evening. It hurt, but not in the way I'd expected. The contractions sent crushing pain through my middle, but there was no tearing, no cutting, none of the horrors I'd forced myself to expect. And then there she was. A nurse put her on my chest, and the tiny warm weight of her there was more than I ever thought I could feel.

"Freya," I said, filling my eyes with her tiny nose, her angry-looking little face, the pursed lips, the damp, matted scruff of dark hair on her head. "Freya." Adam stroked a finger along her cheek, his eyes wide and unbelieving. I knew how he felt. How could so much love be spontaneously generated? How could a body feel so much, be so enraptured with another creature who, moments before, had only existed as a kernel and a germ, and who now, just now, breathed in the world, became the most precious thing in that entire world for her two parents? How?

A COUPLE OF WEEKS LATER, GEOLOGISTS WOULD ASSURE THE WORLD that Eyjafjallajökull had returned to dormancy. Flights over northern Europe had fully resumed, and even though a handful of flights would still be delayed in the coming days, the danger to aircraft had largely passed. The volcanic eruptions that spring had grounded thousands of commercial, private, and military flights. Hundreds of people were evacuated from the area around the volcano. Lava was ejected over a hundred metres into the air, and it sent the temperatures of local rivers spiking. Volcanic ash filled the northern hemisphere for weeks. However, not a single fatality was connected to the eruptions, and no long-term health effects have been linked to the volcano or its clouds of ash.

THREE

We had learned about the Chernobyl nuclear accident in grade three Social Studies class. It had been on the news, so Mlle. Lefebvre must have decided it was best to explain it to us as gently as she could. That's what she called it—a "nuclear accident." I imagined a big barrel of dangerous, luminescent green liquid spilling across the power plant floor, and workers slipping on it and falling. She showed us where Chernobyl was on the big map on the wall opposite the windows. She tapped the spot where the accident had happened, then slowly arced her hand through the air to tap the spot where we were. The effect was meant to show us how far away it was. But I couldn't help picturing the beach ball–shaped globe my mom had bought me. I wondered how far through the Earth it was between the two points. They were both on the same half, I noticed, both above the equator. Was it really that far?

"It was a very dangerous accident," Mlle. Lefebvre said with a pink-lipsticked smile, "but you don't need to worry about it. Very smart people are working very hard to fix it."

Until that moment, it had not occurred to me that I would *have* to worry about it. Sure, I'd heard the story on the news, but I knew where Ukraine was. My grandparents had emigrated to Canada from Ukraine, and it was half a world away. Surely no accident there could ever hurt us here? But something about the determined gentleness in Mlle. Lefebvre's tone made me wonder.

That night, I asked my mom. She was pulling a pan of fish and chips out of the oven as I set three plates and sets of cutlery on the counter.

"The accident in Ukraine? The power plant? Could that hurt us here?"

"If they don't get a lid on it," she replied.

"How?"

Kyle snorted. His job was to heat up some frozen vegetables. He dumped the peas into a bowl, jabbing the frozen lumps with his finger, and shoved it in the microwave.

"Don't forget to add butter," Mom said.

"It's nucular meltdown," Kyle said. "The whole world could go totally Mad Max."

"How?" I asked, playing with a knife I'd just set down.

"Radiation," he said.

"What's radiation?" I snapped.

"It's, like, bad waves in the air," he said, watching the peas go round and round. "It'll turn everyone into mutants or something."

I looked at my mom. "That's not true," I said. "Right?"

"Not quite." She gestured at me to get my plate from the counter. "Eat, eat."

I slipped a spear-shaped fish stick and a pile of fries onto my plate then squeezed a puddle of ketchup next to them. I sat down and bit into a fry. "Is that what they make nuclear bombs out of?" I asked. "Radiation?"

"Yup," Kyle replied.

"Where are the peas?" Mom asked as she set her own plate on the counter. Kyle groaned and went to pull them out of the microwave.

That night, after I'd crawled into bed, I heard my mom on the phone. I caught the words *Vira* and *Petro*. Names, I realized, wondering where I'd heard them before. Her voice sounded tense when she said them.

Moments later, she walked past my bedroom door.

"Mom?" I called.

"You're supposed to be asleep."

"Who are Vira and Petro?"

She hesitated, rubbed a hand against her opposite shoulder and then let it drop. "My cousins," she said at last.

"Why were you talking about them?"

"Go to sleep, Jessica." Her voice hadn't taken on the edge of annoyance yet. I knew it was okay to push. A bit.

"Please tell me?"

She took a slow breath, then finally answered. "I can't reach them," she said at last. "Auntie Maria, Vira's mother, hasn't been able to either."

"Why not?"

Mom was staring over my head at the dark window above me. "Could be any reason," she said. "Except they live in Dymer. In Ukraine."

"That's where Chernobyl is." I felt an odd excitement bubbling up inside me. I knew someone, or at least knew of someone, who might have been killed by the disaster. I knew I should feel sad and worried. I tried to make my face look like that's the way it felt.

"Never mind," Mom said, her gaze snapping back down at me. "Go to sleep."

I didn't go back to sleep, though. I waited until Mom closed herself into the bathroom to get ready for bed, and then I crept out of bed. I snuck through the house, checking the windows in every room except for Kyle's bedroom and the bathroom. I checked that they were shut tight, that there were no cracks where poisonous gases might seep in. I tiptoed back into bed and just had time to pull up the blankets and pretend to be asleep before Mom emerged, her face and teeth fresh from her bedtime rituals. I closed my eyes and repeated the names *Dymer*, *Vira*, and *Petro* in my head as I willed myself to sleep.

A while later, a week maybe, I asked Mom again about Vira and Petro. Her cousins, our cousins.

"Never mind," she said again, her voice flat and unrelenting.

She never spoke of them again.

But all that week I'd lain awake, thinking about the fire drills we had at school. When the fire bell clanged, we'd all stand up, leaving our pencils and notebooks at our desks, and clatter out into the hallway. If it were winter, we'd have to grab our jackets from the hooks on the wall as we passed. The teachers would hush us, but no one could hear it over the clanging red bell in the hallway. We'd press on, not quite running down the hallway, and spill out into the schoolyard. The *mean* teachers like Mlle. Thornton would make their students stand in regulated lines, shushing and sometimes lightly smacking them on the shoulder or the back of the head if they laughed or talked too loud. But the *nice* teachers like Mlle. Fillion or Mlle. Lefebvre would just count us as we emerged into the schoolyard, then count us again on our way back in, letting us mill around and chat, soaking up the excitement of a fire drill. Then when the clanging stopped, we'd line up again, waiting for the signal to file back into our classrooms, invigorated by the brief adventure.

Bomb drills were different.

At the beginning of every school year, we'd have an assembly in the gym. We'd all sit in rows on the floor, facing the stage. Our teachers got to sit in chairs against the wall, angled to face us, to keep the shuffling and chatter to a minimum. I could see my mom sitting in her chair, usually shushing a fidgety student at the end of her row. The vice-principal, Nicole's dad, would start by giving us a talk about school rules. Then someone from the base commander's office would arrive, an officer in dress uniform. For some reason it was usually a woman, even though there weren't that many women enlisted back then. Maybe they thought what she'd have to say would be less scary. As the officer made her way to the front of the room, one of the teachers would follow her with a big map attached to a flip chart.

"*Bonjour, les élèves*," she'd begin. "You are students in a very special school, a school that's part of the Department of National Defence. Your dads and your moms have a very important job to do, and that job is to protect Canadians, to protect our freedoms. Some people have different ideas about how the world should be run, and we don't always get along with those people. And we are the closest military base to those people. We are what you call the First Line of Defence." She'd point to the map, a polar map, showing the world from the top down. CFB Cold Lake was marked with a little blue dot. She'd point to us and then trail her finger across the North Pole to the big red mass on the other side.

"This is the USSR. They are what we would consider a *risk*. It could be that, someday, they decide to attack, and we would have to defend. And as close as we are to them"—her finger trailed back over the pole to us—"we would be the first to find out if there's an attack. So it's up to all of you to understand how to take the proper precautions." With that, she'd nod and stride back to the row of chairs at the side of the gym. I remember on assembly day in grade three, I turned to look at Kyle. He had his head low. He and his best friend Matt were laughing quietly, their faces turned away so the teachers wouldn't see them. I wondered whether he'd heard any of what the officer had said.

That afternoon, we'd have our first bomb drill of the year. Over the intercom in every classroom and down every hallway, a horn would sound in short blasts. When it did, we would slide out of our chairs and under the desks they were attached to. We would each have to sit under our desk, straddling the long bar that supported the seat, our knees or our toes pressed painfully against the front crossbars. Our neck bent low to keep our heads under the desk, our hair held away from wads of gum that other students might have pressed there.

Why would somebody do that? I always wondered. Who would put gum under their desks when they knew that, eventually, they'd have to crawl under there?

During bomb drills, we all had to be silent. Not even the nice teachers allowed a whisper in the classroom until the horn blasts stopped and the intercom speakers crackled to silence. We'd have a drill every couple of months or so. Afterwards, we'd slide back into our desk chairs, feeling dampened. All of the normal excitement and apprehension and joy and resentment of an ordinary day of school would have been extinguished by the suffocating exercise. I thought about the fire extinguishers that firefighters would show us for fire-safety day, the way they smothered the little flames that ate at the cardboard they lit specifically for the demonstration. The white foam whooshed over those flames, dampening their ecstatic fingers.

That's how I felt during dinner the day that Mlle. Lefebvre told us we didn't need to worry about the accident at Chernobyl. Dampened.

OUR LAST BOMB DRILL OF GRADE TWO WAS A WEEK OR SO BEFORE I met Laura. Our moms had arranged for us to play together on the Monday of the May long weekend. Victoria Day. Mom had marking to do. She asked us whether we had any homework left. I didn't—I'd finished it after breakfast Sunday morning, the way I did every weekend. Kyle had grunted a reply, then pedalled off.

Mom picked up the phone in the kitchen. She used the bright voice she normally saved for the school Christmas party, and for when she ran into parents or other teachers when we were out shopping. "Nadine! Is today still a good time for the girls to play?... Sounds lovely. I'll see you soon."

She hung up the phone and looked me over. "Is the outfit I got you for your birthday clean?"

I nodded, my heart sinking. It was a frilly little pink and purple number—a matching T-shirt and cotton pants in a purple-and-pink floral pattern with a little pink skirt that went over top. And matching pink socks with a lace trim. The fabric was soft and stretchy, but every time I even looked at the outfit, I thought, *itchy*. Mom had presented it to me at my last birthday party, pride pinking her cheeks. I'd opened the wrapping, and Stephanie and Nicole had both *oohed* in delight. It looked like the kind of outfit a kid on TV might wear.

"Thank you, I love it," I'd said quietly.

Too quietly, I guess. Mom's eyes darkened, her smile hardened. "Go try it on," she ordered.

Obediently, I took it to my room and put it on. It fit perfectly. I smoothed down the frilled edge on the skirt.

"So pretty," Nicole breathed.

Mom nodded approvingly, then retreated to the kitchen to let me open the rest of my presents. I tucked the lace-topped socks up into the pant legs.

I put on the outfit now, and then looked at myself hard in the mirror. This was who I was to be when I met this girl, Laura. Well, so what. Who even knew what she would be like?

Before we left, Mom pulled my fine, wispy hair into a ponytail at the side of my head.

Even though Laura's house was only a couple of blocks away, Mom herded me into the car. It would only take a minute to get there. No time to ease into it.

"If I don't like her, do I have to call you to come get me?"

"What do you mean, if you don't like her?"

"Well, what if I don't?"

"Why on earth wouldn't you?"

I puffed my cheeks out to cover the sigh that would surely get me a full day of dark looks and short commands. I'd just walk home on my own, I decided.

We turned off the road that flanked the schoolyard onto a street lined with Manitoba maples. When we were younger, Kyle and I used to collect the seed pods and throw them up in the air, watching them spin back down to the ground on their dry wings. *Helicopters*, we called them. Mom pulled up to a small stucco house with an even smaller detached garage. A cracked asphalt driveway ran the edge of the property, from the street to the chipped and peeling garage door. Mom stopped in front of the house. She peered at the scrap of paper where she'd written the address, then back at the house again.

I reached for the door handle.

"Just a sec," she said, letting the car idle. She looked back up at the plain, single-storey home, frowning.

Just then, the front door opened and Nadine emerged, waving us inside. She was wearing jeans and a light green blouse. How strange, I thought, not to see her in her IGA uniform. She lifted her right arm and a small, dark-haired girl slipped under it. Nadine was fair, smooth-haired, but the girl had a warm, deep-tan complexion, and a thick braid sprung out on either side of her head. I knew lots of Native kids, Cree and Dene and Métis, and my classmate Tarek told us on Multicultural Day that his mom was from Morocco. I knew that Black people existed, but this was the first time I'd ever met one. I felt a rush of excitement—it was as though the world I'd seen on TV, the world of Rudy and Vanessa

Huxtable, of Michael Jackson and Whitney Houston, had finally penetrated Grand Centre, Alberta. I bounded out of the car and up to the house.

Nadine laughed. "Come on in, Jessica. You two go on and get to know each other." She beckoned to my mom. "Come, have a coffee with me!" she called.

I turned back towards our car. Mom was hovering by the driver's side door. I watched her put on her determined smile and march up to the house. I turned back to look at my new friend.

Her dark eyes were taking me in. "It's nice to meet you. My name is Laura," she said.

"I know. I'm Jessica."

She nodded, then looked at me for another moment. "Want to come play in my room?"

I followed her through the arch between the living room and her bedroom. I heard Mom and Nadine chatting in the kitchen. Even from there, I could hear Mom's frosty formal tone. Fake-nice. I sighed. She wouldn't be driving me here for another playdate, that was for sure.

"I like your outfit," Laura said as she showed me into her room. It was small. A single bed was pushed against a wall with a small rectangular window that looked out toward the neighbours' house. The bed was completely covered with stuffed animals—so many I couldn't see the bedspread.

I looked down at my clothes. "Thanks," I said. "I hate it."

Laura laughed. It wasn't a mean laugh; it was the kind of laugh that opens up, that invites. "It's really...pink," she said.

"I know." I felt my cheeks flush.

"These are my guys," she said, gesturing to the stuffed animals. "You want to play with them?"

I did.

I picked a green plush frog, and she chose a ratty, floppy-eared bunny. We had them travel through troll country to rescue a princess. Just as the princess, the frog, and the bunny were setting off on a new adventure to find troll treasure, Nadine stuck her head in the door.

"That was your mom on the phone," she said. "Time to go home."

I hadn't even realized my mom had left. I stood up and handed the frog back to Laura.

Nadine led me to the front door, Laura following behind. "We're so glad you could come and play, Jessica."

"Thank you, Mrs...." I murmured, trailing off. I didn't know her last name.

"Oh, call me Nadine," she said, batting her hand in the air as if fanning away my shyness.

"Thank you, Nadine." It felt odd in my mouth—an adult's first name.

Laura waved to me from the living room window as I made my way down the sidewalk, back towards the main road.

When I got home, Mom was cooking hamburger on the stove for sloppy joes.

"Did you have a nice time?"

"Yes," I said, tucking my shoes into the hall closet.

"Think you'll want to play with her again?"

"Yes," I said again, taking care not to say "Yeah," or "Uh-huh." I could sense Mom feeling for a reason not to let me, and I didn't want to risk having her say I was being rude. Rudeness was cause for a privilege to be taken away in our house. Playing with Laura was not a privilege I wanted to lose, especially so soon.

Mom nodded. "See if you can find out what kind of engineer Laura's father is, okay?"

I went to my bedroom without answering, passing Kyle's room on the way. He was lying on his bed, reading an old Archie comic. He didn't so much as lift his head.

AFTER SUPPER THAT NIGHT, KYLE ANNOUNCED HE WAS GOING FOR A bike ride.

"Dishes," Mom replied.

Grunting, Kyle made his way to the sink. He rinsed the plates and handed them to me to load into the dishwasher.

"Can I go now?"

"Is your homework all done?"

"I don't have any." Kyle was standing at the door, poking at his shoe with his toe.

Mom sighed without looking at him. "Back by eight."

He turned and bolted out the door. I heard him pull his bike out from under the steps. Then I heard him say, "Shit." I turned and looked out the kitchen window. Kyle was straddling his bike, next to the car. His back was bolt-straight, and he was staring at the driver's side door, immobile. Slowly, he turned and looked up at the kitchen. He caught my gaze. His mouth opened and closed.

Mom saw me staring out the window. "What is it?" she asked, coming to the sink.

When Mom appeared over my shoulder, Kyle ducked his head and took off, pedalling down the street as though someone were after him.

Mom frowned. She walked to the door and slipped on her shoes. I followed her out to the driveway.

Gouged into the burgundy-red paint of her car door was a long, silvery-fresh scratch. Mom drew in a sharp breath. She clapped both hands over her mouth.

I reached out and traced the long scratch with my finger.

Mom smacked my hand away. "Get inside."

The back of my hand stung where she'd hit me. I grasped it in my other hand. "I didn't—" I started to protest.

"Inside!" she barked. Her lips had set and her voice had flattened. I made my way up to my bedroom, the injustice of it burning in my chest. I thought about slamming the door, but the back of my hand was still burning. Instead, I grabbed my favourite book—*How Does It Work?*, a thick bible of scientific and mechanical explanations with bright photos full of interesting details—and sat in the small space on my floor between my dresser and desk.

Kyle didn't come home until after nine. I'd gotten ready for bed, but hadn't crawled under the covers yet. I sat in my room, listening for the sound of his feet on the steps. Listening to the sound of the kitchen stool easing as my mom shifted in her seat, the *thunk* of her glass on the counter every time she took a sip.

Finally, the slow plodding of his feet on the steps, the sound of the door opening and closing.

I held my breath.

"In here," Mom said icily, almost a whisper.

The creak of my brother's footsteps into the hall. Silence. "It was an accident," he muttered at last.

"And you just took off."

Silence.

Then the sharp *thunk* of a glass set down too hard on the counter. "I have to drive it," she said. "Me. My coworkers see me in that, the parents of the kids in my class. They all see me driving that, and now it looks like… And you can't even stick around to apologize?"

"I'm sorry." It was a fast mumble. Sullen? I couldn't tell.

The creak and ease of the stool as she stood up. "An embarrassment," she said. "An utter humiliation."

She strode down the hall first, slamming the bathroom door shut behind her. Kyle stood, immobile, staring at the door. It was a long moment before he turned and slid down the hallway. I got up and stood at my door. *She meant the car*, I'd tell him. But I waited too long. He slipped into his bedroom and shut the door.

THE BUS DROPPED KYLE AND ME OFF BY ABOUT 3:45 EVERY AFTERnoon. Mom stayed at school, marking and preparing her lessons, until 5:00 or so every day. There was no official curfew, no rule that we had to go straight home from the bus stop, but Kyle and I both knew to be home around the time Mom got in; 5:15 was pushing it.

Laura's house was on my way home from the bus stop. As I walked home one sunny afternoon the week after we'd met, I saw her sitting in the dappled shade of the hedge that separated her house from her neighbours'.

"Hey," I called from the sidewalk. I was on the other side of the street, so she looked around for a moment, trying to follow my voice.

"Oh, hi, Jessica!"

"Want to come play at the playground with me?"

She stood up. "I have to ask my dad."

I waited as she ran inside. She emerged moments later, her father hovering behind her on the steps, his hand holding open the screen door.

"Be safe," he said. "Come straight home if there are strangers there."

"We will," Laura called cheerfully, leading the way toward the school.

I glanced back over my shoulder. Mr. Clayton was watching me. The look on his face made me falter. He was assessing me the way grownups often did—I'd seen them look at me and other kids the same way, weighing our behaviour and our manners, trying to gauge the potential for misbehaviour. But there was something else. *Please,* his eyes seemed to be saying. I stopped. *Please what?* I almost asked.

"Come on," Laura called, and I ran to catch up with her. We made our way across the schoolyard to the playground on the big kids' side of the school. It was much cooler than the playground on the little kids' side. It was made to look like a fort or a treehouse, constructed out of logs and ropes. There was even a rope bridge connecting the two sections.

"We're not allowed to play over here at recess," Laura said.

"How come?" I asked, pushing the bridge with my hand, making it sway. Was it dangerous?

"It's only for the grade four-five-sixes. It's so dumb, though. I've seen them, and they don't even play on it. They just stand around. They should let us play here."

"Yeah," I agreed, trying to sound enthusiastic. I followed her across the rope bridge, gripping the rope railings as the wooden slats bounced and swayed under our feet. She stopped in the middle, braced her hands on the rails, and swung the bridge back and forth, giggling. Then she bolted to the other side. My hands gripped the railings harder, and I did my best to smile when she looked back at me.

"Where'd you move here from, anyway?"

41

"Ottawa."

"Oh." I had expected her to say somewhere cool, somewhere distant, like New York or Los Angeles or Philadelphia. Kyle said his favourite city was Philadelphia because that was where Rocky came from. He kept a *Rocky IV* poster taped to the back of his bedroom door. It showed Dolph Lundgren as a snowy mountain, Rocky climbing up its slopes.

Once the bridge stopped swaying, I remembered my mom's orders. "What does your dad do?" I asked.

"He's an oilfield engineer," she called over her shoulder as she climbed up the net of knotted ropes to a small platform above.

"What does that mean?"

"That's just his job." She sat down on the platform, her legs dangling over the netting to looked at me. "Do you like your school?"

I shrugged. "We have to talk in French all day." If you were caught talking in English at recess or in the halls too often, you'd be sent to the principal's office. I didn't know what happened once you got there, but every now and then, I'd see Kyle slumped in one of the hard wooden chairs across from the secretary's desk. "Do you like it here?"

"The kids are pretty nice. The teachers, too."

I remembered what Nadine had said—that Laura didn't have any friends at school. I wondered if that was true. "Who's your best friend?"

Laura raised and dropped her shoulders quickly, matter-of-factly. "I don't have one yet."

I suggested we pretend that we were on a desert island, defending our fortress from pirates. She agreed readily, hopping down off the platform, and we ran back and further across the bridge, climbing up the wooden towers on either side, until finally Laura stopped, breathless.

"I should go home," she said.

"Me too," I agreed.

She turned and bolted across the schoolyard, sprinting towards home without saying goodbye. I watched her until she halted at the corner of the street, checking for traffic before she crossed. I made my way toward the opposite corner of the schoolyard, wondering whether, for once, Kyle would get home before me.

"WHAT'S AN OILFIELD ENGINEER?" MOM ASKED AS SHE HANDED ME three dinner plates.

"I don't know," I said, my back to her as I headed for the table.

"Is it an actual engineer, or is it a technician?"

I set a place for each of us. "I don't know."

She sighed. "I wish I knew a little more about her parents."

I knew what that sigh meant. "I can still play with her, though, right?"

She shook her head in a way that said *I don't know*. I finished setting the table in silence, not wanting to push it further.

THE DISTANCE BETWEEN COLD LAKE AND CHERNOBYL IS ABOUT 4,900 kilometres. When our class went to the school library one day, I hauled the big atlas off the reference stand near the card catalogue and measured the distance with my ruler. Mme. Poirier, the librarian, helped me convert the distance to kilometres, using the scale at the corner of the page. The distance around the earth is 40,000 kilometres, she told me—almost ten times the distance between us and the nuclear accident with its poison gases.

I waited for a feeling of relief that never came.

began to dream of Chernobyl.

I was standing on a sidewalk, looking at those hyperboloid cooling towers that I thought were the reactors. A dark green sludge oozed out of the towers, flowing inexorably toward me. I would turn to run, only to discover that the sludge had bubbled up around my legs, immobilizing them, fixing me in place. Sometimes, a bomb would whiz across the sky, hurtling toward the tower. Sometimes, the tower itself would just begin to shudder and smoke, turning red before—

In my dream, I would be screaming, but I'd always wake to the crushing silence of my bedroom, no one rushing to see if I was okay.

FOUR

After Freya was born, once they'd checked her over, and me, they put the two of us in a wheelchair as I held her to my chest. She was, to all appearances, perfect. The doctors and nurses seemed satisfied with her colour, heart rate, reflexes, muscle tone, and breathing. No one mentioned her early arrival, and I chose not to ask about it. Once, a nurse came into the room to check on us, and the urge to tell her where we'd travelled nine months before snagged at me, but I bit the words back, letting the medical staff's words of approbation wash over me. Adam followed as they guided us into an elevator, up one floor and to the private room my health insurance had paid for. They set up a fishbowl-looking clear plastic bassinet for Freya, and later that evening, they wheeled in a cot for Adam.

Adam called his parents first, then I called Kyle. Our mom had been dead almost a year by then, so as far as family went, I really only had him to notify. I'd post something on social media later for everyone else, and send an email off to my dad and his wife.

"Welcome to worrying about absofuckinglutely everything," he said when I gave him the news. A hysterical giggle threatened to burst out of me in response, but I managed to pare it back to a low, sympathetic-sounding chuckle.

Kyle had two daughters—Maddie, eight, and Kayleigh, five. They split their time between his house and their mother's. Kyle and Juliet had split up when Kayleigh was a toddler. Juliet was a nurse, and Kyle still worked the oilfields. I often wondered, but never asked, how they'd managed childcare during her shifts and his stints up in the oil patch. Of course, these days there was Zoë. Kyle had moved into Zoë's place just south of Edmonton a year or so before Freya was born. She had a twelve-year-old son, Derek. Full custody.

Kyle wasn't entirely right, though. At first, it seemed he might be. I kept imagining all the horrible things that could befall my tiny, helpless, fragile daughter if we weren't careful enough. The day we came home from the hospital, I carried her up the stairs to our front door. She was in her car seat, and I pictured myself carrying her in my arms. I couldn't stop the image of her slipping out of my grasp and breaking her body on the ruthless cement steps. When I got to the top of the short flight of steps, I set her down gently, away from the edges of the stoop. The horrible fantasy sharpened my mistrust of myself as a mother. What kind of person could possibly imagine such a thing happening to their own baby?

"You carry her in," I said to Adam. I tried to smile a little to make it a kind of ceremony: *I got her this far, now you take her the rest of the way.* Still, he looked puzzled as he slipped the bag with my change of clothes and toiletries off his shoulder to pick up the car seat. Freya made a little squawking noise and opened and closed her hand against her cheek as he hoisted her carefully through the front door.

Days later, I was slicing tomatoes for a salad, and I couldn't stop imagining my daughter lying on the floor next to me, helpless, as the knife slid off the counter and pierced her soft body. I set down the knife slowly, placing it behind the cutting board, far from the edge, and went to find her and her father.

Adam was half reclining on the couch, holding Freya to his chest as he watched reruns of a '90s sci-fi show. Freya's eyes were closed. I reached out to stroke her cheek, my fingers grazing her upper lip to feel for her warm breath. Her hand flew up in the gesture we had nicknamed the "Surprise Kitten" after a viral video that had recently made the rounds.

Adam frowned, jiggling her little bottom to soothe her. "You woke her up."

"I didn't mean to," I lied.

As I prepared to load her into the car to get groceries, I worried that her car seat might not latch into the seat or her stroller properly, that she'd be ejected through the windshield or onto the hard pavement.

"I forgot my wallet," I lied to Adam. "Can you load her up?"

I ran inside and waited a second before returning to check his work. He was waiting in the passenger seat. "You don't trust me," he said.

"Of course I do," I answered as I pulled away from the house.

He stayed silent, his face turned away from me, until we reached the grocery store. I wanted to insist, to reassure him, but the truth was, he was only partly wrong.

As I fell into bed each evening for a few hours' sleep, I was beset by the grimmest fantasies—what if I was so overtired that I put my daughter into the oven instead of the chicken? What if I forgot her in the car in the baking sun? What if I set her down in the dirty laundry hamper and then dumped the works into the washing machine? Who was I, after all, to take on such a precious charge? What in my life had prepared me to keep this perfect, defenseless creature safe?

How had I qualified for motherhood?

OF COURSE, NONE OF THOSE HORRORS I IMAGINED BEFELL US. One night in the middle of summer, I awoke to my daughter's cries as I had already done more times than I could count. I rolled out of bed, sluggish, and carried her from her bassinet to the chair by the window. As she nursed, I breathed in the warm, sweet scent of her and I realized that I was happy—*happy*—that she had woken me up because it meant I got to be with her, holding her. I gazed out into the dark, still street, the lights casting a hazy bluish glaze over the houses and cars and sidewalks, all of which seemed entirely peaceful and untenanted, and I felt suddenly as though we were alone in the world, she and I, and we were free from everything that pulled us away from each other.

I hadn't planned to nurse her. Or rather, I'd been prepared to fail at nursing her. I'd heard the stories of "nipple Nazis" at the hospital, nurses who insisted that mother breastfeed, no matter how painful or difficult it was. I'd steeled myself for what I imagined was an inevitable confrontation, prepared to unleash my well-researched dissertation on "fed is best." But, to my surprise, nursing came naturally to me—to both of us, Freya and I, right from the start.

It was at these times, in the middle of the night, when I got up to feed her, that I realized that we were a contained universe. She needed me, and I could give her everything. Everything that her tiny body was, apart from Adam's initial genetic contribution, came from me. And sitting there that night, looking out into the stillness of our neighbourhood, I felt that need so powerfully. I almost laughed out loud—the elation filled me as I realized I wasn't failing her. Not by a long shot. I was all she needed, and she was all I needed. I couldn't remember ever having felt so safe or serene before. And soon, as the hormones subsided, so too did my dark imaginings.

In fact, I settled into a kind of bliss. That was the only word for it. When Freya bleated at night, needing a breast or a diaper change or just the contact of our skin on hers, I'd feel a soft, eager glow at the thought of holding her, of looking at her tiny, perfect face. When she sprayed me with an explosive shit during a diaper change, I laughed heartily at her performance as Adam grimaced, offering halfheartedly to help clean us up. And although it took me a few days to get used to the odd, urgent suckling at my breast, I soon came to love those quiet, tender moments with her.

Bliss.

I hadn't prepared for bliss.

I felt as though I finally understood what I hadn't seen throughout my pregnancy—the connection, our bodies linked. I could feel what she needed, I sensed her in every moment. How had I missed it when she was growing inside me?

One evening, we were cleaning up after supper. Adam held Freya as I slotted the plates into the dishwasher. She let out a flat, fretful wail. He patted her bottom, a gesture I'd come to recognize—checking her diaper—though the pat told him nothing. He turned, headed for the change table in the bedroom.

"She just wants to be bounced," I said.

He looked at me—not disbelieving, exactly. More tying to decipher our connection, Freya's and mine. "Yeah?"

I held my arms out, and he passed her to me. Her cry rose in pitch, insistent. I held her close and bobbed up and down with her. Her cries lowered, taking on the rhythm of our bouncing, and finally tapered off. Adam watched us, his eyebrows raised. I saw him again the way I knew him way back when we'd first met, puzzling over his assignments. I felt as though my lungs had expanded, making more room for the delight of that moment.

None of this was close to what I had expected. I'd braced for the worst—I'd worried about her, certainly, but also about me, about what kind of mother I'd be, especially if the depression I anticipated materialized.

But in the end, there had been no depression. Just bliss, as I contemplated this tiny girl who was suddenly everything to me, who spoke to me more clearly than anyone I had ever known. At first, the idea that some great sadness might come upon me nudged at the corner of my thoughts, and I braced for an all-consuming despair and helplessness, but over time, I realized it wasn't coming. And I gave in to the bliss, trusting it to last.

OVER THE NEXT COUPLE OF YEARS, IT WAS ADAM WHO CALLED "Careful!" if our daughter crawled too near the stairs or reached for a lamp cord plugged into an outlet. It was Adam who tried to keep her corralled on blankets when we took her out to play on the lawn, who brushed the handful of dirt from her hand before it made its way into her mouth. It was Adam who read the parenting books, downloaded the apps, set mealtime alarms to try to keep her on a regular feeding schedule, bought all the safety paraphernalia to secure the cupboards and drawers she might try to open.

Me, I watched her; I felt her, knowing when she was safe, knowing without thinking when I should pick her up, move her out of harm's way, knowing when she was absolutely fine. It was Adam who worried about absofuckinglutely everything, not me.

Instead, I took her on adventures. First, during my mat leave, then after, on the weekends. I took her to the art museum and on ferry rides across the harbour. I let her put handfuls of grass and soil into her mouth, wanting her to know the taste of her world. I let her pet the cat, her tiny face lifting in delight at the softness of the fur, as Adam hovered, fretting about teeth and claws. I kept sugar and dyes and artificial flavours out of her diet, throwing kale into her blueberry smoothies and handfuls of sunflower seeds into her puffed wheat breakfast cereal, but on our adventures, I let her eat ice cream for lunch, even though it made her squirrelly and stubborn all afternoon. Though the initial hormonal bliss faded by the time I stopped nursing her, it was joy I felt with her. Not worry.

BEFORE I HAD FREYA, I'D CHAFED AT THE IDEA OF TAKING PARENTAL leave. I'd proposed to Adam that we split it, but he pointed out that our income would be slashed if he took time off. It was true. His benefits wouldn't pay him for the time off, so his income would be reduced to the Employment Insurance rate. Not that we were suffering, but it was difficult to fathom a drastic decline in income. So I took the full maternity leave.

To say I loved my job would be inaccurate. There were days that I found the company, my coworkers, my staff intolerable. But the work itself—I could lose myself in the work for hours. I would become immersed in the technical specifications of a control system, and it was as though my entire self—my body, my mind, everything—dissolved entirely, and I became whatever problem I was working to solve. It was an almost delirious state, and I craved it. When something—a coworker bustling past my desk, reminding me it was time to go, my cellphone ringing, the sound of laughter in the hall—pulled me out of it, I'd feel a sharp regret, as if waking up from a pleasant dream. In another life, I might be a drug addict. It had always been this way. I couldn't imagine being away from my work, trading it for a slurry of unallocated hours.

But I did. Freya and I would nap together, she on my chest or in the bassinet next to our bed. When the weather was good, we went for walks around our neighbourhood. I hadn't done that since I was a student. Back in my university days, I used to force myself to take breaks from studying and wander around the wealthy neighbourhoods in the South End. Most of the Victorian and Edwardian homes I'd fallen in love with back then were still standing. Many had hardly changed, in fact. So as Freya dozed in her stroller, I'd walk, feeling as though I were coming home from far far away.

I felt an odd sense of freedom, then. Not the claustrophobia I'd so expected. And during that time, it was Adam who tried to impose an order in our home.

"She needs a routine, Jessie. How are we ever going to be able to enforce bedtimes and mealtimes?"

"She's an infant." I shifted her from one breast to the other. Adam looked away, the way people did when I nursed her in parks or cafés. There was a time I might have been hurt by his polite squeamishness, but right then, I felt there was something right in the way he was giving up his claim on my body—giving it up to Freya, I thought. "She's way too young to have a bedtime."

"That's not what the research says."

"Fine. You put her to bed then."

And at seven thirty that evening, he did. He tucked Freya into her bassinet and I stayed downstairs on the couch, even though I had gotten in the habit of heading up to bed for a few hours' sleep around eight or nine. And, to my surprise, she slept. She didn't fuss or call for me. I stayed waiting on the couch for her to cry, and she slept peacefully until after ten.

"Not bad," Adam said.

"You're not the one who's up all night with her," I snapped as I made my way up to our bedroom to soothe her.

When she was six months old, he asked if it was time to introduce solid foods. I felt the suggestion like a blow to the chest. Up until that point, everything she was, everything that made her up, had come from me.

"I'm not ready to stop nursing," I said.

"Did I say to stop nursing?" he asked. "I just said it's time to *start* solid foods. Also. In addition to the milk or whatever."

Then, as Freya's first birthday drew near and the end of my parental leave loomed, it was finding a daycare. "You're not going to stay home with her forever, are you?"

In truth, I had blocked the idea of my leave's end from my mind. I wasn't considering either going back to work or staying home. "I'm not ready to think about it."

"These places have wait lists. We might already be shit out of luck."

But when he suggested getting a sitter for the evening and having a night out, I dug in my heels. Freya was nine months old then. "She's not going to trust a stranger. She'll cry all evening, and I'll be miserable, knowing she's crying."

"You don't know that for sure," he said, but then he dropped it. There was no sitter, no night out.

I did go back to work at the end of my year's leave. And as I was packing up my breast pump that first week, grumbling about having to use it in the office, having to close myself up and draw the blinds and attach this stupid vampiric device to my boobs, he suggested I stop nursing. I didn't answer, just stared at him in response. He dropped it.

And soon, he stopped making suggestions, stopped trying to nudge us along the parenting trajectory. He left most of the decisions, big and small, to me.

He knew, just as I did, that I understood best what our daughter needed.

FIVE

I spent most of the summer before grade three playing with Laura. I eventually met her father. Although Nadine had insisted right away that I call her by her first name, Laura's father never introduced himself to me. I just called him Mr. Clayton. He was a tall, quiet man who seemed to work a lot. His skin was darker than Laura's, and his hair, like hers, curled tightly. I seldom saw him, even on the evenings Nadine invited me to stay for supper. When he was home, he tended to slip away into the basement or the master bedroom whenever we came inside to play. Nadine would ask us questions about our games or tease us when we came in with dirt streaked on our faces and knees, but Mr. Clayton seldom said more than "Hello." I never did ask him what an oilfield engineer did.

Laura and I ranged around the neighbourhood. She seemed content for me lead her about. I wasn't used to that. At school, I mainly did whatever Nicole or Estelle suggested. But if I asked Laura whether she wanted to go to the playground behind the school or the forest at the end of her street where some kids had built a fort, or to the pond behind the high school where ducks would swim to the shore, hoping for gifts of bread crumbs, she always agreed and followed me happily.

One afternoon, Laura and I walked down to the creek that lay beyond the last houses a couple of blocks behind my house. We were hunting frogs. She didn't really want to go, I could tell, but she hadn't argued when I'd suggested it. She didn't like to touch the frogs. She'd recoil if I held a hand out to her clasped around a cool, squishy body squirming tenderly between my fingers. She held the bucket, a blue plastic beach toy, its bottom covered in creek water and leaves we'd picked to keep the frogs comfortable. I'd wade into the lazy trickle in my rubber boots, capturing the creatures in my hands. Laura waited on the bank, holding out the bucket to receive my catches. She kept a count of the frogs, naming each one.

"I think this one will be...Dapple," she said as I dropped in a small, brownish-green fellow.

I climbed up onto the bank. We sat together on a patch of soft moss and examined our haul.

"What do we do with them now?" she asked.

"Let them go, I guess."

She set the bucket down a few feet away and cautiously tipped it over with the toe of her sneaker. Most of the frogs leaped out right away, breaking for the creek, but a few stayed behind, crouched among the leaves that clung to the bottom of the bucket.

"Bye, Dapple, you can go home now," Laura murmured. I reached my hand in and scooped out Dapple and another straggler, depositing them on the grass nearby.

Just around the corner, Kyle appeared, riding his bike along the rutted dirt path that bordered the creek. He stopped next to us, setting his foot down on the ground for balance. "Mom says it's time to come home," he said.

I was looking at the spot his front tire had stopped. The spot where Dapple had been moments before. "Okay," I said.

He turned and rode off. I made myself look at Laura as she stood and brushed the dirt from her pants. She hadn't noticed, it seemed, where Kyle's bike had stopped. She'd already lost track of the frogs she hadn't wanted to catch in the first place. "See you," she said cheerfully, following Kyle down the path.

A sick heaviness had invaded my belly. I tried not to, but as I stood up, I looked down. There was Dapple's crushed body smashed into the dirt. I could see the tracks of Kyle's bicycle tires where they'd run over him.

I felt sick the whole way home.

THAT EVENING AFTER SUPPER, KYLE AND I RETREATED TO THE basement. Mom was watching a TV movie in her bedroom. Kyle and I watched a Disney cartoon. I headed up to my room before Mom called down that it was bedtime—I wanted to read my book, a novel in a series about a junior scientist who solves mysteries. As long as I was in bed before Kyle, Mom probably wouldn't bother enforcing my nine o'clock lights-out.

Shortly after nine, Kyle had closed himself into his bedroom. My door and Mom's were still open, and the flickering light and soft voices from her TV spilled out into the hall. I was just finishing my chapter, getting ready to turn off my light. Then, from the basement, a muffled thump. A jolt of fear tore through my body—it gushed from my head down my arms, ending in a pricking sensation in my hands. I froze in bed, listening hard. A second thump, less distinct than the first, but my nerves were tuned in. I tried to find my voice to call for my mom, when I heard her sit up in bed. She snapped the TV off. The hallway turned dark and silent. I sat up.

Mom appeared in her bedroom doorway. She was stilled dressed in the slacks and blouse she'd worn to school. She wavered in her doorway, and it was her uncertainty that reignited the shock of fear in me.

Kyle's bedroom door opened. Mom unfroze, then, and waved urgently to him. "Into Jess's room," she whispered. "You two stay here."

"No way," Kyle said. He slipped back into his room. I heard his closet door open. I got out of bed and crept to the doorway, careful not to let the squeak of a floorboard alert whoever was downstairs. Mom held out her arm and I huddled into it.

Kyle emerged from his room with his baseball bat. He stood in front of Mom and me, and I realized how much he'd grown that summer. He was taller than Mom, and even though he was still skinny, his arms and legs looking a little too loose, not quite articulated to his narrow torso, he somehow seemed menacing in that moment. He wasn't quite crouched, but his shoulders were curled inward, coiled, the bat held at shoulder level. He crept slowly down the hall toward the stairs. Mom tapped my side, her hand fluttering and nervous, to tuck me in behind her as she followed.

We crept down the stairs, single-file, to the spare bedroom at the back of the house. The door was closed, as it always was, to keep the dust out.

Mom and I stood back, her hand still pressed lightly to my side, keeping me behind her. Kyle hesitated a moment, his hand hovering above the doorknob, and then his muscles uncoiled. He snapped the door open and sprang into the room, the bat cocked and ready to strike.

Nothing.

Then another soft thump, this one from the still-closed window.

The streetlight beyond illuminated the branch that had fallen. That side of our yard was dotted with poplars. Mom always lamented how brittle they were, how they weren't good hardwood like maple or oak, which wouldn't grow this far north. I guess she was right. A branch had fallen against the house, and the wind played among its leafy extremities, thudding it softly against the vinyl siding and the windowpane.

Kyle's body loosened. His shoulder muscles unfurled, his arms sunk, and the bat clattered to the ground.

Mom made a sound like a sputter. She took a long step into the room and crushed Kyle's lanky frame into a fierce hug, pressing her face into his shoulder. He looked over at me, a little askance, I thought, and then his free hand came up and patted her uncertainly on the back.

Without withdrawing her face from his shoulder, Mom jutted one arm out to me: a command and a request all at once. I joined them, and she pulled both of us into a long, crushing hug. Her arms felt like poplar boughs, I thought. Hard and brittle.

At last, she let go with a sort of *Ugh*, an acknowledgement of our unfounded fears. "Okay," she said. "Back to bed."

We followed Kyle up the stairs, but with Mom at the back of the procession this time. She snapped the spare bedroom door shut behind her, and before we retreated to our bedrooms, she gathered us both into her arms once again and crushed us together, just for one quick second, before retreating to her room.

"Goodnight, my kiddos," she said.

I looked at Kyle. He looked back at me and shrugged one shoulder. "Night," he said and slipped into his room.

Afterwards, as I lay in bed, I imagined that I had been the one to retrieve a baseball bat, to lead us down the stairs. I imagined that some-one really had broken into the house, and that I fended him off, fought him back by swinging the bat, by growling, "Get out of my house!" as I swung, edging him back up out of the window, sending him fleeing down the block. I imagined my mom looking at me with admiration, saying, "I wish I had been brave like you when I was your age."

That night, I dreamed of Chernobyl.

ONCE GRADE THREE STARTED, LAURA BEGAN TO DISSOLVE FROM MY life, just a little, but still enough for me to feel her absence. Over the summer, we'd seen each other almost every day. We'd slept over at each other's houses a handful of times, and it seemed natural to have my days so entwined with hers.

But then, as soon as the Labour Day weekend closed, our lives took a hard turn back to the routines of school. Kyle and I were back to trudging to and from the bus stop, to bagged lunches of sandwiches and soup, apples, and granola bars instead of handfuls of cheese and soda crackers, or bowls of cereal poured hastily when we burst into the house at two or three, ravenous from a day of ranging wild about the neighbourhood. Now it was homework and alarm clocks, recesses at the monkey bars or the painted pavement with Nicole, Estelle, and Stephanie. It was striving hard to be the best in the class at every sub-ject (or every subject that counted, anyway), but refusing to allow my traitor tears summon Madame's tender looks when Nicole beat me on math tests.

Laura had almost slipped entirely out of my life when one evening, Mom announced Laura and her parents would be coming to supper on Sunday.

Kyle looked up from his plate. "Why?"

"What do you mean, why?" Mom snapped. "Because it's nice to have company sometimes."

"We never have company," he said. And he was right—sometimes Janet, our school secretary, would catch a ride home after school with Mom—she lived just a couple of blocks away, and it seemed her car was always broken down. The two of them would sit on the back deck or at the kitchen counter, sipping rye and Cokes, but she never stayed for supper. Her visits never had anything to do with Kyle and me.

That Sunday, Mom had me take out the good plates. Our everyday plates were a mismatched set—some were white with little olive-green flowers around the edges, and some were a heavier tan-coloured ceramic with brown and yellow flowers in the centre. A few had chips in the rims. But we kept a matched set in the buffet—they'd belonged to my grandmother, and they were lighter and thinner, printed with delicate bunches of pink-and-blue flowers, and rimmed with a pink stripe like a bow. I always thought of them as the Christmas dishes—we'd use them for Christmas dinner, then put them back away for the rest of the year. But I was setting them out now. I'd cleared the crocheted tablecloth and fruit bowl off the dining room table, replacing them with a light-blue cotton tablecloth and matching napkins. Kyle and I normally did our homework at the dining room table, so I'd had to clear away our notebooks and pencils, too.

Mom had Kyle at work in the kitchen, peeling potatoes. I'd started the job, but Mom had peered into the pot of cold water and scoffed. "Come on," she said, pointing to narrow slivers of brown peel that still clung to the white flesh. She called Kyle up from the TV room and assigned him my task. She nodded approvingly as he peeled each potato to a flawless whiteness, and told me to set the table.

He glared at me as I retrieved the utensils from the kitchen drawer.

Mom made roast chicken, mashed potatoes, and green bean casserole, then set out cookies from the bakery on Main Street—the real bakery run by the old German couple, not the bakery counter inside the IGA—for dessert.

At five o'clock, the doorbell rang. The sound made me feel very stiff suddenly, very formal. No one ever rang the doorbell. Our friends just knocked. Janet usually just walked in, calling "Halloooo!" as she kicked off her shoes.

Laura was wearing a dress. It wasn't the kind of frilly dress I'd seen her wearing to church. It was made of purple T-shirt material, and the slim blue waistband fell to her hips. Still, I glanced down at my own jeans and sweatshirt, wondering if I should have dressed up. Mom hadn't told me to, but now that seemed to be a misstep. Mom was wearing one of her school outfits, a long skirt with a blouse. Nadine was wearing a skirt, too, and the knot of Mr. Clayton's tie peeked out over the collar of his tan sweater.

As they came inside, Laura's father handed my mom a bouquet of flowers and a bottle of wine. "It's good of you to have us," he said, and I thought for a moment he must have practiced saying that; it sounded so smooth and formal.

"You didn't need to do that, Philip, Nadine!" Mom said. I could feel her eyeballing the jeans me and Kyle were wearing. I slipped away to put the salt and pepper shakers on the table.

Mom put the flowers in a vase and brought the food into the dining room, setting it down in the centre of the table. We all sat down, Mom, Kyle, and I on one side of the table, and Laura's family on the other. Laura's father—*Philip*—held out his hands. Nadine and Laura each clasped a hand and reached out to me and Mom. I reached out automatically. Though we never said Grace, I'd grown to enjoy the tradition when I had dinner at Laura's house. But Kyle glanced around, confused, his hands planted in his lap. Mom gave him a tiny, urgent nod and we all held hands for a moment around the table. Laura and her family had their heads bowed, their eyes closed, and after a moment, her dad murmured, "Amen." The rest of us mumbled it back to him and then Mom, forcing a bright smile, held the bottle of wine out to Laura's parents. The adults each had a glass, and Laura, Kyle, and I filled our wineglasses with apple juice.

At first, the only thing the adults talked about was the food, passing it back and forth around the table, encouraging us kids to try some, to have a little more, then praising the dishes, mentioning that the recipe for the green bean casserole had been my grandmother's. Then there was a lull.

"So, Philip," Mom said, "you're an engineer?" I realized that in all the times they'd greeted each other during sleepover drop-offs and pickups, they'd never really said much to each other.

He nodded, chewing a mouthful of chicken. "Oilfield engineer," he said.

"What do you think of this nuclear power business?"

He shook his head, disapproving. "Chernobyl. Could have seen that coming."

"Oh?" Mom asked.

"An unstable power source in the hands of a corrupt government?" He frowned, shaking his head once again. "Unavoidable. Natural gas, that's the future. It's cleaner, safer. And the oil industry, that's where the jobs are. Kids just out of high school, even some of the ones never finished school, can make a good living on the rigs, as long as they're hard-working. And there are other jobs, too. Careers in geology, chemistry, physics. Trades. Engineering."

Mom nodded. Then she glanced at me. I looked over at Kyle, expecting him to have that closed-off look he always got when Mom talked about careers and education and stuff like that. But he was looking at Laura's dad, his eyebrows raised, his fork stopped in mid-air.

I looked back to Mom. She was smiling again, and this time it was her real smile—softer, not forced. "Jessica wants to be an engineer when she grows up."

Laura's dad looked at me, his eyebrows raised in the exaggerated way that adults do when they want children to know they're impressed. "Do you?"

"Yes," I said. In truth, Mom had suggested it to me, and I'd never really considered the matter one way or the other. She'd brought home a big hardcover book from the school book fair. It was called *What Will I Be?* On the cover, there were drawings of a yellow-haired boy dressed as a doctor with a stethoscope, a firefighter, a police officer, and a scientist with a bubbling test tube. In the book, the boy tells a bunch of different stories, each starting with "I will be a…" "I will be a lawyer." "I will be a carpenter." "I will be a teacher." "I will be an engineer." Mom had sat on the couch and beckoned me over. We'd read several chapters together, and when we got to "I will be an engineer," Mom had put her arm around my shoulders and squeezed me tightly to her. "You can be an engineer," she'd said. "You're smart enough, you can be anything you want." I'd rested my head against her shoulder and nodded, looking at the picture of the smiling boy designing a suspension bridge in a city studded with skyscrapers and puffy green trees.

A few years later, I would say the words aloud for the first time: "I'm going to be an engineer." I was in grade eight then. In September, the guidance counsellor, Mr. Desjarlais, came to our classroom. He handed out a booklet for us to fill out, an aptitude test. I filled in the bubbles on the test sheet, feeling a bit uneasy about a test that didn't have right or wrong answers. The following week, while we all worked on assignments in class, Mr. Desjarlais brought each of us, one by one, to his office for career counselling.

I sat down across the desk from him, and he opened up a manila file folder with my name printed along its edge. It held much more than just my aptitude test, I could tell.

"You're a very strong student, Jessica," he said, closing the file to smile at me.

I was the best student in my class. The year before, I'd switched to the English Junior High program, and my class was bigger than Nicole's French program. But still, as I collected math and science tests, English and social studies assignments with 90s and 100s on them, I was confident that I'd have no trouble keeping ahead of her in math any more. For the last year of elementary school, we'd been neck-and-neck.

"Have you ever considered becoming a teacher?" Mr. Desjarlais asked.

I thought of my mom, of her stiff politeness when we ran into her students' parents in town. I thought of the marking she often brought home with her to finish after supper. I thought of my classmate Brian Mason, who balled up little bits of paper and threw them at the teachers' backs until they became red-faced and sputtering. "No," I replied.

"What about a nurse? Do you think you might want a career when you're finished school?"

I remembered Mr. Clayton at the dinner table, the easy confidence in his voice when he'd said that natural gas power plants were the future. I thought about my mom telling me I could be anything I wanted. "You're smart enough," she'd said.

"I want to be an engineer," I replied.

Mr. Desjarlais smiled. It was the kind of smile I'd seen adults give to little kids who say they want to marry their brother or become an astronaut when they grow up. "Well, good for you," he replied. "There aren't many lady engineers, I don't think. And you'll have to study very hard."

"I will."

He sent me back to class and told me to send the next student in.

AFTER DINNER, MOM SENT KYLE, LAURA, AND ME DOWNSTAIRS TO play while she and Laura's parents shifted into the living room. Kyle asked if he could go out to play, but Mom shook her head. "We have guests."

Kyle watched TV while Laura and I sat on the floor with a box of dolls. Laura had brought them—I didn't have a lot of dolls, but she had a lovely case of costumes, and we liked to each choose a doll and dress her up, mixing and matching the outfits that came as a set, making jewelry out of pipe cleaners and Christmas ribbon.

"What are you going to be when you grow up?" I asked.

"Hairdresser," she said matter-of-factly. "Like my mom."

"Your mom's a cashier, though."

Laura shook her head. "Not really. That's just cause she hasn't found a job in a salon yet."

I thought of Nadine's hair, how it was always smooth and stylish, either done up or curled around her face. And Laura's hair, too, was always braided or tied back differently, often held up with shiny plastic bauble elastics or sparkly barrettes or even ribbons braided right into her hair. I'd never seen Nadine or Laura look messy-headed, the way Mom and I both did on days we didn't have school. I wondered what it must be like to be able to make yourself so neat and stylish all the time.

One day, not too long after our dinner with the Claytons, Laura came over after school. We were playing in the backyard as we waited for Mom to come home. We were trying to weave together a wall of thin branches to make a screen to hide us from the street. I heard Mom's car pull into the driveway. I knew I should go in, but I didn't want to yet. I handed Laura a branch and sharpened my ears.

I didn't have to wait long. Mom went inside, then banged back outside almost immediately. I could feel her anger in the sound the door made as it slammed behind her. "Kyle and Jessica!" she bellowed. "Get in here and help me with these groceries *now!* I am not your servant!" And the door slammed again as she went back inside to wait and fume.

A flush of embarrassment washed over me. I glanced quickly at Laura, and I could see she felt it too. She kept her eyes on the ground as she brushed the dirt off her pants. "Bye," she mumbled as she slipped away back to her house, where her parents never screamed at her for all the neighbours to hear.

"Where's Kyle?" Mom demanded as soon as I came inside.

"I don't know," I mumbled.

She glared at me as though it were my fault he'd gone. She jabbed her finger at the car. "Help me with those groceries," she snapped.

A tiny mutiny rose in my chest. I followed her, scuffing my shoes against the sidewalk.

As we unloaded the groceries from the car, I told her, "I want to be a hairdresser when I grow up."

Mom shook her head once: a hard, quick gesture. "Not with your brains," she replied. "No way. You're going to university." She handed me a bag of bread and breakfast cereal and I followed her up the stairs into the house, wishing I had the courage to push back harder.

SIX

I'm dreaming of Laura. She's about eight years old, the same age she was when we first met, and she's dressed in one of her doll outfits—a tulle skirt with a denim jacket, and a necklace of red-and-gold curled Christmas ribbon. She's standing at the door of Freya's room now, peering in.

"Shut the door," I say, "You're going to wake her up."

Laura looks at me and shakes her head. "She needs to do a bomb drill," she says. "You need to get her under the bed."

"I can't. The bandages." I can see them now and they're massive, a stiff white bundle wrapped around my daughter's poor, fragile leg. They won't fit under the bed, they're too bulky. And if I try, it'll hurt her. The wound will open up. A bomb drill will tear her open.

"It's your job. You're not doing it right, though. You were supposed to focus on natural gas."

"Nuclear power is safe," I tell her, launching into my reassuring practiced tone, even though all I want is to push past her, to get her away from Freya's room, to close the door tight. "We can't rely on fossil fuels forever."

"Tell that to Kyle."

Then before I can react, she steps into Freya's room and closes the door. I try to follow her in, but the door is locked. I want to pound on it, to yell at her to get away from Freya, but I can't make any noise that will wake my daughter. She needs her rest. She needs to heal. So I push on the door, I try to turn the handle, but it slips in my fingers. I can't get in. I'm trying, but I can't get to Freya.

I WAKE UP ON THE COUCH. I FEEL THE HAMMERING OF MY HEART AT the base of my throat. The breathless panic, the sliding between the dream and the waking. It was like the sleep paralysis I used to get sometimes in university, especially mornings after I'd stayed up too late studying. I sit up on the couch, focusing on the pricking feeling on the backs of my hands. I push away the blanket and creep in to Freya's bedroom, opening the door as softly as I can.

She's snoring a little. She usually doesn't do that. It's probably because of the medication, but still I find the sound comforting. If she's snoring, she's sleeping. If she's sleeping, she's breathing. I allow myself to kneel by her bed, to press my nose to the fabric of her pyjamas, just at her shoulder. Faintly, faintly, she still has the same sweet, yeasty scent she had when she was a baby. I hardly ever notice it on her anymore. I breathe it in.

But when she shifts, turns her head to the side and rolls her arm away from me, I stand and edge out of the room. I leave her door open and retreat to my own bedroom, leaving my door open, too. I know I should charge my phone, but I don't want to see how many messages Adam sent while I was asleep. I'll call him tomorrow, I promise myself.

As I pull the covers up over my shoulders, my ears tuned for the sound of Freya's voice, or a cry or a cough or a whimper, I remember Laura as she'd looked in my dream. I realize I'd given her Freya's face. Laura's dark skin and eyes, Laura's tightly curled hair, but Freya's features, her expressions. I try to remember Laura as a child, bring her own face to my mind, but I can't do it. I only have Freya's to draw from.

FOR YEARS, MY FRIENDSHIP WITH LAURA FLOURISHED IN THE SUMMER and then waned in the school year. Once we got to grade ten, we were finally in the same school, but by then we already had our own set of friends, our own circles. We ended up taking a couple of classes together, and when we did we'd claim a pair of desks side by side, but I was taking all advanced academic courses and Laura was only taking advanced English.

At first, I tried folding her into my social life. Stephanie had a car, and most weekends, she'd come pick us up and drive us to the mall. It wasn't much of a mall—a handful of dowdy shops, a food court with a grim little coffee counter and a sandwich place, the whole thing anchored by a newly built grocery store on one end and a home improvement store on the other. They'd built the thing in a farmer's field on the edge of town a couple of years earlier. Still, for a teenager, it was a draw. We'd get coffees and occupy one of the tables in the centre of the food court. Sometimes, we'd pretend to shop in what we called the Old Lady Store across the hall—a clothing shop filled mainly with pleated pants and cardigans with little flowers embroidered on them, sarcastically suggesting outfits to each other as the saleslady glowered.

One day that fall, I asked Stephanie to stop by Laura's on our way. I ran up to the front door. Mr. Clayton answered, greeting me politely before calling Laura.

"We're going to hang out at the mall," I said. "Come with us?"

Laura opened her mouth to answer, but Mr. Clayton looked up sharply from his book. "No," he said quickly. "Laura, you cannot *hang out* at a mall."

I saw her shoulders drop just a fraction, as though his words had slung a heavy bag on her back. "Sorry," she said, shrugging.

"It's okay," I replied quickly, forcing a smile and trying to decode the atmosphere that had filled the living room with her father's interdiction.

She closed the door softly and I returned to Stephanie's car.

We saw even less of each other by the time school ended. I headed to Halifax to enroll in the engineering program of the technical university, and eventually she headed to Toronto to work. It was years before we reconnected.

I'd learned about the engineering program in the fall of grade eleven. My math teacher, Mr. Glubish, had nominated me for a full scholarship to attend a Youth in Science program in Ottawa. For a full week, I stayed in a dormitory with other students from all over Canada. We spent our days combing through museums, and we stayed up all night, talking to other smart kids, kids who didn't know who we were at home, who our parents and brothers and sisters were, what kinds of neighbourhoods we lived in. It was glorious.

I met a boy, Simon, from Antigonish, Nova Scotia. He was the first gay person I'd ever met. He was shy and polite, but he had a wickedly funny sense of humour. He could pick out someone's flaw, cut it away from them with the precision of a surgeon, and somehow make fun of it without reducing the person themself. He teased me about my fine, wispy hair, about my fashion sense (I had brought an extensive collection of plaid flannel). He was wicked, but not mean. He made you laugh with him, drawing you into the joke. Not like Stephanie, or some of the other girls I'd gone to school with, who could eviscerate you with a word. He was funny, but there was a camaraderie, a kindness, even, beneath his joking. I was utterly in love with him.

After supper one evening, we went out into the little courtyard behind the cafeteria to talk. I sat down on a bench and he lay down, his knees hooked over the armrest and his head in my lap.

"Do you like where you live?"

I didn't answer right away. If he'd asked me that question at the beginning of the week, I'd have said "Sure," and I would mostly have meant it. After all, I liked the lake with its beaches and its long boardwalk. I liked the campgrounds and the trails. My teachers liked me. I had friends—Laura, for sure, and Stephanie, Jason, and a few other friends from school. Hanging out with Stephanie and her crew was a constant dance of who's-on-the-outs, which of us had done something to incur the secret wrath of the others. When we'd reached high school Stephanie had unfurled, becoming our grade's social regent, with all the little tyrannies the title conferred. Nicole had gone on to the French high school in Bonnyville, and Estelle's dad had been transferred to Petawawa a couple of years earlier, leaving the top social spot open for Stephanie, who was more than happy to assume the crown. Being part of her court didn't lead to any deep bonds of friendship, but it was a comfortable enough social arrangement. For the most part, I was pretty good at keeping the moving target off my own back, mainly by sidestepping the barbs and gossip aimed at whoever was the outcast of the moment. I could credit Mom and Kyle for that—my skill in staying out of arguments, and in the relative good graces of everyone involved.

But then, there were no museums at home—not really. There was the small Pioneer Museum at the edge of Cold Lake and the Avionics Museum on the base—a disused hangar filled with fighter plane parts. Nothing that interested me. There were no universities, and I would certainly have to leave after grade twelve to study. I knew every restaurant, every business and café and bar. There were no new places to discover. Before this trip, I'd always been vaguely apprehensive of big cities. When we went on shopping trips in Edmonton, Mom was constantly reminding us to stick with her, not to wander off and get lost or abducted and sold into sex slavery. Not that I really believed that would happen. But here in Ottawa, cities seemed not to be places of vague threat, but places where things could happen. Unexpected things that could turn out to be good. Like sitting here, in this little concrete courtyard with its boxed-in trees and shrubs, with this smart, funny, beautiful boy resting his head on my lap, making me feel, for the moment, utterly indispensable, even though he would never kiss me or slip his hand up my shirt the way the lacklustre boys I'd dated back home had done.

I ran my fingers through Simon's brown curls, pushing them back from his face. He closed his eyes and turned his face into my hand. "No, I don't like it," I said. "Do you?"

"God, no." He looked up at me. "So, how're you getting out?"

"When I go to university, I guess. I'm going to study engineering."

"I'm going to be an architect," he said. "I'm going to Halifax to study, then I'm leaving Nova Scotia forever, and I will never go anywhere near Antigo-nowhere again." Then he glanced across the courtyard at a girl from Montreal. She was wearing worn brown brogues under her wide-leg jeans. "You steal those shoes off your grandfather's corpse or what?" he called. She laughed and threw an apple core at him.

That conversation was all I needed. As soon as I got home, I asked the guidance counsellor for a university catalogue for the Technical

University of Nova Scotia. Even though I still had a year of high school left, I started picking out my first-year courses.

MY FIRST FEW MONTHS IN HALIFAX, I EXPECTED TO RUN INTO SIMON. I looked for him on the TUNS campus, in the cafés and pubs downtown, on the streets and in the halls of my residence, but I never saw him again. Instead, I met Adam.

I was in the low study hall of the library, sitting next to the narrow window at the end, working on my physics assignment. The answers were coming together neatly, and I paused between questions, admiring the tidiness of the problems and solutions, the way that the numbers came together in predictable ways. The orderliness to it.

Adam came in and sat at the end of the table. He was slight, blond. He was only about my height, 5'7" (though in his early twenties he'd suddenly have a growth spurt and gain another full inch, making his first set of suits and dress pants too short at the ankle). His straight, fine hair was parted off-centre and fell over one eye. He glanced shyly at my physics textbook as he pulled his own out of his bag.

"We're in the same class, right?" he asked, his voice just above a whisper in the dead-quiet study room.

I nodded.

He gestured helplessly at the assignment sheet. "Do you get *any* of this?"

"All of it," I said.

His eyebrows shot up. It occurred to me that I might have lied and we could have gone for coffee and commiserated, flirted, then shifted the conversation to social topics. Not that I wished I had said that. I only recognized it as a conversational option. Recognized it and dismissed it. "Do you need help?"

He blinked quickly, surprised. "Yeah, actually."

I glanced at the boy at the other end of the table. He was glaring pointedly in our direction, giving us a stern look over his thick, wire-rimmed glasses.

"We'd better go somewhere else," I said.

We packed up our books and he followed me back to my dorm room. I had a single room. It had been a source of contention between my mom and me—not the cost of it. I was paying for it anyway, or I would be, once I started repaying the student loans I'd taken out to cover my tuition, books, dorm room, and meal plan. My entrance scholarship had barely scratched the surface. Engineering was an expensive program. But she'd told me that her roommates had truly been the best part of her university experience.

"Those were the best years of my life," she said, "because of those girls. You wouldn't believe the fun we had!"

It's not that I'd discounted the possibility of having fun. I fully intended to enjoy my time at TUNS. I expected to meet the same kind of people I'd met during my week in Ottawa—quirky, smart, brave, ambitious. But the guidance counsellor and my teachers had warned me how tough my Engineering program would be.

"More than half of first-year Engineering students end up either dropping out or flunking out," Mr. Glubish had told me. "Don't you dare be one of them."

I didn't intend to be. So I decided on a single dorm room. Mine had extra desk space where the other bed would normally be.

That was where Adam and I set up. I'd never really thought of myself as much of a teacher. But he bent over the work, listening to me so seriously as I explained the formulas we had to use. He got through most of our assignment before our Intro to Engineering class that after-noon, then without even asking, followed me back after class was over.

As we were packing up to go to the cafeteria for supper, he leaned over and gave me a one-armed hug. "You're saving my life," he said. He was half-leaning against the desk, his chin down and his soft-looking hair flopping over his eyes. The word *wistful* popped in my mind. He looked wistful, as though a soft wish were blowing through him, so tender he couldn't touch it for fear it would collapse.

I kissed him. His lips stayed closed, and he hesitated a moment before he pulled back.

"I have a girlfriend. She goes to Acadia," he said, naming the university in Wolfville, a few hours away.

I looked at him. He had soft, full lips. They were partly open, as though he were waiting for my permission to—what? To stay loyal to his girlfriend?

When I'd kissed him, his lips had tasted sweet, like fruit-flavoured lip balm.

"Okay," I replied. "See you in class."

He finished packing up his books. At the door, he turned back and looked at me. "Thank you," he said. "I mean it, really." And he left, shutting the door behind him.

I SAW HIM IN CLASS A FEW DAYS LATER. IT WAS IN ONE OF THE lecture halls that hadn't been updated since the fifties. Engineering students from all specializations had to take Intro to Engineering, so they crammed us all into the sloped, wood-panelled cavern with a rickety lectern and scratched blackboard at the front. The professor droned in lightly accented English over a hollow-sounding PA system. About half the students were scribbling furiously, trying to write down everything he said; a bunch were nodding off in their hard-backed seats, elbows perched precariously on the fold-down tables. The rest of us listened, either with looks of utter incomprehension or—like me—with the calm knowledge that the professor was merely summarizing the assigned reading. No need to take notes. It was all there, in our textbook.

Adam was one of the furious scribblers. He and I both sat near the middle of the room. He was in the centre of the row, and I usually grabbed a seat near the aisle. I hated the idea of being caught, pinned in the middle of the crowd, if a fire broke out or something. Could happen, in that outdated room with its dried-out wood panelling and mid-century wiring.

Near the end of the class, Adam caught my eye. He gave me a quick smile and a little wave. It was sweet—like he'd caught himself being too eager and deliberately dialled it back.

I stood and waited for him in the nook by the door at the end of class.

"I was going over my physics notes, and it actually makes sense now," he said. "I owe you big time." He'd slung his bag over his shoulder, but he was holding his books to his chest, like a shield.

"Want to come over to work on next week's assignment?"

He nodded quickly. "Yes, please."

This time, he was the one to kiss me. We were still sitting at my little desk. It was wider and longer than the desks in the double bedrooms. It gave me enough room to set up my clunky desktop computer at one end and my textbooks and notepad at the other, but it was a squeeze to fit two chairs (one borrowed from the common room down the hall). Our knees kept pressing together. At first, Adam would shift away self-consciously, but soon, he left his right knee lightly touching mine. After a moment, I felt the tension leave his muscles as he focused on the work.

And we *were* working. There was no question I was a stronger student. Adam struggled to grasp the basic theories, wanting to simply plug in a formula to solve a problem without considering which one he was using, or why. But as we talked over the assignment, I could sense an easing in his mind, an opening toward the beautiful logic of the science, the orderly reasoning that guided the solutions. He was still making mistakes, but when I pointed them out, he was quicker to understand why they were the wrong answers and where his thinking had gone astray.

It was when he finally started solving the problems correctly on his own—asking me for confirmation that his solutions were right, instead of directions on how to find the answers—that he relaxed.

I felt a ballooning in my chest. It was a familiar feeling—I had felt this way whenever Laura and I spent time together. The simple pleasure of enjoying an activity with someone else.

I hadn't really felt this way with my friends at school. That was really more of an arrangement of convenience, people to pass the time with. They were a faction, a squadron. We banded together for our mutual security. And even my friendship with Laura had dwindled over the last couple of years, I realized. I wondered when the last time had been that I'd actually had fun with someone I liked. Still, I'd never shared a moment like this over schoolwork with someone else. Before university, the better students, even the ones I was friendly with, had been unacknowledged rivals. Even then, no one I knew would ever admit to loving homework.

But here, now, with Adam, I felt a moment of deep kinship. It was like touching another human being, skin-to-skin, for the first time in years. Or ever. I felt my throat tighten a little, had to blink hard against the tears.

That's when I saw him looking at me. I saw the decision in his eyes. He leaned forward and kissed me, softly, on the mouth.

His body pulled toward mine, a gravitational force. No, electro-static, I reflected, feeling the sparking as his hands grasped my backside, pulling my hips to his.

We fucked on the rickety plastic chair I'd dragged in from the common room for him to sit on. He was already inside me when I pulled our shirts off, his then mine. It was clumsy; I remember murmured apologies, my elbow clipping his nose as I peeled our clothes away, our foreheads bumping together awkwardly as we leaned in for an ill-timed kiss, but it was intense and blissful, too.

I'd had sex before. My first week in the dorm, with a student who lived the floor above us and who seemed cuter in the dim lights of the residence party than he did the next day in the cafeteria. And before that, during my last year of high school, I'd had a boyfriend for a while. A convenient boy named Jason who'd found his way into our friend group the year before because he had a few classes with Stephanie. We kissed at lunchtime, watched movies in his parents' basement or mine, had urgent, inexpert sex a few times in the back of his parents' car. But it turned out that he and Stephanie had started making out after school just before Christmastime, and in January he broke up with me to date her. I was offended at the betrayal, of course, but not particularly bereft to lose him. It did make my social standing a little more precarious, though, and not just in our group of friends. I stopped going to school dances that winter.

I never asked if it was Adam's first time. I thought about the girlfriend at Acadia, and I guessed that you wouldn't decide to do a long-distance thing if you weren't either sleeping together or weirdly religious. But I didn't ask whether he'd broken up with her, or whether he intended to. And he never mentioned her again.

SEVEN

Adam and I dated all through university. A lot of our classmates moved into apartments in their second year, either with roommates or their girlfriends or boyfriends. Adam found an apartment a few blocks away from the university. It was the top floor of an old Victorian house. Each of the three floors had been divided up into three-bedroom apartments with one small bathroom each, a living room at the front of the building, an eat-in kitchen, and a narrow hallway that ran down the centre, connecting the string of rooms. He was living with two other Engineering students: two guys from China, Ping and Yanhua, and a student from Weymouth named Dennis.

Adam had met Ping and Yanhua in his first-year classes, and he'd played hockey against Dennis in high school. Their apartment was always tidy, but never clean. Each of them kept their books and clothes scrupulously put away on the shelves and dressers in their own bedrooms. Dishes were washed and stacked in the drainer next to the sink, though they seldom made it back into the cupboards. I doubted any of them owned a broom or mop, or that anyone had ever bought any kind of cleaning solution when they trekked to the grocery store at the end of the street, carrying their canned and frozen dinners and sugary cereals home in their backpacks.

Sometimes, when I spent the night, I'd catch Dennis, Ping, or Yanhua casting furtive looks between me and the overfull basket of dirty towels in the bathroom, or the kitchen stove.

No way.

I was still living in residence. I had to keep my own room tidy, but the cleaning staff came through twice a week to scrub the shared bathrooms and the common room, and once a week to vacuum the thin industrial carpets in the halls and bedrooms, and to swipe disinfectant over the little sinks and mirrors behind our doors. I had a meal plan and ate decent food prepared by the cooks in the cafeteria. I was not interested in taking care of these lost boys.

Most nights during the week, I stayed alone in my dorm and Adam stayed in his apartment. I often studied until late in the evening, and I appreciated the solitude to keep my marks up. But the weekends were always an uneasy compromise.

"My bed's bigger," Adam said, and it was true. But while I stuffed my sheets into one of the washing machines in the small laundry just off the common room every Monday, Adam's bed faintly carried the sharp scent of sweat and sex.

Near the end of our second year, Adam started to ask where I'd be living the next year. He always came at questions like that from the side.

"So," he said one day between classes. "So." We were sitting across from each other at a small table on campus. It was a common area fringed with a sandwich stand and a cheap coffee counter. Some of the tables were occupied by students chatting between classes, some were like ours—covered in books, the sites of impromptu study groups. At the end of our first year, Adam had chosen civil engineering, while I'd specialized in electrical. We didn't have any more classes together, but Adam remained in the habit of asking me for help whenever he didn't understand his assignments. And I didn't mind—it let me dip into his specialization, satisfying my academic curiosity.

He cleared his throat. "So," he said one more time.

"Oh my god, what?" I asked, setting down my pencil.

"So, I was wondering where you're going to live next year."

I shrugged. "Residence."

He nodded. "I was thinking about getting a smaller place. Fewer roommates."

"Good idea."

"So?" He cleared his throat, fiddling with the pencil I had just set down.

I looked at his face, feeling the way I often did with him—an ambivalent mix of irritation and indulgence. "So?" I repeated.

"So, you ever think of getting an apartment?"

"Not really," I replied. I knew where he was going, but I wasn't going to lead him there.

He let it alone for a day or two. Then as we sat on the couch in his apartment, takeout containers from the university cafeteria on our laps and a couple of glasses of cheap red wine on the chipped coffee table, he started again. "So."

"So."

"So, do you think you might want to…think about getting an apartment?"

"Eventually," I said.

"What about next year?" He reached over and took my hand, his fingers laced between mine. He kind of tugged at my fingers, then lifted it up to kiss my inner wrist. He knew I loved that.

I let go of my breath. It made the same kind of groaning noise my mom always made when she was about to say no. The sound—her sound in my throat—caught me off guard. "It seems like a lot of hassle," I said.

"I can find a place," he said quickly.

"Not just that. Like cooking and cleaning and stuff."

"We'll share the work."

I looked around his apartment dubiously. It was the end of the school year and all three roommates had lost their previous commitment to tidiness. We'd had to move a couple of T-shirts off the couch and a dirty plate and glass from the coffee table before we settled in.

He saw me looking. "Everyone thinks it's the other guys' mess," he explained. "No one wants to clean it up." He gave me one of his bright smiles: goofy, half-teasing, half-earnest. I pressed my body into his warm, lean frame, and wished that Yanhua weren't just down the hall, making his supper in the kitchen.

"It'd have to be a two-bedroom," I said at last.

He looked at me quizzically.

"We need an office, a place to work," I said.

His smile broadened. He took our Styrofoam containers and set them on the table and leaned over, kissing me hard.

I laughed. "Yanhua," I reminded him in a whisper, wishing I could just peel off my shirt and jeans right there. He grabbed my hand and pulled me up. He was already undoing his jeans as we ran down the hall to his room.

WE ENDED UP FINDING A ONE-BEDROOM-PLUS-DEN IN THE BASEMENT of a house in the North End. Adam didn't love the idea of a basement suite or having to buy a bus pass to get to campus, but he confined his objections to asking "Are you sure?" a half-dozen times. But the two-bedroom suites closer to the university were either out of our price range or in old houses in disrepair.

Adam's favourite was on the top floor of what looked like a converted church. It was the biggest apartment we looked at. A long set of wooden stairs led from the gravel driveway up to a small deck with a brown wooden door that opened onto a kitchen and eating area. Beyond, there was a small living room and a narrow hallway that angled around the bathroom on the other side of the wall, down three steps to a big bedroom that looked out onto the street.

"We could fit two desks in here, easy," Adam said. He looked appreciatively at the high ceiling and the wide window. It was the type of window you'd normally see in a living room—three-paned, no opening. Bedrooms were supposed to have an egress, I knew, a way of escape in case of fire. It was code. And in the bathroom, an ordinary electrical socket was mounted above the sink, not six inches from the counter. No ground fault interrupter—no security against electrocution. I hadn't seen a single smoke detector in the place, though there was a suspicious-looking circular mark in the paint of the crooked little hallway.

"No," I said flatly. "No way."

The basement suite was newer, its wiring and smoke detector and windows all unobjectionable. The landlord had even affixed a fire extinguisher to the wall in the corner of the kitchen, next to the fridge. This place was clean and neat, and I didn't have to worry about rats in the cupboard. Plus, the den gave us a space to set up two small desks, back-to-back.

AS SOON AS WE WERE MOVED IN, OUR APARTMENT FURNISHED WITH pieces from Value Village and Zellers, we invited my mom to come for a visit.

"I just saw you," she said over the phone. I could hear her thunk her glass down on the table.

It was true. I'd spent the summer at home. I'd gotten a decent-paying job at the town library and moved back into my old bedroom to save money. It hadn't been too bad. Much better than my first summer home.

That first summer, Mom had found out that Kyle was in Cold Lake. He was working a rig just out of town, and staying with a girl in one of the low brown apartment buildings along the highway on his days off.

We drove past that building on the way to the grocery store, and every time we went by I saw her glance at it, and felt the air in the car go sour. She'd be tense for hours afterward, poised to snap at me for a jacket left on the back of the dining room chair or a plate forgotten on the counter. It was like being a kid again, except that without Kyle at home, I knew that her bitterness would be aimed at me every time.

But my second summer home, Kyle was back to working the rigs in Fort McMurray, and unless someone in town happened to mention him, or unless Mom found something of his around the house—a photo, a sock under the couch—his presence never pressed on us at all to sour Mom's mood. And even though her voice would still sometimes go flat, her cold rage creeping throughout the house for an hour or two if I didn't keep up with whatever she'd decided was a fair share of the housework that particular day, she was mostly relaxed and easy. Easier than I'd never known her to be when I was growing up.

When she drove me to the airport in Edmonton that last week of August, she'd hugged me tight and said, "I can't wait to meet this Adam of yours. He sounds like a real good guy."

And so, when we bought a cheap futon for the study, I asked Adam if he'd mind if I invited Mom out for a visit.

Adam had looked startled, as though he'd suddenly discovered there was a quiz he hadn't studied for. "She's not gonna be freaked out about us?" he asked.

"What do you mean, us?"

"Like, living together."

I stared at him, trying to understand where this sudden panic was coming from. "She knows I live with you."

His eyes widened. "She does?"

"Of course," I said. Then the penny dropped. "Wait, don't your parents know?"

He shook his head quickly, vehemently, his hair falling back and forth across his forehead. "No. No way. No."

"What did you tell them?"

He looked down at his feet. There was a small hole forming in his right sock and he curled his toes under, as though to hide it from me. "I told them I got a two-bedroom apartment with another student." He looked back up at me. "Which is true."

I shook my head. "They're going to find out," I said. "Might as well tell them."

"I will," he said, his voice wavering just a bit.

MY MOM DIDN'T END UP COMING OUT TO VISIT, NOT THAT YEAR. I saw her again at Christmas. I was home for nearly two weeks. Every evening after supper, I'd call Adam, or he'd call me, and I'd retreat to my old bedroom so we could talk quietly. He told me about his parents' place in Wolfville, about holiday celebrations with his aunts and uncles and cousins.

"Who do your parents think you're talking to every night?" I asked.

"My girlfriend."

"They know about me?"

"Yeah," he said. "I showed them some pictures. They know you're the top student in our year."

"I'm not, though," I said. In fact, I was in the twelfth percentile, based on my academic results from the previous year.

"Close enough."

My mom tapped on my bedroom door then. I called for her to come in, but she just stood, smiling, in the doorway. "Say hi to Adam for me," she said.

We'd been having a great visit, she and I. She was softer than she'd ever been during my childhood. We went two weeks without any of her flat, heavy anger, and no more than a handful of sharp words. It occurred to me that this must be how other people my age were with their parents. No waiting for the inevitable yet unpredictable anger. No wondering what might set her off or bring out that icy disapproval. It was nice.

The truth was, she had started softening before I'd even finished high school. Except for that first summer when she'd learned Kyle was in town, things between her and me had been gradually easing. Not all at once—in fact, for at least a year after Kyle had left home, she was icy and brittle almost all the time. I felt like I lived in a perpetual state of high alert, never sure what would set her off—it could be a clump of mud that had stuck to my shoe and then let go, making a crumbling mess in the hall closet, or my coming home late on a Friday night, even though she'd never set me a firm curfew, or a tone of disrespect she heard in my voice when she called me up for supper and I told her I'd be there in a minute. Then, her voice would slide from a sharp command to a snarl, vicious and feral, her hand shaking as she jabbed at the air, pointing in the general direction of the infraction, whatever it was. One time, when I'd forgotten my promise to fold the clothes in the dryer, I remember thinking, This must have been what it was like for Kyle.

I imagined the relief he must have felt, being away from it all. Was that what he felt, though? Or was there guilt, too, when he thought of the rift? I'd never been able to figure out where his resentment ended and the regret began when it came to him and Mom.

He was halfway through grade eleven when he took off. He'd just turned seventeen. I was almost fourteen. Grade eight.

That year had been rougher than usual between them. There must have been some moments of detente, but I don't remember them. I only remember the unstable hostility—his resentment, her impatience—that broke all too often into shouting matches. Usually, he wouldn't actually shout. Her voice would rise up into its angry roar, and he would growl back at her. Most of the time, his face was averted from hers, his gaze on the TV or the window, his dinner plate, a plant in the corner, anything that wasn't her or me. But during their fights, he would lock eyes with her. His voice almost dropped in volume, as well as timbre, as he growled his rebuttals to her accusations—but his eyes: those, he raised. In them, I could see his anger was as hot as hers was cold.

One Saturday morning in January, I was still in bed. First-term report cards had gone home the day before. Kyle had thrown his on the kitchen counter. I'd turned it over, glancing at the barely passing marks. I wondered whether his leaving it there had been a provocation, or simple carelessness. I went out with my friends right after supper, staying out as late as I dared. When I got back, it was almost midnight, and the report card was still on the counter.

She must have found it the next morning, though. They were already fighting about it when I came out of my bedroom.

"I don't care," Kyle was muttering, his jaw tight, eyes locked on her. An open dare.

"How are you ever going to get into university? What school would have you?"

"I'm not going to university."

"The hell you're not," she shouted. "Do you think I worked and sacrificed for you to be *nothing*?"

"Right. I'm nothing. What are your friends gonna think?"

"At this rate, you won't even get into trade school, and do you know what they'll think? They'll think I'm just another trashy single mom who can't take care of her kids. Is that what you want?"

"Are you stupid?" By now, Kyle really was raising his voice. He was almost shouting. I don't think I'd heard him shout in anger since we were little—and certainly never *at* Mom. I felt frozen in the middle of the hall, halfway between my bedroom and the bathroom. I felt my heart hammering away and the heat rising up my neck and into my face, as though I were the one shouting, as though Mom's rage were directed at me, not him.

"What did you say?" Mom roared back at him.

"I said, are you stupid? I've been telling you forever that I'm not going to university or college or trade school. As soon as I graduate, I'm getting a job and I'm moving out."

"Where?" she scoffed. "Where are you going to live on a high school–graduate salary?"

"As far as I can away from you!"

Mom raised her hand. He didn't blink, didn't move. It felt like forever, but they just stood there, frozen, it seemed—her, poised to strike and him, daring her to.

Finally, he barrelled past her. He grabbed his parka and stuffed his feet into his running shoes. I felt the walls shudder as he slammed the door behind him.

Her arm sank slowly, her body still wound up with the tension of the blow that never fell. Before her hand reached her side, I slipped into the bathroom and locked the door.

I waited until I heard her going down to the basement to do laundry, just as she did every Saturday morning. I quickly dressed and pulled my hair into a low ponytail.

"I'm going to Laura's," I called before I slipped out the back door. She called up a question in reply. I wasn't sure what she said, but I pretended not to hear her, walking away from the house as quickly as I could.

It was cold. Really cold. The trees were still coated in hoarfrost—an intricate sculpture of ice crystals clinging to every branch and glittering in the weak winter sun. It was beautiful and ominous. When you saw hoarfrost, you know the day would be biting. I hadn't grabbed my mittens or hat, and before too long, the tips of my ears, my knuckles, and my fingertips were burning cold. I pulled my hands into my coat sleeves and pressed them to my ears, wondering where Kyle had gone and whether he'd dressed any better for the weather than I had.

Laura and Nadine were only a little surprised to see me. Up until a year or so before, Laura and I had frequently turned up on each other's doorsteps, especially on weekends. These days, we tended to spend more evenings together, but it wasn't all that unusual for me to drop in.

"You're just in time," Nadine said. "Pancakes are ready."

If we had pancakes at home, I cooked them. Mom never bought instant mix, so they were homemade. I much preferred Nadine's from-a-box variety. They were lighter, fluffier than my own. Laura and I each had four.

We were just clearing our plates away when Laura's dad emerged from the bedroom. Laura and Nadine were in their slippers, but Mr. Clayton was already dressed in tan slacks and a blue golf shirt. "Nice to see you, Jessica," he said, as though he were expecting to find me in his kitchen.

I followed Laura to her bedroom. Even though she would be fourteen on her next birthday, her bed was still covered with her "guys," the massive collection of stuffed animals. I knew from years of sleeping over that she had a nightly ritual, carefully setting them, one by one, on the narrow patch of carpet between the foot of her bed and the wall. Only the worn, patchy-furred bunny, Hoppy, stayed with her while she slept. Whenever I stayed the night, she'd pull the camp mattress out from under her single bed and I'd sleep next to her. In the morning, as soon as she got up, she'd make her bed and I'd hand her the guys, one by one, as she placed them carefully on her bedspread.

Now, she shifted them over to make a spot to sit. I sat where I always did, on the floor between the door and the dresser. It was comfortable to lean up against the white-painted wood.

"Your mom and Kyle?" Laura asked.

86

"Yup," I replied. "Bad one."

"Sucks," Laura said.

"Sucks," I agreed.

I called Mom to tell her I'd be staying the night at Laura's.

"You know, I'd like a little more notice," Mom snapped.

"Sorry."

"Don't you need an overnight bag?"

"No, I'm good," I said.

"Fine. Be back in time to get your homework done."

"I will."

"*All* of it," she barked. As though she needed to remind me.

"I will," I said again.

"Let's go rent a movie," Laura suggested as I hung up the phone. She lent me mittens and a hat, and we walked down to the Blockbuster. We rented a handful of movies and stayed up past midnight watching them. Laura's parents joined us for the first couple, a romantic comedy and a cop movie. Nadine made us all popcorn served in small matching plastic bowls. After they went to bed, Laura stayed up with me to watch a horror film I'd been looking forward to, one that was just released on VHS, even though she hated horror. We watched a Disney cartoon before we went to bed so she wouldn't have nightmares. It was nice, except the tiny pit in the bottom of my belly every time I thought about going home.

EIGHT

I don't know when Kyle came back to the house, or whether he and Mom fought again, or where he told her he was going. I don't know if she tried to stop him. I only know that by the time I got home on Sunday, he was gone. Really gone.

The house was eerily still when I came through the front door. If the car hadn't been in the driveway, I would have assumed Mom had gone out. I slipped down the hallway toward my room. I stopped on my way past Kyle's room. His bed was stripped, the mattress and the pillows bare. Even the comforter was gone. It was strange—Mom always washed the bedsheets on Sunday, it's true, but as soon as she stripped the bed, she'd take a clean set of sheets out of the linen closet and lay them on top of the comforter. It was our job to re-make our beds.

I checked my room. Clean, folded sheets sat on top of the comforter, which was neatly folded down to the foot of the bed.

I went back to Kyle's room. That's when I noticed how spare it looked. Usually, you'd find a pair of clean-enough jeans draped over his desk chair, a hat on the bedpost. But there was nothing, no clothes anywhere. And the top of the dresser looked emptier than usual. I couldn't pinpoint what, exactly, was missing, but I was sure there had been more stuff there before. A chunk of uneasiness, hard and heavy, was forming in my chest.

I made my way downstairs.

Mom was in the laundry room, folding Kyle's clean sheets. Behind her, something bulky was tumbling in the dryer.

"Homework," she snapped by way of greeting.

"I was just about to start." I didn't want to ask, didn't want to crack open her brittle rage, but I had to. "Where's Kyle?"

She gave a kind of half-laugh, bitter and sharp. "Oh, he'll be back soon."

I hesitated. I knew better than to push it… "Okay, but where *is* he?"

She gave the fitted sheet a hard shake, snapping it in the air between us.

"Homework. Now."

I went back upstairs to gather my schoolbooks. I pulled open the hall closet. Kyle's winter boots were gone, and his sneakers. His parka, his favourite corduroy bomber jacket, not warm enough for the January weather, both gone.

I sat at the dining room table and tried to focus on my chemistry assignment. I heard Mom stomping around in the basement, rage-cleaning.

At dinnertime, she dumped some canned spaghetti sauce into a pot on the stove. She under-cooked the noodles, leaving them stiff and a bit crunchy. She only pulled two plates out of the cupboard. We ate in silence, then I stood to clear the plates and wash the pots.

Kyle didn't come home that night. In fact, he didn't come home at all. At dinner on Monday I tried asking my mom again where he was, but she just glared at me and told me to mind my own business. She slouched around the house, her anger palpable, and I did my best to stay out of her way.

Wednesday, Janet came by for a drink after school. I stayed in my room but cracked my door to listen to their conversation. That's how I learned where Kyle had gone.

"He's working on an oil rig in Fort Mac," my mom said, sounding as though she were biting through every word. "Can you believe it? What kind of outfit would hire a seventeen-year-old boy?"

"Lots of jobs up there for anyone strong enough to work them."

My mom laughed, a bitter, derisive little bark. "Just wait and see how long he lasts. Work ethic has never been his strong suit."

Janet made a sympathetic noise. I heard the hiss of the pop bottle opening as Mom poured them both another drink.

HE DID LAST, THOUGH. HE STARTED OFF AS A LABOURER, WORKING up in one of the camps in northern Alberta. His days off, he stayed with his friend Devon, and Devon's father, in their small house in Cold Lake. They both worked the oilfield—Devon since he'd graduated a year and a half earlier. I ran into Kyle coming out of a fast food place a few weeks after he'd left.

"Hey." He gave me a bit of a smile.

The smile made me mad. What was there to smile about. "Where've you been?" God, I sounded like Mom.

"Working," he said. "I make good money, too."

"Great," I said. "Meanwhile, I'm stuck with Mom and her shitty temper."

His smile faded. He looked down at the grease-stained paper bag in his hand. "Not much I can do about that."

"Thanks a lot," I muttered, pushing past him on the sidewalk.

The next time I saw him, spring was just arriving in all its muddy, dog-shit-smelling glory. I was walking home after school. A slightly battered-looking blue pickup pulled up next to me. I tensed. But the driver's window rolled down, and I recognized his voice.

"Get in," he said. "I'll drive you home."

I stared at him. "Whose truck is that?" I asked.

He was grinning. "Mine."

I got in, even though I was only a block or so from home. He cranked up the stereo, blasting Metallica for the half-minute drive to the house. Mom's car wasn't in the driveway yet. He pulled up front and put it in park, but didn't cut the engine. "You coming in?" I asked.

He shook his head. The grin was gone now. "Nope."

"You should try to talk to her."

He frowned. "She should try to talk to me."

We sat for a minute, not saying anything. Then he forced a smile. "She still do the vacuum thing?"

I smiled back, even though it wasn't funny. In fact, I could feel a wobbling in my chest that threatened to turn into weeping if I let it.

Whenever Mom was mad at us, really mad, and not ready to let it go, she'd vacuum—either late at night or early in the morning. She wouldn't come into our bedrooms, but she'd ram the heavy, noisy machine up against our closed doors as she went over and over and over the hall carpet. If we dared tell her we were trying to sleep, she'd snap that it *must be nice* to have time to sleep, not to have housework to do. As though normal people did housework at five in the morning.

"Yeah," I said, even though it wasn't true. She hadn't done the vacuum thing since Kyle had left.

He gave a kind of half-laugh. It sounded like a sniff, really. I could tell it was forced.

I opened the door. "Thanks for the ride," I said. I waited a second for him to answer, but he didn't say anything. As he drove away, he stuck his hand out the window, a half-wave goodbye.

But he did come by again the next evening. Mom was browning hamburger and onions for meatloaf and I was sitting at the table doing my homework. We heard footfalls on the back stairs, and Mom went to see who was at the door. I figured it was Janet, so I didn't look up until I heard his voice.

"Hi, Mom."

She was standing in the doorway, one hand against the door frame, the other on the handle, as though she were blocking him from coming in. "Are you back for good?" she asked.

"Just wanted to see how you were doing," he said. His voice was unusually soft. I tried to remember the last time he'd spoken to her without a sullen edge to his words.

"I take it that means no."

"I'm back to work tomorrow," he said.

"And how long are you going to keep this up?" Her voice was flat, the same way it always was just before it rose in anger.

"It's a good job," he replied. "I make good money."

91

"Sure," she scoffed. "I bet they're willing to pay high school drop-outs a lot of money."

There was a silence. I could feel him weighing his words, deciding whether or not to snap back at her. I thought he would. He usually did, and before you knew it they'd be all-out snarling at each other. Not this time, though. Instead, he just called, "See you, Jess" over his shoulder. Then, in a flat, heavy voice, "Bye, Mom." And he was gone.

He kept working up on the oil rigs. As he got to know the equipment, he went from a labourer to a driver. Whenever he came back on his days off, he'd manage to find me in town. Usually, he'd pick me up in his truck and we'd drive a bit, not saying much, before he finally dropped me off again.

Before I finished high school, though, Kyle stopped coming back to town. He and Devon rented an apartment in the north end of Edmonton, and that's where he'd spend his days off. He called me every few weeks or so, always right after school when he knew Mom wouldn't be home yet. We usually talked about his job, or the money he was making, what he was saving for. He wanted to buy a new truck, then a snowmobile, and eventually a townhouse of his own.

Mom and I didn't talk about Kyle. In fact, I don't think she talked about him at all, with anyone. I'm certain she didn't talk *to* him. And the first few weeks after he left, she was a simmering rage, ready to erupt at the slightest provocation. Whenever I was home, I felt constantly on my guard, always ready for her bursts of temper. But after a time, things eased between us.

One afternoon, a month or so after Kyle left, Mom got home early from school. I'd just arrived home myself, and at the sound of her boots on the stairs, my guts plummeted. I rushed to the porch to put away my coat and backpack before she had a chance to snipe at me for leaving them in the middle of the floor.

"Come on, get in the car," Mom said.

I froze, my coat in one hand, backpack in the other. "Where are we going?"

"It's a surprise."

It's a trap, replied some dark part of my brain. But I tucked my bag away in the closet and slipped my jacket and shoes back on and followed her to the car.

She took me to the optometrist's, a little converted house just off main street. The receptionist smiled when we came in, and I took a seat in the waiting room, once the living room, back when this was a proper house.

After a moment, Dr. Edstrom, the optometrist came out. "Good to see you, Jessica," she said, smiling. She held out her arm, guiding me back into her office. Mom followed me, carrying both of our coats over her arm.

"Well, then," Dr. Edstrom said as I steeled into the chair. "Contact lenses, is it?"

"Um?" I looked at my mom for confirmation. She nodded, smiling. "Yes?"

Dr. Edstrom tested my vision, even though I'd just had my regular checkup a few months before. She fitted me for a pair of lenses.

"Tint?" she asked as she finished up.

I looked at my mom again. It was hard to predict what she'd find objectionable, in poor taste. But she just smiled and raised her hands, a magnanimous gesture. "Up to you, Jess."

"Can I have green?" I asked.

"You can have green," Dr. Edstrom replied.

"Thanks," I said.

My mom beamed.

As we drove home, I thanked her again. "I did not expect that," I said.

"You look so pretty when you're not hiding behind that hair and those big dowdy glasses," she said. "It's about time you start letting people see your face."

"Okay," I said, afraid she'd press me to get a haircut, too. She'd often urged me to try bangs over the years. Thankfully, she didn't that day. I showed my appreciation by pulling the front of my hair back every day for the rest of the week in the little butterfly clips she'd bought me a while ago that I hadn't yet used.

Without Kyle at home, Mom's anger eased. She seldom raised her voice anymore, and even when I left dirty dishes on the counter, or came home later than she expected, or wore the Beastie Boys T-shirt she hated to school, she'd restrain herself to snapping at me. It was nice, actually. I felt at ease at home in a way I never had before. But I knew that it was because Kyle was gone, and I felt guilty, as though I were betraying him by enjoying his rift with our mom.

I MET ADAM'S PARENTS WHEN I GOT BACK TO HALIFAX AFTER THE Christmas break in our third year of university. I flew in January second, but there were a few days before the new term started. Adam's parents drove him back from Wolfville, where he'd spent the holidays with them. They were staying overnight in a hotel downtown before driving back, and they invited us both to have supper there with them.

Adam buzzed around the apartment nervously as I got ready. I was wearing a dress printed with burgundy velvet roses. The material was warm and stretchy and relatively comfortable. It was nice, but not too fussy. He watched as I pulled it on and gave a quick, nodding approval. The gesture irritated me, as though he had final say on my outfit. I half wanted to change into jeans and my favourite sweater, which was starting to sag a little at the elbows. But I didn't.

I'd never really done the meet-the-parents thing before. I'd always known my high school boyfriend Jason's parents—they owned a pizza place in Grand Centre. Jason had never taken me to dinner with them, though whenever we did go to the restaurant to eat with friends, his mom or dad would pull a chair over and sit for a moment at the end of our table, asking us about our plans for the evening.

This was different. Watching Adam buzz around me as I got ready, I wondered whether I *should* feel nervous. I didn't, though. Adults usually liked me—a byproduct of being a good student.

Dinner went well. Adam's parents had what I'd come to recognize as small-town manners: they smiled a lot, but they didn't reach out to shake my hand or hug me. They told me to call them by their first names, Gayle and Gary. They said all the ordinary polite things: "It's so nice to meet you"; "I've heard so much about you"; "Adam never told us how pretty you are." Gayle was just a little too imperious to the waiter, almost rude. She demanded a glass of white wine, rather than ask for one, and she never looked him in the face or said "please," though she did give him a perfunctory "thank you" when he brought her drink, and later, her meal. Gary made a show of looking over the menu carefully, as though his practiced eye might detect a lapse in quality. My mom would love them, I realized. They would seem to her the epitome of good breeding.

Adam's nervousness never really subsided. I started to feel bad for him. I kept catching him watching me, as though I might—what? I'm not sure what kind of faux-pas he was expecting from me. The evening did get a little dicey when Gayle asked me about my living arrangement.

"Do you like living in residence, Jessica?"

"I did," I replied, spearing a small bite of pan-seared Atlantic salmon. "I'm in an apartment this year."

"On your own?" Gayle asked.

"With a roommate."

I watched an uncomfortable flush colour Adam's cheeks, but thankfully for him, Gary changed the subject, asking me about school. I told him about the power systems course I was taking that term, and we floundered a bit, trying to find common ground—Gary was an electrician. In fact, he owned a residential electrical company. I discovered that his technical knowledge was rusty, and did my best to lead the conversation back toward his business. But he seemed genuinely interested in my studies. He kept asking Adam whether he understood power systems, and Adam would remind him he was studying civil engineering, not electrical. Gayle, for her part, kept trying to pull Adam into the conversation by asking him about his classes, but neither Adam nor Gary were particularly interested, so we talked mainly about my studies.

"That's a real smart gal," Gary said as Adam hugged his parents goodbye in the hotel lobby. "You're going to have to work hard to keep up with her."

"A boy as smart as our Adam can keep up just fine," Gayle said, folding Adam into a tight hug.

Gary shook my hand and clapped me on the shoulder and Gayle pulled me in for a quick, loose hug.

"They really like you," Adam said, his body exuding relief as we walked home.

"That's good," I said carefully. Until he said that, I hadn't realized that he'd worried they might not. I felt unnerved, as though there had been a ticking bomb in the corner that I hadn't noticed all throughout dinner.

He stopped me on the sidewalk and pulled me in for a long kiss. He wasn't usually one for public affection. In truth, I wasn't either, but this was nice.

"I like them, too," I lied.

He twined his fingers around mine and we walked home, taking our time and enjoying the unseasonably warm, dry evening.

NINE

Freya wakes me at seven, calling out to me in a little voice. I bolt out of bed, feeling a flush of guilt at letting myself fall so deeply asleep. I didn't think I'd slept—it felt like I was awake every few minutes—but I must have.

Ever since she was a baby, Freya has been able to jog me wide awake with the tiniest sound. Even when she cries out in her sleep, I feel as though I've received a jolt of electricity right to my core. I'm wide awake, listening for the next sound, poised to dart to her room.

This morning, though, I don't wait. I'm out of bed and at her bedroom door in two steps; I push it open slowly so as not to startle her.

"How are you feeling?"

"It hurts," she whimpers, suddenly looking much younger than her nine years.

"I know, sweetie," I say. "We'll get you some medicine."

"I have to pee."

I help her up, holding on to her on her right side so I don't accidentally bump against the incision. She leans against me and we shuffle slowly to the bathroom, trying not to jolt her or put any weight on her left leg.

When we get to the toilet she pauses for a second, and I can tell she wants to do this on her own, but she can't. I help her, holding her clothes gingerly away from the surgical dressings. Afterward, I help her over to the sink to wash her hands.

She looks at me in the mirror. There are hollows under her eyes. I can see the pain in her face. "Can you carry me?" she asks, her voice tiny.

I scoop her up carefully, making sure not to touch the dressings. She leans her head into my shoulder, and I wonder when she last did that. I press a kiss into her hair set her down in a kitchen chair.

She says she's not hungry, but she hasn't eaten in over a day. She had to fast before the surgery. Was it only a day ago she was complaining about wanting some cereal, telling me in her growling pre-teen voice how hungry she was?

Her painkillers have to be taken on a full stomach, though, so I get her a glass of orange juice and a piece of toast with butter and honey. She has her snack in little sips and bites. "Thank you, Mom," she says as she pushes the plate away, a couple of crusts left behind. I'm touched. She's never been great at remembering her manners unbidden.

I hear my phone buzz. It's on the coffee table, where I left it last night. I try to suppress the irritation that bubbles up. It's only natural that Adam would want to know how she is, I remind myself.

"Do you feel like talking to your dad?" I ask. "Let him know how you're doing?"

She nods quickly.

This time, when I pick her up, she stiffens and whimpers. "Sorry, I'm sorry," I say, shifting her carefully in my arms. I set her down on the couch. She pulls a blanket over her legs as I dial Adam.

"Here," I say, handing the phone to her before he has a chance to answer.

"Hi, Daddy," she says, and her face lights up with a soft smile. I try not to feel hurt or jealous that he can always bring that kind of joy out in her when she and I spend so much time sniping at each other.

I should call Kyle, I think as I head back to the kitchen to make some toast and coffee for myself. He'll want to know how she's doing.

NEITHER ADAM NOR I WENT HOME THAT THIRD SUMMER. I WAS DOING a work term with the local power company and Adam was retaking a couple of his winter courses. He'd managed to tell his parents the truth about our living situation in April.

"Jess and I are living together," he'd slipped into the middle of a phone conversation. There was a pause as his mom or dad asked him something. Then he said, "We moved in together this year." There was another pause, then a "Yeah, yeah," before he started talking about his summer classes. He didn't mention he was taking them because he'd failed the first time.

We stayed in our apartment that year, our last of university. Then we graduated the following spring, earning our iron rings to symbolize our responsibility as engineers. Adam was worried he'd have to retake his geotechnical engineering course, but he managed to scrape by with a C-.

I got a job at Maritime Energy, the regional power company. Every year, they invited graduates of the engineering program to apply for junior engineer positions. I sent in my résumé and my transcripts, and the following week, they invited me to their downtown Halifax offices for an interview. I brought a copy of my senior project on microcontroller-based control systems for vapour-detection devices. The professor had given me an A. He pulled me aside after class to tell me that he never assigned A+ on principle, but that if he did, my project would have earned me one. I smiled tightly, wondering if he'd told the same thing to the guys in my class.

I went shopping the week before my job interview, putting a few things on the credit card I'd applied for back in my first year but seldom used. I hated the idea of debt, but my student loans had all but run out and I had only been able to work part-time the previous summer, reshelving books in the library, since the work placement (for which I got academic credit, but not a paycheque) took up most of my time. Still, work clothes seemed like a good investment. I picked out a grey knee-length skirt and a pair of dress pants. I figured that if I bought a blazer, a couple of blouses and sweaters, I'd have a full week's worth of outfits. I could buy more once I got a job.

"Fancy," Adam teased me as I hung the clothes up in my closet.

"Aren't you going to buy a new interview outfit?" I asked him.

"I have a suit," he said, gesturing to the black polyester number he'd had since high school. He was in the midst of what would turn out to be a final growth spurt—he wouldn't reach his full height of almost 5'9 until a year later. Already, his ankle and wrist bones protruded from the cheap suit material. He caught me staring at it in our closet. "They're not hiring us to be pretty, Jess."

I never got a chance to talk about my control system project at the job interview. The interviewer was the senior manager in charge of the Risk and Compliance Group. He started by asking me about my program choice.

"Most girls choose chemical and materials engineering, or else civil," he said. "What made you pick electrical?"

I felt my mouth clench around the word *girls* and forced a smile. "I'm interested in control systems," I said, gesturing at the copy of my report, which sat under his coffee cup on the desk between us. "I'd like to work on control systems in power plants." In truth, I wished I could have worked in the control room of power plants decades ago—the huge generator boards and turbines, the indicator panels and strip chart recorders. The army of technical workers monitoring the manual control stations. Not that I didn't like the newer, streamlined computerized systems. I did. They were certainly safer, and there was a much smaller margin for human error. If Chernobyl had had an automated control system governed by state-of-the-art software, people would still be living in Pripyat officially, swimming in the pool, riding the Ferris wheel, and visiting their dead parents and grandparents in the cemetery. And in fact, the nuclear meltdown at Three Mile Island had been a driving force behind the newer, digital systems, which reduced the possibility of human error and ensured that all systems—even those less likely to experience failures—were continuously monitored.

I started to tell the interviewer (his name was Douglas Johnson) about my interest in averting accidents through an elegantly designed, meticulously monitored and maintained control system, but he was already on to his next question.

He leaned back in his chair. The sunlight from the window behind him caught his thinning light-brown hair, illuminating his pink scalp.

"With your marks, you could be in a graduate program," he said.

"I might go back for a Master of Engineering someday," I said. "But I want to get some career experience first."

"What about an MBA?" he asked.

"Uh." I was caught off guard. Had he mixed up my résumé with someone else's? "I don't…"

He waved off my floundering response. "Have you considered going back to get an MBA?"

"No…why?" I'd practiced for this interview, researching all the types of questions an employer was likely to ask an engineer-in-training. I'd practiced responses for each one. I was even ready to tell him which graduate engineering programs interested me most. But was I even interested in an MBA? This was a question that hadn't been listed on any of the websites or pamphlets from the university's Career Development office. Was this how Adam felt when he wrote an exam, I wondered.

Douglas gestured at me, a sweeping motion that began at my black leather ballet flats and ended at my side-parted low ponytail. "You're put together, Jessica. You're very nice-looking, you're well-spoken, you have a very professional demeanour. You're the kind of engineer I can put in a room with a client. People like you don't come around very often. With an MBA, you could have my job in under ten years. Is that the kind of career move that would interest you?"

"I hadn't really thought about it," I replied. "What I'm really interested in is the work, you know. The engineering, the design and implementation."

"Sure," he said. "You have to get to know the process before you can sell it to the client. I respect that. Still, consider it."

"Okay," I said, even though I wouldn't. "Thanks."

As I walked to the bus stop, the anger flared within me. He hadn't even *looked* at my report. He hadn't asked me for my transcripts, or talked about my technical competencies. If he wanted someone with an MBA, why had he bothered to interview me at all? What a waste of time.

I sat at the back of the bus, feeling my anger simmer to a dark self-pity. Was that what employers needed now—a business degree, on top of an engineering degree? I wasn't even all that sure I wanted to go to graduate school. I meant what I'd said: I was eager to get to work, get real-world experience. I was done with the theoretical world of university. I wanted to delve into the things I'd studied, to turn my high marks into something real, something that marked the world, making something that people did or used better, safer, more practical in some way. Was I going to have to go back to school before I even had a chance at a decent job?

I trudged into our apartment to find that Adam had decided to surprise me with a celebratory lunch. He'd made grilled cheese sandwiches, and the kind of herbed tomato soup that comes from the deli fridge instead of the canned food aisle of the grocery store. Even though it was the middle of the day, he'd put a handful of tea lights on a side plate in the centre of the kitchen table. He handed me a bouquet of multicoloured daisies as I came through the door.

"Congratulations on your first interview!"

"A little premature," I grumbled. His face fell, and I immediately felt bad. "But thank you."

"You'll get the job," he said as he led me to the table. "I know you will."

"I won't," I replied, then added, "but thank you" again.

Adam had just been hired as a warehouse labourer for a heavy equipment–supply company. He was hoping to make some engineer and construction contractor contacts there. He'd be starting work on Monday.

Over lunch, I asked him how he'd manage to start those conversations. "Are you just going to walk up to the first engineer who comes in the door and ask, 'Are you hiring any junior engineers?'"

"Sure," he said. "Why not?"

He looked so sweet and hopeful, it made me smile. And he probably would, wouldn't he, I thought.

Late the following afternoon, just before dinner, Douglas Johnson called the apartment. Adam answered, and when he handed the phone over to me his eyebrows were raised in excitement.

"Jessica, I want to offer you a position. I'd like to see what you can do on the job."

"What kind of work would I be doing?" I asked, imaging myself in a control room of a power plant, making notes on the systems, designing upgrades and streamlining processes. I felt a tingle in my hands, an eagerness to delve into the guts of a system.

"We need some folks on a coal-fired power plant retrofit to start," he said.

"Coal?" I felt a sinking disappointment. I wanted to work on cutting-edge plants—nuclear, geothermal, solar and wind. Coal plants were dinosaurs.

"Up in Amherst," he said, naming a small town near the New Brunswick border.

"Amherst?" I repeated. That was nearly a two-hour drive away.

"We'll give you a living stipend. Some of the guys stay in a motel near the plant, a couple others got in together on an apartment. Your call."

Adam sat next to me on the couch, grinning like a fool, nearly vibrating with excitement. I tried to give him a little smile, even though this was not at all what I'd been hoping for.

"Anyway," Douglas continued, "you can come into the office Monday morning and we'll get you all set up. Have you out at the plant by the beginning of next month. Sound good?"

"Sounds good," I said. It didn't.

"Great. Glad to have you on board."

After he hung up, I realized that I hadn't thanked him. Nor had I explicitly accepted the job offer, or even asked about salary.

Adam gave an excited *whoop* and threw his arms in the air before he planted a big kiss on my lips. "I knew you'd get it!" he said.

I smiled, trying to feel excited about the job. After all, some of our classmates who graduated the year before were still looking for work. And who knew how long Adam would be at the labourer job. I was lucky, wasn't I?

TEN

I was assigned a small desk in a two-person cubicle in the Halifax office. Another junior engineer sat at the other desk. He had dark eyes and longish black hair that grazed his collar, but not in an unkempt way—he looked like he might be a college rocker, the kind of guy who might play an electric guitar in a three-piece band that played mostly ballads. His name was Yash.

I could tell that Yash wasn't thrilled at sharing the tiny workspace, but he was gracious about it. He smiled and shook my hand when Douglas introduced us, then helped me move my desk over a bit so we could both sit comfortably without bumping into each other. But I wouldn't be there long, anyway. As Douglas had promised, I was soon getting packed up and ready to work on retrofitting a dinosaur of a power plant whose mere existence was a blight on everything I'd ever hoped for in my career.

In the weeks before I left for Amherst, I hadn't really planned on getting settled into the office in Halifax. I didn't bother putting photos or inspirational posters in my cubicle, the way most of my coworkers did. After all, I wouldn't be spending much time there. And anyway, this was work. I didn't need pictures of Adam or trinkets to distract me.

There was a woman about my age, Esmé, who was interning in PR, though, and who seemed to take my stark workplace as a personal affront.

"You're giving me second-hand depression," she said, her *e*s and *r*s belying an Edinburgh accent.

"Well, you don't have to look," I replied, peering at a technical report on my computer screen.

"Hard to look away," she replied tartly.

The next day, just before lunch, she plunked a nobby-looking little succulent in a bright orange ceramic pot on my desk. "There," she said, sounding very satisfied with herself.

"It's going to die," I said, nudging it toward the corner, out of the way.

"Don't fucking let it, then."

I laughed, despite myself.

Of course, the plant died while I was working in Amherst. It took me a long time to throw it out, the bright orange pot with its desiccated corpse inside making me feel a vague guilt and happiness all at once.

Douglas gave me the numbers of some of the guys who were renting an apartment together, but I remembered Ping, Dennis, and Yanhua, and how they'd look longingly at me every time their kitchen sink filled up with dirty dishes. I realized I'd never had a female roommate. I wondered what it would be like to share an apartment with Esmé. Or Laura. I thought of the few girls in my program at university. I'd viewed them as competitive, unfriendly. I wondered now if that had been true, or if that was how they'd seen me.

I chose the motel. And it was there I did most of my work, setting up my laptop at the tiny desk near the window. I'd head over to the power plant almost every morning, and the project lead, a balding, middle-aged senior engineer named Sam who didn't like to use any more words than he absolutely had to, would brief me on the progress, then send me back to my office/motel room with my assignment for the day.

The first time I met Sam, I could see his disappointment at being saddled with me as his junior engineer. It was my first morning in Amherst; I'd driven up from Halifax the night before in a sedan I bought from a used car dealer in the North End the week before. Sam met me at the front gate. He was wearing a light blue short-sleeved dress shirt with a dark-blue tie. I immediately recognized him as the kind of engineer who still wore ties he'd bought two decades earlier but would be shocked to discover that his wardrobe was outmoded.

I pulled up to the gate and rolled down my window.

"You Jessica Manchaky?" he asked.

"Who else would I be?" I heard the tone after the words left my mouth and I forced what I hoped was a light-hearted smile as I held out my ID.

"Hmm." He shifted his gaze from my face to my car, taking in the silver-grey paint edged in rust, the long, boxy frame, the sagging uphol-stery of the back seat. "Okay, then. Park over there," he said, gesturing to a row of spaces on the other side of the gate. He gave the guard a little wave, and I pulled forward to sign in before I parked my car and officially started the first day on site.

A CONTROL SYSTEM'S JOB IS TO MONITOR AND REGULATE HOW EACH of the components in any given system work. It's the conductor of an orchestra, the commander of a starship. A power plant's control system regulates the boiler, turbine, generator, and all of their auxiliary systems. It keeps the plant from melting down, and it keeps the electricity flowing.

The Cumberland Generating Station began operating in 1981. It was built in response to the soaring oil prices of the 1970s. To keep the cost of electricity low, the province of Nova Scotia decided to put its massive underground coal stores to immediate use, building a handful of new coal-fired power plants. It used a Japanese-designed distributed control system, or DCS, which relied on a network of autonomous con-trol systems to monitor each component of the generating station. Like earlier, non-computerized control rooms, the control and monitoring of each system was centralized in a single room, but unlike pre-DCS control systems, digitization allowed operators to monitor and operate several systems from a fixed point. Computer screens had replaced the panels and switches that required operators to be stationed around the control room to monitor each component. But if computerized DCS control systems were cutting-edge in the 1980s, by 2000, they had fallen far behind. The new supervisory control and data acquisition (SCADA) systems could connect to all of the systems in a plant and monitor them remotely; they could connect all of the discrete components of a control system, even allowing those from different manufacturers to communicate with each other. SCADA systems were allowing power plants to take a leap forward in reliability, efficiency, and security.

As a student, I'd dreamed of getting the chance to work in a pre-DCS control room. There was a romance to the workers keeping a watchful eye on the displays and manually operating the switches and panels. I imagined there would be something intrepid about modernizing those systems, moving them into the digital era. But there was nothing romantic about the 1980s-era DCS technology—patched here and there with a more recent computerized component—of the Cumberland control room. There was a faintly musty smell to the cinder-block-walled, windowless space. Even the furniture was outdated, the chair upholstery worn and snagged, and the wood veneers of the desks cracked and peeling. I imagined that even Sam held open the door for me with an air of faint defeat. Though, he might perhaps still have been reeling in his evident disappointment with me.

"How old are you?" he'd asked as we walked down the brown-tiled hallway toward the control room.

"I graduated this spring," I replied. Let him do the math.

"Welcome to Cumberland," he'd said, opening the door to give me my first view of the control systems I'd be working to modernize.

I'd worn my dress pants and a blouse that day, and my slip-on flats. On the drive up, I'd wondered whether I should have bought some pumps. Would heels make me seem more professional, I'd wondered, or would they serve as a bright neon sign announcing *Lady Engineer on Site?* I was glad I hadn't. Sam and I were the most dressed-up people in the plant that day. He was the only one with a tie, and the only woman I saw was a janitor wearing coveralls as she mopped the hallways.

We walked a lot that day. Sam toured me around the plant, walking briskly as he pointed out the turbines, generators, and electrostatic precipitators.

Sam was staying at the motel too. We made a plan to meet at the plant each morning, then use our rooms as offices to work for the rest of the day. Space in the power plant was cramped, with no dedicated offices for the members of the retrofit team. He made no mention of the possibility of carpooling between the plant and the motel, and I certainly didn't bring it up.

That first night I sat in my motel bed, a crime show keeping me company, and called Adam. I'd spent my whole first paycheque and dipped into my credit card funds to buy myself a car, a cellphone, and my work clothes just before I'd left for Amherst. Things I needed to show my employers and their clients I was a proper grownup. The small phone felt strange in my hand. I'd never had one of my own before.

Adam answered on the first ring. "So, how is it?"

"Good."

"Yeah?"

"Yeah." I could hear the TV on in the background where he was. Home. Our apartment. It was a sitcom—I could tell by the laugh track.

"You still coming back for the weekend?"

"Why, you make other plans already?" It came out sounding a lot more bitter than I'd intended.

"No, no. I just miss you."

I sighed. "I miss you, too."

AFTER THAT FIRST DAY, IF SAM WAS STILL DISAPPOINTED IN ME, HE didn't show it. In fact, by the end of my second week, he actually seemed impressed by my work. For me, those two weeks had been a brisk routine, not altogether unpleasant, of getting up early, fitting in as many work hours as I could, and returning to the hotel room early enough to get some rest and call Adam, but not so early I'd be bored in my dull quarters. I was proud of the work I'd done, and especially of my growing intimacy with the plant and its control systems. It felt like an early friendship, a gradual opening up between Cumberland and me.

"Good thinking," Sam said as he went over some of my modifications to the project plan. "Impressive efficiencies."

I felt a flush of pride, but I didn't say anything. Instead, I just nodded and turned back to my computer screen.

"Are you going to Smitty and Dinidu's tonight?"

Smitty and Dinidu were the engineering technicians who shared a two-bedroom apartment in Amherst, instead of staying at the motel. Were they working on some aspect of the project at their apartment? Was I supposed to be there?

Sam saw my confusion. "Dinidu is going back to Halifax next week and Smitty's giving up the apartment. They're having some kind of shindig. They invited the whole project crew."

"Oh." The whole project crew? No one had said anything to me. "I'm not sure."

"Drive over with me," Sam said. "It'll give me an excuse to cut out early if I have to drive you back."

"Okay, then." Instinctively, I wanted to refuse his offer—it seemed weird, like hanging out with your teacher. I'd never been one of those students who liked going for a beer with my professors after class. It had always felt unseemly to me somehow. But after all, I reasoned, I was showing up to the party essentially uninvited. It would seem less rude if I came as Sam's guest.

We agreed we'd meet at his room at seven. I put on a pair of jeans and a blue-and-grey-striped sweater. I'd never seen either Smitty or Dinidu wear so much as a collared shirt at work; I doubted they'd be expecting anyone to dress up. I knocked on Sam's door at exactly seven. He opened it up and emerged in a pair of jeans, a black T-shirt, and a well-worn black leather jacket. I could almost see what he'd looked like in his twenties. Without his usual Dilbert uniform, he looked a lot looser. Some women might even find him attractive, I realized.

"Ready?" Sam said as he led us to his car, a new-model coupe.

Even though it was early by the time we got to the apartment, the party was already thumping. Grunge rock from the nineties was playing on the stereo at a level just below what the neighbours might reasonably see as provocation to call the police. I recognized a few employees from the power plant, but most people there were strangers to me.

I set down the bottle of wine I'd brought on the kitchen counter. Smitty, a round-faced engineering technician with a brush cut and thick glasses, greeted me with a bowl of chips. I took a handful.

"So, you're moving into the motel with us?" I asked.

Smitty nodded. "Sucks. This place is sweet."

I nodded politely, wondering where Smitty lived in Halifax to make this bland two-bedroom apartment with worn carpeting and decades-old appliances seem sweet. "Yeah, I'm sure you'll miss it," I replied. I looked around for a glass and a wine opener. No luck.

"Oh, check it out!" Smitty gestured to the living room. Dinidu was sitting on the end of the coffee table, tuning an acoustic guitar. As he started strumming, someone cut the stereo. He wasn't bad. Not great, but not bad. He played "Sweet Caroline" first, all of us singing along with him, the "Bah! Bah! Bah!s" reaching a joyous crescendo in every chorus.

A woman I didn't know, someone from town, I supposed, sidled up to Dinidu. She was pretty in a hard kind of way, a couple of years older than me. She had chunky blond streaks in her brown hair and her eyelids were done up in smoky, dark shadow. Dinidu gave her a quick wink over his shoulder as he started to play "Summer of '69." We all sang along to that one, too. Watching Dinidu flirting with the woman made me miss Adam all of a sudden.

But it was fun, singing along with everyone to Dinidu's inexpert but enthusiastic guitar playing. Between songs, I watched another party guest fumble through kitchen drawers and cabinets until he found glasses and bottle openers. I followed him, pouring myself a healthy glass of the red wine I'd brought. There was a warm glow in my chest that was only partly from the second glass.

As Dinidu started in on "Have You Ever seen the Rain," I realized Sam was standing behind me. I gave him a smile. He smiled back and gave me a chummy nudge with his elbow. He was a good guy, I thought. Pity I hadn't realized earlier.

The small living room was full of people, and more seemed to be trickling in all the time. Before long, Sam was pressed up behind me, and I was pressed into a woman with big blond curls. At first, I didn't notice the hand sliding along my belly, and when I did, I thought it was an accident in the crowded room. But then the hand slid under my sweater, then down into my pants. It cupped me, a finger suddenly fumbling, searching. I froze.

Sam leaned in, kissing my neck. I turned away, freeing myself from his hand. He gave me a lazy smile as he sang the next verse, low. I smiled back, quickly, instinctively, then shuffled a few steps to the side.

"Watch it," the blond said.

I mumbled an apology and made my way to the door. I hesitated for a second, wondering whether I should say goodbye to Smitty and Dinidu, whether they'd think it was weird if I just left. I wondered whether I should tell Sam I was going. He wouldn't be looking for me, would he? I glanced back toward him.

I could tell by the way he was swaying that he was drunk. The realization struck me as a relief. He hadn't meant it, not really. He probably wouldn't even remember it tomorrow. At the same time, the sight of him in his black T-shirt, hair flopping down over his forehead as he shuffled just off-beat, made me feel slightly sick. I slipped out the door.

I walked a couple of blocks before I called up the local cab company whose number I had providentially saved in my phone before leaving Halifax. I asked them to pick me up at the convenience store I could see on the next street corner. I walked there quickly, then waited next to the door. My legs and arms were buzzing like I'd been electrocuted. There was nowhere for the energy to go. I couldn't stand still, but I couldn't leave. I wanted to start walking, just walk back to my hotel, but I knew it would take close to an hour. Anyway, it wasn't sensible to go walking by myself on a Friday night. Anything could happen.

Finally, the cab came. I sat down on the saggy back seat, grateful the cab driver wasn't the chatty type.

When I got back into my hotel room, I deadbolted the door behind me. I tried to shake off the jumpy feeling, and the heavy sickness that clung to me whenever the image of Sam drunkenly swaying to the music came to my mind. He hadn't meant it, I reminded myself.

That's when I noticed I'd missed a call from Adam. A wave of sorrow hit me then. Sorrow and guilt. How could I not have reacted? Why hadn't I pushed Sam's hand away? Why had I let that happen?

I peeled off all my clothes and dumped them into the empty liquor store box I was using as a laundry hamper, then took a hot shower.

IF SAM REMEMBERED WHAT HAD HAPPENED AT THE PARTY, HE DIDN'T show it on Monday. He met me at the plant as usual, looking like himself again in a yellow dress shirt and brown tie. I felt a wave of embarrassment. Was it weird that I had just left? Should I have said something? Then I felt a rush of anger at myself. After all, what else should I have done? Let him grab me? Yell at my boss? He was drunk, he probably didn't even realize what he was doing. And I remembered how, when we'd met at his motel room, I'd thought that he wasn't so bad looking after all. Maybe he'd noticed. Maybe I'd given him some sort of signal without meaning to.

I wondered if I should say something about leaving him at the party. But he didn't mention it, and neither did I. We talked about the system specifications for the turbine and then I went back to my motel room to work.

As I stared at my laptop screen, my tongue found the sharp edge of my front tooth. There was a little ridge. It had always been there, I suppose, but somehow, right now, I couldn't stop worrying it with my tongue. I found myself losing focus as I probed the uneven edge of my tooth, my tongue becoming raw and my jaw tight and sore. I'd tell myself to stop, to forget about it, to focus on my work, but a minute later I was at it again, my tongue rubbing away at the tooth until I tasted blood.

All day, I kept thinking about Adam. Every time, a wave of guilt washed over me. I kept wanting to call him and tell him about the party, but I didn't. Maybe on the weekend, I reasoned. But I didn't end up telling him. Not that weekend, or any weekend after. I'd spent Saturday and Sunday holed up in my motel room. I ordered takeout. I worked. I watched TV. I didn't leave in case I ran into Sam. And I didn't call Adam. Instead, I let his call go to voicemail and then, half an hour later, I sent him a text to tell him I was working.

It didn't take long before I was able to excise the party from my thoughts. After all, Sam was himself again—his tie-wearing, work-focused self. It was as though I'd had an embarrassing dream about a coworker, nothing more.

I n 1979, a reactor at the Three Mile Island Nuclear Generating Station experienced a partial meltdown. A minor fault in a secondary system set off a chain reaction. At first, operators in the control room didn't understand what had gone wrong, or how big the problem really was. They misread the control system user interface and didn't realize that a valve in the primary system was stuck open, leaking radioactive coolant.

The world watched the accident unfold. They shook their heads and muttered about the dangers of nuclear power. They longed for the days of safe, natural coal- and oil-fired electricity.

The nuclear energy sector was also watching carefully. Three Mile Island became a cautionary tale. Mechanical failure and human error caused the accident, but poor control systems design kept the damage from being checked. After Three Mile Island, control rooms were designed to monitor the types of issues that human operators are prone to miss. Digital monitoring systems don't get distracted or fail to keep an eye on secondary systems. They keep track of everything all at once—even the systems that are not likely to lead to catastrophic failure. Digital control systems don't miss early warnings.

ELEVEN

I try not to listen in on Freya's call with her dad. I clean up in the kitchen, washing out the coffee pot and loading the breakfast dishes in the dishwasher. I hear her laughing at something he said. My heart lifts for a second before I feel a sudden clutch of jealousy that he'd been able to make her laugh, then guilt. What kind of mom doesn't want her sick kid to laugh?

I hear her say "Goodbye, I love you too," and then seconds later, "Mom?"

I make myself pause, as though I weren't listening. I carry the dishtowel out of the kitchen. "What's up?"

"Can I watch TV?"

"Sure." I go to find the remote, noticing her eyebrows shoot up in surprise, but she gives a cool nod, as though she expected to be allowed screen time right after breakfast. I load her streaming channel and hand her the remote, already wondering what I'll do when she gets bored of watching her shows.

Freya has never been great at sitting still.

By the time she was enrolled in school, we'd already figured out that a suite of activities would be necessary to keep her energy levels manageable. This was not how I'd planned to parent, managing schedules and constantly ferrying her back and forth between school and sports, music, or arts activities. But you do what you have to do to keep your kid, your adorable, bright, funny, unrelenting offspring, from driving you completely fucking insane.

I remember the day I first realized that something had shifted between us, that she didn't look at me in the same worshipful way she once had. That she didn't *need* me the same way she had. She was almost seven, and she'd been invited to her first sleepover. Her friend from school, Aisha, was having an overnight birthday party. Freya had asked me to buy her new pyjamas for the occasion, and she'd chosen a simple green-and-purple-striped set. I'd suggested a pair that had her favourite cartoon characters on them, but she refused to consider them, declaring them "babyish."

I'd dropped her off at her friend's house, chatting for a moment with Aisha's mother at the doorstep. We exchanged phone numbers.

"If you change your mind about spending the night, just ask Aisha's mom to call, and I'll come right away to pick you up," I said, reaching for a hug.

But Freya shrugged me off, rolling her eyes for Aisha's benefit. "I *won't*," she said, "don't worry about it."

I forced a laugh, glancing at Aisha's mom for her reaction. I wanted to snap, "Tone!" at Freya, but I felt suddenly then that we were in a cold war, she and I, and I didn't want to be the one to escalate it. Instead, I called a feeble "Love you" to my daughter and left.

And she was right. There was no call to pick her up that night.

So we enrolled her in soccer and a handful of other activities throughout the year to manage what we called her "squirreliness." She didn't love soccer; we figured that out a week in. But she also refused to go back to softball, and we needed her to have a physical outlet. Adam and I didn't agree on a lot these days, but we were both on board with keeping her in a sport.

"It's boring," she whined after the first week of soccer practice.

"The games will be more fun," I replied. But what did I know? I'd hated gym class in school, and I'd never played any team sports.

"No, they won't," she grumbled. She looked at me hard, daring me to argue. Why did she do that? It had started pretty much as soon as she could talk.

"We'll see," I said, keeping my voice even and cool.

She was quiet for a minute, but she stayed in the kitchen with me, running her fingers along the edge of the counter. I could see where this was going. I tried to tamp down my annoyance, which was already rising, anticipating her next move.

"What's for supper?" she asked at last. She was watching me batter the haddock fillets as she said it.

"Poop on a stick," I said. Our old joke. It used to make her laugh.

She narrowed her eyes. "I hate fish."

"Since when?"

"Since always."

When she was younger, Freya was better at baiting me into an argument. Or I was worse at avoiding one. Since then, I'd figured out how to sidestep. But I'd also figured out that she wouldn't be cut loose so easily.

"Fish is gross."

She wanted me to tell her she was being rude. She wanted a reaction. It's what she did: tried to bait me into losing my temper. I'd never been able to figure out why.

Just a couple of years ago, I would be snapping at her by now. I'd demand she be more polite, more appreciative of the meal I was cooking. And she'd dig in, complain about the carrots and the potatoes. Maybe even say something rude about my shirt or my hair. *Why do you let the white show like that? It makes you look old.*

And I'd be hurt, and I'd tell her so, but I'd snarl it at her. *That was rude and hurtful and unacceptable.*

I'd demand an apology. She'd refuse. I'd send her to her room. She'd stomp off. I'd wait five minutes, then ask if she was ready to apologize. She'd say no, or just refuse to answer. She'd stare at me, her eyes ablaze, and I'd suddenly be reminded of Kyle. I'd want to walk it back, but I wouldn't know how—not with her constantly raising the stakes. How could I let her get away with it? I couldn't. I'd take away a toy, her favourite dress. I'd take away screen time and our evening story. All the while, I'd be getting angrier and angrier, and I'd hear my mom in the flatness of my voice, feel her in the tightness around my mouth. And then the anger would turn inward.

Finally, finally, I'd land on a consequence that dissolved Freya into teary remorse. She'd hold out her arms instantly, demanding a hug. And, once she'd apologized to my satisfaction, I'd hug her, relishing the urgency of her affection, but also the depth of her remorse.

And then I'd feel shitty. What kind of mom is happy that she finally made her kid cry? Hours later, I'd stare into the darkness of my bedroom, guilt and regret swirling in my chest, pulling up every old memory of things I'd done wrong, and my mind would chew on those all night long.

Was that the way Mom had felt with us, I wondered. Did she feel bad when she finally broke us down? If she did, she never showed it. There was always a palpable triumph in the way she looked at us when we finally backed down. Especially Kyle—not that he backed down often.

Every now and then these days, Freya could still goad me into anger. But most of the time, I was able to suppress my irritation. To deflect her provocations instead of meeting them dead on.

"Fine," I said to her comment about the fish. "You can just have potatoes and carrots." I wasn't going to call her on her rudeness, but I also wasn't going to make her a separate meal.

Out of the corner of my eye, I watched her puff herself up, looking for another target. But then she gave up. I saw the defiance melt from her shoulders, watched her jaw relax. She leaned into me.

"Do I have to play soccer?" she asked, her voice soft.

"You have to try it," I said.

"What if I don't like it?"

"Then we'll talk."

She wrapped her arms around me, hugging me tightly. It made making supper difficult, but I didn't complain.

I went to her first game. So did Adam. Yash came, too, and we sat together, our lawn chairs on the sidelines, glad to have the game to talk about. Yash brought a little insulated bag full of cold sparkling water. I accepted a lemon-lime and sipped on it as I watched Freya run.

She was playing defence. The first half of the game, she made an acceptable show of following the play up and down the field, trotting halfheartedly after the other players. But soon, she'd be distracted by a scab on her elbow or a plane flying over the horizon until her coach shouted at her to get a move on. Then she'd let her arms flop and roll her head back dramatically. *Do I have to?*

After the game, the team did a little cheer together, then formed a line to slap the other team's hands. Freya's team had lost badly, so her teammates slouched down the line while the other team tripped along merrily. Freya trudged. As soon as the coach released the players, she spun and continued dragging her feet over towards us.

"Soccer's stupid," she said.

"You did great, kid," Adam said. "I was really proud of you."

Yash nodded. "You've got potential. I can tell. You know, I played defence in university," he said. "I had a soccer scholarship."

A momentary flicker of interest crossed her face. She turned her eyes to Yash, as though she were trying to detect a trick or a lie. As if Yash ever lied. "For real?"

"Absolutely," Yash replied. He gave her a raspberry water.

She actually smiled at him. But only for a second. "Soccer makes my leg hurt," she said. "Right here." She pointed to her left femur, up near the hip.

"You're just using muscles you're not used to using," I said. "You have to build them up."

"Melinda says my legs are really strong," Freya replied, naming her gymnastics coach. Freya loved gymnastics, but classes didn't start up again until October. Soccer was meant to bridge the gap until then.

"Different muscles," I said.

She did her huge *Do I have to?* gesture again. She'd been doing that since she was three. Her dramatics back then used to make me call her my "threenager." Everyone said that she'd grow out of it by the time she started school. She never had.

Of course, she'd fought me when I tried to take her to soccer practice later that week. "I hate it," she grumbled when I told her to get her shoes. She'd been the same way with violin lessons at first. Not that she ever really got excited to practice or attend her lessons, but eventually she'd stopped stalling quite so much. And she loved performing. Every recital, she absolutely glowed onstage, and for days afterward, too. But the first couple of months, you would have thought we were sending her off to have her hair tweezed out, strand by strand.

"You said I didn't have to do it if I hated it."

"I said we'd talk."

By the second week, she'd focused her efforts. "It makes my leg hurt," she said, clutching her upper thigh. "Really, really bad."

"Get your shorts on," I snapped. "Now." I'd started getting her ready a half hour early because of her intensifying stall tactics.

When she was like this, I'd have to force myself to remember it wasn't *always* like this with us. The previous winter, a classmate had gone to New York to see *Hamilton*. Suddenly, Freya was entranced by the idea of live theatre.

"Mom, can you take me to see a Broadway show?" she'd asked me over dinner one night. "Please?"

I'd ended up getting us tickets to see a showing in Montreal. We went by train—I splurged on a sleeper car, and we'd curled up in the lounge car together, watching *Into the Woods* on my iPad. Not that I was a big fan of theatre—I'd seen a few plays in university and hadn't minded them, but musicals always grated on me. It seemed so implausible every time the cast broke out into song that I was pulled right out of the action. But now, I fell under the spell of my daughter's delight.

I bought us both new dresses to wear for *Hamilton*, and she positively glided into the theatre, the pale blue skirt rustling around her ankles. When the show ended, she bounded to her feet, applauding, pulling me up from my seat to join her. And after, as we walked back to the hotel, she leaned on my arm and quizzed me intently on my favourite parts of the play.

I clung to that memory now as I forced her cleats on, her feet unresponsive lumps. I could feel her anger surging down her legs like a current.

The following week, I took advantage of Freya's time at her dad's to put in some long hours at work. Jordan, the cybersecurity engineer

Maritime Energy had hired last year, was working at the nuclear plant in Mispec, just outside of Saint John, New Brunswick. The control and safety systems there were from the late 1990s—not too bad. It was a bit of a Frankenstein's monster, with some patch-ups and additions over the last twenty years, but we certainly had worse in operation. Jordan was doing a cybersecurity audit of all Maritime Energy's plants, starting with nuclear. It was a shared position, reporting to Nuclear, General Risk & Compliance, and to Admin, too. Not ideal. I'd have wanted a dedicated cybersecurity unit.

"I don't love the security levels here," he said, his voice echoey over my car's Bluetooth. It was close to seven and I'd finally left the office for the night. I could almost feel the white-painted cinder-block walls of the plant closing in around him.

"Okay, so what do you need to start *liking* them?" I asked.

"I'm gonna need a team up here."

"What's a team?"

"Three guys? Computer engineers, maybe a programmer."

I snorted. "Not likely." I'd had to persuade my bosses that Jordan was a smart hire. They'd wanted me to fold cybersecurity into my existing duties. It wasn't that they didn't care, they said, they just didn't see the value of a dedicated specialist. A power plant's safety and control systems aren't internet-connected. Logically, there's no way for a hacker to break into the systems and stop them from performing their safety functions, or to put the control systems into an unsafe state. Not from outside the plant, anyway.

That's not to say there aren't vulnerabilities. Someone could implant bad code into the systems before installation—in software development, or in transit. And depending on the physical security at the plant, someone could break in and upload a malicious code. A logic time bomb, for instance, to cause a safety system failure at a designated date and time. Imagine a program, for example, that shuts down the essential service water system at 4:00 A.M. on March 28, the anniversary of the Three Mile Island accident, allowing the temperature of the core to mount to dangerous levels... An unlikely scenario, but not impossible. And not something I'd necessarily be able to detect—nor would anyone else on my team. If that happened, would I be like one of the engineers at Chernobyl, chasing an impossibly hopeless solution to a ballooning disaster, or would I be like the engineers at Fukushima Daini, frantically but effectively cobbling together a solution to a situation no one had foreseen? I'd do anything in my power to avoid ever having to find out. So I pushed my supervisor for a dedicated cybersecurity specialist. Enter Jordan.

"What can you get me?" he asked. Typical. He didn't even report to me. Technically, our positions were laterally equivalent.

I sighed. "I don't know. I'll see tomorrow."

"Sounds cool," he said.

"Cool," I parroted, trying to reflect his breezy tone back to him.

The next morning, Adam called me just before Freya's soccer practice. I was at my desk, looking through my project plans to see who we could shift to Mispec. Jordan wasn't going to get three computer engineers, that was for sure. He might have to make do with a couple of technicians—one had some coding experience from a previous job.

"She says she hates it," Adam said.

I sat back in my chair and closed my eyes. "Yeah?"

"She says it makes her leg hurt." Since we'd split up, the word "sidle" popped into my mind whenever he spoke. Adam never approached any subject directly. But I knew if I told him to just spit it out he'd sputter and make excuses, and it would take even longer to get to the point.

"Yeah, I've heard that one, too."

"What do you think?"

"I *think* she doesn't like soccer and wants to be back in gymnastics."

"You don't have to say it like that," Adam grumbled.

Like what? I thought it, but I didn't say it. I just wanted to get back to my work. "What do you think we should do?"

"I don't know," he mumbled.

"We can take her out of soccer."

"No," he said quickly. He knew as well as I did how impossible Freya got when she wasn't getting enough exercise.

"If you find another sport that's taking registrations now, let me know."

"Hmm."

"Listen," I said, doing my best not to snap. "If you come up with a better idea, you let me know."

"Yeah, okay," Adam said.

"Tell her I love her," I said before he could hang up.

"I will."

I knew he wouldn't. The worst thing was, it wasn't even malicious. Adam just let things slide out of his mind. Anything he didn't think was important. What was the point of getting mad about that? He wouldn't remember the next time. I often wondered how he managed to do his job at all. His job as an engineer and, a spiteful little voice deep in my head whispered, his job as a father. He couldn't do what I do. He didn't know how.

TWELVE

I drove back to Halifax Friday night, a week after the party at Smitty and Dinidu's. Things had been pretty much normal at work. Smitty had moved into the motel, but I didn't see any more of him than I had before. I didn't see anyone outside of work.

Not that I had been social at all before the party. I pretty much only went back and forth between work, my room, and a handful of restaurants with decent takeout menus in town. The only difference was that before the party, I didn't think too much about it. Afterwards, as soon as work was over, I felt like I'd turned on a set of sensors. I wanted to make sure that if I left my room after hours, I wouldn't run into Sam or Smitty or anyone else from the plant. I got delivery instead of takeout. And when I did go into town, I felt like I was constantly scanning the perimeter. The tip of my tongue often felt raw. The sting would signal me to the fact that I'd been worrying the rough spot on the back of my tooth again. As soon as I noticed that, I'd also notice the tightness in my jaw, a clenched ache that would soon begin working its way up into my skull.

Not that I was scared of running into any of them. It just seemed so unbearably awkward, after what had happened. It was one thing to see Sam at work, to talk about the project. When we were both in work mode, I could pretend that everything was the same as it always had been. But the thought of running into Sam after he'd changed out of his outdated professional wear, when he might look more like he had at the party, when I might have to remember how I'd thought, just for a moment, that he was kind of a good-looking guy, sent a jolt of revulsion through my gut. So I stayed in my room as much as I could.

It felt good to be driving back to Halifax. The highway was broad and bright. I could suddenly get more air into my lungs.

Adam took me out for a late supper. We went to our favourite pub, not far from our apartment. I had a couple of beers and felt loose and silly. We laughed the whole walk home, I don't even remember about what, and then had sloppy sex on the living room couch before watching a movie late into the night.

The next morning I got up first, as I usually did. I made a big pot of coffee and sat at the kitchen table, reading a tech magazine I'd subscribed to back in university. Adam kissed my cheek when he got up an hour or so later, and the gesture seemed so hokey, so sitcom-coupley that it made me smile.

"So," he said, sitting down with a coffee and a bowl of cereal.

"So." I put down my magazine and started at him pointedly.

"So, I noticed Maritime Energy is hiring," he said, stirring his cereal.

"Yeah?"

"They're looking for civil engineers for an infrastructure project in Dartmouth."

"Okay." I carefully picked my magazine back up and pretended to read it.

"I was gonna apply." I could feel him trying to catch my eye.

"Good idea." I turned a page mindlessly.

"So."

I resisted the urge to mimic him. *Sooo.*

"I thought. Could you maybe. Could you say something to your boss for me?"

I set the magazine back down and took a sip of my coffee. It was cold already. "I don't really know who does the hiring."

"What about Douglas? He interviewed you, didn't he?" Adam had set down his spoon and he was staring at me with a look so open, so hopeful, that I had to look back down at my magazine.

"Yeah, but he's the team leader for Risk & Compliance, not Infrastructure or whatever."

"But you could ask him who is? Maybe he can tell them I'm applying."

I took a sip of my coffee. "Mm," I said, hoping he'd take that as a yes.

"So, you'll talk to him?"

"I'll do my best."

His shoulders dropped just a little. All of a sudden, I remembered Sam, and how he looked in his T-shirt and leather jacket, and how I hadn't said anything. Why hadn't I at least told him *no*? The guilt rose up in me at once, prickling my skin like static electricity. And just like that, I couldn't stand to look at Adam, or his oversized bowl of cereal, or his sad, drooping shoulders. I stood up.

"Where you going?" he asked.

"To the bathroom," I snapped. "Can't I even go to the fucking bathroom without letting you know first?"

"Yeah, of course," he stammered.

I stomped out of the kitchen.

The next morning, I headed back out to Amherst without having to go into the Halifax office at all. In fact, I wouldn't be back in Halifax again until weeks later, after they'd finished hiring the new engineers. I felt a flush of guilt when Smitty mentioned the new guys one morning. But I never talk to Douglas outside the office, I reasoned. It would be weird to just call him up out of the blue and ask him to hire my boy-friend. Weird and unprofessional.

I worked on the Cumberland project for four months before I was transferred back to Halifax. Sam stayed on in Amherst to wrap things up.

IN NOVEMBER, THE COMPANY HOSTED ITS ANNUAL HOLIDAY PARTY. They rented the small ballroom of a waterfront hotel downtown. There were hors d'oeuvres and an open bar. The invitations said "black tie," but Yash told me no one would be in a tuxedo. "Most of the guys won't even bother with a suit," he said. He was right. Most of the men were in dress pants, a dress shirt, and a tie, and several of the women wore dresses I'd seen them wear to the office.

I'd bought a new dress, a cocktail dress, I supposed. It was knee-length and sleeveless. If the material were less shiny, I'd have been tempted to put a blazer over it and wear it to work.

Adam wore a black suit he'd bought recently for job interviews. It was the only one he had that was long enough in the sleeves and pant legs, not that he cared much. He kept pulling at the cuffs. I could tell he was nervous. I just hoped that he and Douglas wouldn't end up talking about the job I *hadn't* recommended him for.

When we got there, Smitty, Dinidu, and Yash were all chatting at the bar. Smitty had brought his fiancée, a pretty woman who wore a dark red dress with little straps, a matching headband in her shiny black hair. Her eyes were expertly lined with little black wings, and her skin positively glowed. I fought the urge to find a mirror to check my own reflection.

"This is Denise," Smitty said, beaming just a little.

I shook her hand, then remembered Adam. "This is my boyfriend, Adam," I said to them.

"I'm a civil engineer," he blurted with a wide smile.

Denise rolled her head in mock exasperation. "So you're *all* enginerds?" she asked. "Everyone but me?"

"What do you do?" Yash asked.

"I'm a teacher up in Indian Brook," she replied, naming a Mi'kmaw community outside of Halifax. "Fifth grade."

"Are you Native?" Adam asked.

She didn't answer, taking a sip of her drink. I felt at once protective of Adam, wanting to explain he hadn't meant anything by the comment, and irritated by his social clumsiness.

Fortunately, Yash filled the silence. "How about you, Adam?" he asked, giving my boyfriend an easy, welcoming smile. He was good with people, I realized. I wondered whether Douglas had tried to talk *him* into an MBA program.

"Oh, I work for King's Equipment," Adam replied. "I'm still looking for an engineering job."

"Did you see the postings with Gallant up in Eastern Passage?" Yash replied.

"No?" Adam said, tilting his head.

The bartender gestured to us then. Smitty, Denise, Dinidu, and I all shifted away, but Adam ordered a beer. Yash followed him, still talking about the job postings. Without the two of them, the rest of us sank into a kind of awkward silence.

"Jess, I heard you were in Amherst with these guys?" Denise asked at last.

"Yeah, for a while."

"What was that like?" She gave one of those smiles that's meant to invite good-natured gossiping among women. I knew I was supposed to complain about living in a motel, working with so many guys, being stuck in a small town. But none of those things had bothered me. I'd never be able to maintain the fiction.

"It was good," I said. "I studied control systems in university, so it was interesting to be able to implement some of that. I hope I get to work on one of the nuclear plants someday."

Denise frowned. "Those are pretty dangerous, aren't they? I mean, the radiation and all that?"

"It's one of the safest, most renewable fuel sources out there," I replied.

"Really, though?" Eyebrows raised, she gave me the kind of look I imagined she gave her students when they gave a wrong answer—a kind of *you-know-better* stare.

"Depending on how the uranium is mined, nuclear power can be as clean and completely renewable as solar power. Only more reliable."

"Huh," she said. I could tell she didn't believe me. "Don't you think we need to shift to renewable energy, though?"

"Like solar?" I asked. "Solar power produces four times as much carbon emissions than nuclear, and you need four hundred and fifty times more land for a solar farm. Four hundred times more land for wind power."

"Wow," she said with an awkward little laugh. She took a long sip of her drink.

I fought the urge to talk about uranium extraction processes, emissions, reductions in waste volumes. I made myself smile instead. We slipped into silence.

Adam and Yash came back then. They were laughing about something.

"Here you go," Adam said, handing me a glass of white wine.

"Thanks," I said, even though I didn't really like white.

Adam and Yash were talking about a superhero movie that had been in theatres that summer. I hadn't seen it—I'd still been in Amherst when Adam had gone, and anyway, I couldn't stand superhero movies. They seemed to solve every problem by developing a new superpower. It seemed lazy to me. While they were gushing about the film, I saw Sam come in. He was standing with a woman who looked to be about forty—his wife, I assumed. She was wearing a floor-length gown, and her hair had clearly been done professionally. Sam himself was wearing a dark suit with a white shirt and a dark blue tie. He and Adam were probably the most formally dressed men in attendance, except for Douglas, who was the only one who'd actually worn a tuxedo.

And there was Douglas now, making his way over to greet Sam and his wife. As Douglas chatted with her, Sam looked over our way. He gave me a little wave. I sent him a quick smile back. A reflex, a social convention.

"We should go soon," I whispered to Adam as soon as the conversation lulled.

He looked at me in surprise. "Why?"

"This is so dull," I replied.

He nodded, his smile fading.

I waited until Sam and his wife moved away from the door before I started our goodbyes. Before we left, Adam and Yash exchanged email addresses so that Yash could send Adam the job postings they'd been talking about.

"Those guys are really cool," Adam said as we left the hotel.

"I guess." I scanned the sidewalk in both directions, an excuse about having dropped something ready, just in case.

"You're lucky," he said. "Bet it's a nice place to work."

"It is," I agreed, trying to give him a smile. The surging revulsion in my stomach made it too hard.

THIRTEEN

That Christmas, I managed to talk my mom into finally coming out for a visit. Adam and I went to a furniture store in Dartmouth and ordered a nice couch that folded out into a reasonably comfortable double bed. We still had a two-bedroom, but the second room was our office (though he almost never used it, except to store his old university textbooks). We picked out some sheets I thought Mom would like, and a small lamp.

A week before her flight, Mom called to say that she'd booked a hotel a few blocks away from our apartment. "I don't want to put you out," she said. "Let the hotel staff take care of me so you don't have to."

I breathed in slowly through my nose, fresh laundry on my lap. "Okay." I snapped a tea towel once, twice, trying to shake out my irritation.

Adam looked confused when I told him the news. "She knows we have a spare room, right?"

"Yep." I picked up another tea towel from the basket and folded it in half once, twice.

"And she knows we were planning on having her here."

"Yep." The tea towel sat in a lumpy, uneven square. I snatched it up and refolded it, smoothing the edges crisp with the flat of my hand.

A worried furrow appeared between his eyebrows. "Did you tell her she wouldn't be putting us out?"

"There's no point." I handed him the stack of tea towels to put away. He stared at them for a moment, as though they might hold the answer.

We agreed that I'd pick her up from the airport and drive her to our place. I would make us dinner—Mom had always liked my borscht. It was one of the few dishes I regularly made from scratch.

She emailed the day before to tell us that we should go out for dinner instead. And that she'd just take a cab from the airport to my apartment.

"No cab—I'll come get you," I said. At least she didn't fight that point.

Her flight landed late in the afternoon. "Where's this Adam of yours?" she asked by way of greeting. She reached out for a hard hug before I could answer.

"He's waiting for us at the apartment," I replied.

"What a shame," she said. "I can't believe you haven't introduced me yet."

As we loaded her suitcase into the trunk of my car, she asked me to take her to her hotel first. "I want to take a shower and do my hair before we go out," she explained. "Airplanes always make me feel so *blah*."

"Adam's waiting for us so we can eat," I replied.

"You know me," she said. "I never take long to get ready."

I gritted my teeth and sent Adam a text: *Running late.*

As we drove toward Halifax, Mom chatted about Cold Lake. "You remember Roy Allen?" she asked.

I made a non-committal sound. The name didn't sound familiar, but I wasn't interested in a refresher course.

"Passed away last spring. Pancreatic cancer. It was awful for Cheryl. The kids didn't even make it home on time."

"That's too bad," I said weakly, scrolling through my mind for kids I'd known with the last name Allen.

"And Debbie Wachowitch? She has Parkinson's."

"Oh no," I murmured, turning down Robie Street.

She chattered on, giving me a long list of deaths, divorces, and bankrupt businesses. Some of the names, I recognized. I made enough sympathetic sounds that she didn't stop to give me anyone's history.

"You know what?" Mom said as I turned down the street to her hotel. "Your poor Adam is sitting at home, getting hungry. Let's not make him wait. Let's head straight to your place. I'll make supper with whatever you have in the fridge."

"I don't have much, Mom," I said, my patience finally wearing thin. "Why don't we just go out for supper, like we planned."

"Jessica." Her voiced hardened. There it was. "You can't expect me to sit in a restaurant, looking like this. And you can't expect your poor boyfriend to wait while I get ready. I didn't think you were this inconsiderate."

"We'll get takeout."

She made a scoffing sound. "Waste of money," she snapped.

I breathed in slowly. "And a restaurant isn't?"

"Fine," she said, fixing her gaze straight ahead. "You obviously have your mind made up."

I turned the car toward our apartment. She didn't say anything else for the rest of the drive. When I parked in the lot behind my building, she stood stonily at the trunk. I realized she wanted her suitcase, and I wondered whether she'd decided against the hotel after all. As I reached for the bag, she snapped, "I've got it," knocking my hand out of the way.

But as soon as I opened the door to our place, she was all smiles and warmth once again. "I can't believe I had to wait this long to meet you!" she exclaimed, folding Adam into a giant hug. Then she set her suitcase down on the kitchen table and unzipped it.

"I hope you like them," she said, handing Adam a pair of leather moccasins lined with soft rabbit fur. I could see some wrapped Christmas presents tucked in there, but these were unwrapped, a nice-to-meet-you gift.

"Thank you," he replied, admiring the beadwork.

I reached into the basket above the fridge for our stack of takeout menus.

"That's quite a collection," Mom laughed. "Does she never feed you?"

Adam laughed nervously, not daring to answer. He cast me a sheepish look.

"Pasta?" I asked, flipping through the menus. "Or burgers? Donairs? Sushi?"

"You pick," Mom said.

"Japanese?" I held the menu up towards them.

"Anything is fine with me," she said.

Adam just gave a quick nod.

I chose a few items and called in the order while Mom enthusiastically grilled Adam about his family, the town of Wolfville where he'd grown up, his job. He kept casting me incredulous little glances. I'd told him about her temper, about the frosty silences in our house growing up. It was clear he was having trouble reconciling her warm demeanour with my accounts of my childhood.

"Be right back," I said, pulling on my coat.

"Where are you off to?" Mom asked, looking up.

"Get supper."

"Oh no!" She said it as though I just told I'd spent all day baking a cake, then dropped it on the floor. "I thought they delivered!"

"Nope. Not this place."

"Well. Drive safely."

"I will." I cast Adam a quick look before I left. He was already wearing his slippers. He'd be fine.

After a supper that Mom merely picked at ("I think I like Chinese better"), I drove her to her hotel.

"I really like this Adam of yours," she said. "He's kind. You can tell right away that he's kind."

"Yeah, he is."

"And you? Are you good to him?"

"Yeah, Mom." I kept my eyes on the road.

"Because you don't want to lose someone like that. You have to put in the effort."

I could feel the blood rush to my face. "Okay, Mom."

She was quiet a moment. Then finally, she reached over and put her hand on my arm. I had to fight the urge to pull away. "Just promise me one thing," she said.

"What?" I asked warily.

"You'll get married *before* you have kids."

I was speechless. Married? *Kids*? Where the hell was that coming from? "Mom, we're not—"

"I'm not asking for me, I'm asking for you," she said, her hand still gripping my forearm. I could feel her looking right at me. "You can take my word for it; you don't want to hear the kinds of things people have to say to a single mother."

"I'm not single, Mom. Or a mother."

"I'm just asking you to plan ahead. Can you promise me that? Please."

I pulled up to her hotel. "Here we are," I said, still looking straight ahead. It would be so easy to just agree, to promise, I knew. It would put an end to this conversation. But I wasn't going to do it. I couldn't give her what she wanted anymore.

Finally, she sighed. "All right, then. Promise you'll think about it."

"Goodnight, Mom."

"Goodnight, Jessica. You know I'm only bringing it up because I love you."

"Love you, too."

MOM STAYED JUST OVER A WEEK. WE HAD A SMALL CHRISTMAS IN OUR apartment, and I roasted a chicken for the three of us instead of a turkey. After the drive in from the airport, there were no more flashes of cold anger. Mom doted on Adam, and he beamed under the attention.

"So, you think she likes me?" he'd asked the first night, when I'd returned from dropping Mom off at the hotel.

"Sure does," I said truthfully, trying not to sound bitter, and failing.

Fortunately, he didn't seem to notice. He nodded, looking like a golden retriever. I sank into the couch and turned on the TV.

Her flight left the morning of New Year's Eve. She waited until the night before to ask about Kyle.

Adam was in the kitchen, washing the supper dishes. She and I were in the living room, sipping boozy hot chocolate. She made a show of steeling herself, sitting back in the chair and gripping the armrests. "Have you heard from your brother?" she asked.

As far as I knew, she and Kyle hadn't spoken since he left to work on the oil rigs. But she asked me about him from time to time.

"Yeah, he called a while ago," I said.

"And?"

"Not much new."

She nodded, then sighed as though she'd just gotten through a difficult but necessary task. Her grip on the chair eased, and she picked her mug up again.

I'd lied, of course. Kyle and I spoke on the phone once or twice a month, giving each other the news of our lives and ending each call with a quick *Love you,* and *You, too.*

Kyle had called at the beginning of the month with bigger news than usual. He was apprenticing as an operating engineer, meaning that he was looking at a hefty pay raise running the big equipment out at the camp. And he'd bought a condo in Leduc, just south of Edmonton. His girlfriend Juliet had moved in with him. She was pregnant, due in June.

I knew I'd eventually have to tell Mom she was going to be a grandmother. But I didn't want to get to that just yet. And I didn't want to run the risk of having her decide to call up or drop in on Juliet and stress her out while she was pregnant.

Kyle, for his part, never asked about Mom, and I didn't bring her up.

Adam came with me to take Mom to the airport. She hugged both of us, and she cried a bit. When she was through security, I felt a lifting and an easing in my chest.

ADAM CALLED ME HALF AN HOUR INTO FREYA'S SOCCER PRACTICE.

"Did she stop stalling?" I asked. "Did you actually get her there?"

"Jess, I think we should make Freya a doctor's appointment."

My heart lurched. "What? Why? Did she hurt herself?" I imagined her falling, twisting an ankle or breaking a leg, and Adam nonchalantly taking her home and calling to ask me if we should book a doctor's appointment, rather than taking her straightaway to the emergency room.

"She's got a...bump," he said.

"What did you mean, a bump? Did she hit her head?"

"No, just a bump. On her leg. The one she says hurts."

"Well, what happened?" I snapped. "How did she get it?"

"I don't know," Adam replied. "It's just a bump. Up near her hip."

"Just a bump." Something sank inside me. "You mean a lump."

"Bump, lump," he said. "I think a doctor should check it out."

I reached for my keys. "I'll come get her."

"No, don't," Adam said, sounding a lot firmer than usual. "She's fine now. She's playing video games. I just think we should make a doctor's appointment."

"I'll do it," I said.

"You sure?"

"Do you even know her pediatrician?"

"Well," he mumbled, the surety in his voice dissolving, "you could give me the number."

"I'll take care of it."

After I hung up, I felt as though my hands and feet were buzzing. I couldn't sit still. I needed something to do. I went to get the broom—I'd noticed the front hall floor was a bit of a mess earlier, but suddenly I was standing there, staring off into space, the broom useless in my hand. I put it away.

I reached for a dishcloth to wipe the already clean counter when the sob bubbled up in my throat. Lump, I thought. Lump, bump. What other kinds of lumps were there? There had to be other kinds, right? Other kinds of bumps that turned up on kids, but weren't—*that*?

I couldn't say the word, not even in my head.

I could look it up on my phone. I could do a search for different causes, I could look at outcomes, treatments, recovery rates. I could get a sense of what we might be looking at, what we could expect.

I couldn't, though. I couldn't be thinking of Freya, my Freya, and spell out words like *lump* or *bump* or *tumour*.

Or *cancer*.

I put my head down on my hands, still resting on the counter, holding the damp dishcloth, and I sobbed.

dream of Chernobyl. Only now I'm in the control room, observing the test that shut down Reactor Four. I watch as the xenon builds up in the fuel rods, poisoning the reactor. I watch as steam voids form, increasing the power input, launching a positive feedback loop as more water turns into more steam, generating more power. I call out a warning, but the only words I know are useless: *Lyubov. Pysanky. Nalysnyky.* What good are a few words, food and holiday fripperies and empty professions of love learned from ancient family members I barely knew?

The core temperature rises. I need to prevent the SCRAM—to stop the emergency shutdown that will trigger an explosion. I can see the AZ-5. Emergency shutdown. It was just a few steps away. I just have to guard it, to prevent anyone from pushing it. But somehow, the room has filled with dark green sludge, gluing my legs in place. I cannot move.

Somehow, the Soviet engineers slosh through the sludge like water. One is almost at the AZ-5 button. He is reaching for it. I have to stop him.

Slava Ukraini! I called uselessly. *Heróyam sláva! Holubtsi!*

The engineer looks at me, uncomprehending. Why have I never learned how to say "stop!" in Ukrainian?

He pushes the button.

The shuddering sound and the burning light come from the sludge that binds my legs.

I wake up alone, in the crushing silence of my bedroom, no one to rush in to see if I'm okay.

FOURTEEN

In January, Adam followed up on the job ads that Yash had recommended. By mid-month, he'd had two interviews, and by February first he had a new job as a junior engineer for a residential construction firm.

We had been planning a trip to Europe for the following summer. We'd visit Scotland and England, where Adam's family was from, then travel through France, Belgium, Germany, and Poland to get to Ukraine, flying home out of Kyiv. But Adam wouldn't be able to take more than a week off at the new job, and it just wouldn't be long enough. Both Adam and I were curious to see the countries that had produced our ancestors.

I didn't know a lot about my paternal family. My father was gone by the time I could talk, and Mom certainly never talked about him, but Kyle remembered him. His last name was Jacobs, so maybe English— almost certainly Jewish, originally, though Mom never brought up religion. But my Mom had Ukrainian grandparents on both sides. Her grandfathers' names were Manchaky and Koval. They'd immigrated to southern Alberta in the early twentieth century, fleeing the Soviet regime that enveloped their homeland and in search of the pockets of Ukrainians who had made the prairies their home for a generation. And, of course, she still had great-aunts and second cousins in Ukraine. Aunt Maria. Vira and Petro. Though no one had heard from them since Chernobyl.

Growing up, we used to go down to Pincher Creek to visit our extended family sometimes in the summer. We always stayed in the same motel near the only mall in town. Mom told me that the first couple of times we drove down, we stayed at her parents' house, but as far back as I could remember, they were in a seniors' home, sharing a bedroom that seemed stuffed with too much furniture, too many pictures, and too many knick-knacks. Too much memory. It was hard to breathe in there, the air was so heavy with it. My grandparents, Baba and Gido, spoke in a rolling mixture of English and Ukrainian, and my Baba was forever asking Mom to make her some good *holubtsi*. Of course, my mom was never much for cooking, but sometimes we'd stop at the Ukrainian restaurant and grocery in Edmonton on our drive down, and she'd pick up a big tin pan of the cabbage rolls my Baba loved so much. Mom never explicitly said she'd made them, but Kyle and I knew better than to mention it.

Mom had a couple of aunts and uncles in Pincher Creek, and we'd stop in for brief afternoon visits. I don't remember much about them, except that they all seemed to live in bungalows that smelled of cabbage, and Kyle and I were always bored. We'd have to sit still in fussy living rooms while these old people we couldn't tell apart asked us the same questions: what grade were we in, did we do well in school, what were our favourite subjects, did Kyle have a girlfriend? We'd answer each question with Mom throwing death glares at us, willing us to remember our manners, and to sit still and not squirm too much until the visit was over.

My grandparents died when I was nine; first my Baba, then just a few days later, my Gido. It was in November, right in the middle of the school year.

Mom had gotten home before us that day. She almost never did, so it was a shock to see her car in the driveway. She was sitting at the kitchen counter, her head on her arms.

"Mom?" I asked as I hovered in the hall.

She lifted her head. She'd been crying, I could tell, but she wasn't anymore. "Take your boots off," she said.

Kyle came in the door behind me then, and I nodded my head toward Mom to tell him something weird was going on, and not to kick his boots off so they hit the wall or drop his bag in the middle of the hall or anything else that might set her off. He frowned and put his stuff away neatly and quietly for a change. Then we both just stood in the kitchen, waiting for her to say something.

The corners of her mouth pulled down and trembled. "Your Baba's passed—" she gulped, and tears leaked from her eyes, down her cheeks. "Your Baba's passed away, and it doesn't look like your Gido has much longer," she said before she fully dissolved into tears.

Kyle gave me a helpless look and we both edged toward her, offering her an awkward family hug. She threw her left arm around Kyle, her head still pressed down on her right, and she clutched my forearm with both hands and sobbed. Kyle and I were trapped, and by the look on his face, he was as terrified as I was.

WE DROVE DOWN FOR THE FUNERAL IN THE MIDDLE OF THE WEEK. We didn't stop for Ukrainian food in Edmonton. We stayed at the same motel we always did, Mom and Kyle in the double beds and me in a cot under the window.

I'd never been to a funeral before, and it wasn't what I expected. It wasn't in a church, but a funeral home. There were no caskets, just a big framed picture of Baba and Gido from a few years back, and another one from their wedding, back in the 1940s, and a picture of my Uncle Arthur, who had died of polio when my mom was little. He had been twenty, a university student. My Gido sometimes used to slip and call Kyle "Arthur," especially in the last year or so. There were two big brass jars in front of the photos filled with flowers.

It seemed as though everyone else at the funeral was old, very old. I remember the tripping, tumbling sound of their language, Ukrainian. Even now, when I hear those dancing Slavic consonants, I can see the red tablecloth embroidered in gold and green that always covered my grandparents' table, first at their house and then at the nursing home. The sounds of the language make me taste butter and cream, and smell the sweet sharpness of garlic and cabbage and fried onions. I think that Kyle, Mom, and I must have been the only ones there who didn't speak Ukrainian.

After the service, everyone got up and moved to the next room, where food was waiting. *Pyrohy*, those little dough crescents filled with potatoes, garlic, and cheese, served under a mountain of buttery onions fried until they were sweet and golden; and *kubasa*, the mouth-watering smoked garlic sausage; *nalysnyky*, little crêpe packages of tender cottage cheese filling topped with rich cream and dill; and, of course, the *holubtsi* that filled the space with its smell as soon as the tinfoil over the buckwheat and ground beef cabbage rolls were rolled back.

Mom, Kyle, and I stood, uncomfortable, as everyone passed by us to give their condolences on their way to the food table.

"*Dyakuyu*," Mom said to each person, and Kyle and I repeated the word after her. *Thank you.*

When it seemed that everyone had passed by, we followed Mom to fill up our plates with the familiar comfort foods. We still went to the farmers' market every Saturday to buy a feast of Ukrainian food for the weekend. And at Orthodox Easter (which usually fell a week or two after regular Easter), Mom would sometimes try her hand at *nalysnyky* or *holubtsi*, buying the *kubasa* and *pyrohy* (vulgarly labelled "kolbasa" and "perogies") at the grocery store. There weren't many tables at the funeral home, so we ate standing up, awkwardly balancing our plates in one hand.

"How come you don't speak Ukrainian?" I asked my mom.

"I speak a little," she replied.

"Yeah, but not like everyone else." There were a few people who seemed to be about Mom's age at the funeral, and even they were talking to each other and to the older folks in Ukrainian.

"My parents—your Gido and Baba—didn't want us to," Mom said. "They wanted Arthur and me to be real Canadians."

"Canada's supposed to be a multicultural country, or whatever," Kyle said, spearing a whole *pyrohy* and stuffing it into his mouth.

"A mosaic," I added, throwing in the term we'd learned in social studies.

"Not everyone feels that way," Mom said as she cut a cabbage roll in half with the edge of her fork.

After my grandparents' funeral, we didn't go back to Pincher Creek, and the Ukrainian I heard was limited to the familiar food-words. I realized, as Adam and I planned our trip to Europe, that I'd missed the sounds of Ukrainian words and phrases, floating, as they had, in the periphery of my life. Until they didn't. I was looking forward to seeing Ukraine, to immersing myself in the language and the foods and the culture of my grandparents. Mom had said that they came from a small village near Kyiv, but she wasn't sure which one. I decided just to adopt Kyiv as my ancestral home.

FIRST, WE PLANNED TO POSTPONE OUR TRIP FOR A YEAR OR TWO. But it was hard to get more than a week off at the same time. We talked about taking a shorter trip, maybe just England and France, but I wasn't ready to give up on a trek across Europe. On seeing Ukraine. I wanted to match the sounds and smells and tastes from my childhood, the things I hadn't experienced since my grandparents and the ancient aunties and uncles had died—I wanted to match them to something real, a true place. I wanted to feel myself within it.

I tried not to get impatient with Adam as he struggled to settle into work as an engineer at last, after nearly two years of working in warehouses and sending out countless résumés. Then, in the first few years of his new job, he changed departments a handful of times before leaving for a better offer with another company. He never seemed able to take the block of vacation time we wanted to explore Europe properly. We put it off another year, then another. In the end, it was nearly a decade before we finally booked the vacation we'd always planned.

In that decade, it seemed like so much had changed, and so little, at the same time. We'd given up our apartment in Halifax and moved across the harbour to a house in Dartmouth. We got a cat. But our friends, our neighbours, my brother had had kids in that time, and it seemed to change who they were. Us, we were the same. I moved up in the ranks at Maritime Energy, and Adam cast about, trying on a handful of jobs and companies. But finally, he seemed to find a position he was comfortable with, and a supervisor who allowed him to book a long late-summer vacation.

It had been a heavy year, and in the weeks before our departure, we talked about postponing.

"Are you sure you want to go?" Adam asked as he handed me the little box from the top of our closet where we kept our passports and birth certificates. "I don't want this trip to be sad."

"I think so," I replied, running my thumb over the embossed cover of my passport. I imagined handing it to a customs official overseas, getting it stamped with irrefutable corroboration that we had been *somewhere*, he and I.

"You think so?" I could feel his eyes on me, searching. I didn't meet his gaze.

"Yes," I said. "I'm sure. We need this." I looked up and forced a smile.

And so late that summer, we left, carrying our losses with us across the Atlantic.

We started our holiday in England, wending our way east through Europe. We began in London, feeling the excitement of the weeks ahead of us coursing through our bodies. We did a frantic series of tours—the Tower, Buckingham Palace, museums and Shakespeare's Globe—before taking a train north, making our leisurely way through northern England and Scotland. We stopped booking tours then, opting instead for aimless, tranquil walks through cities and villages, and long afternoons in pubs, sipping beer and eating rich food. I wish I could remember what we talked about during those days—we always seemed to find something to say to each other. We always made each other laugh. I don't know what we were laughing at.

As we left England, taking the train farther and farther east, I found myself getting impatient, wanting to see Ukraine. By the time we'd left Paris, I noticed that we'd stopped laughing so much, and more and more silence filled the spaces between us in the trains, the hotels, the cafés. Finally, we arrived at the Kyiv train station with its soaring glass ceilings.

I looked at Adam as the train pulled to a stop, feeling a tight, goofy, ecstatic smile pulling its way across my face.

He frowned. "What's so funny?"

"Nothing," I said. "I don't know." I thought suddenly of those dogs who "smile" when they're nervous, and how it wasn't really a smile at all. Sometimes, a smiling dog will bite, catching you off guard because you thought you were getting along so well, you and that dog.

For the Kyiv leg of our trip, we'd booked a hotel on the east side of the Dnieper. Most of what we wanted to see was on the west side, but hotels there were a lot more expensive.

As we left Berlin, I had floated the idea of a tour of Pripyat and Chernobyl to Adam. I wanted to see those places for myself, to replace the images from my dreams something real. A sanctioned tour of the town and the power plant would be pretty mundane, I reasoned to myself. An unusual place, for sure, but one that had been sanitized enough to present it to the public as a tourist destination. Adam, however, was uncharacteristically adamant when I brought it up.

"No way. That can't be safe with all the radiation."

"It's perfectly fine to spend a few hours there," I replied. "Most places are measuring under three microsieverts an hour."

"It's creepy," he replied. "People died there."

"People have died everywhere," I said. "Literally everywhere." I reached for his hand, hoping I could woo him into changing his mind.

"You know what I mean," Adam said, pulling his arm close to his body, his hand out of my reach. "I'm not going."

I thought I might be able to change his mind once we got to Ukraine. I was wrong.

"No chance," he said every time I brought it up.

Fine, I decided. Even if I did finally manage to talk him into it, he'd just make us both miserable all day.

"IS THERE SOMETHING ELSE YOU WANT TO DO?" I ASKED OUR SECOND day there. We were walking down a busy street that ran along the east bank of the Dnieper, scanning the ugly concrete buildings for a likely spot for lunch. "I could just book a tour for myself."

"If you really want to," he said. I did, but first, I made plans for us to see something together. We took a cab across the river to see the Kyiv-Pechersk Lavra monastery. I tried to talk Adam into taking transit, but he spent so much time trying to research routes and make contingency plans, I eventually abandoned the effort.

"What if we get on the wrong bus and get lost?" he asked. "We don't speak Ukrainian. We might not be able to find our way back."

"If we were going to spend all our money on cabs, we might as well have stayed in the old city," I snapped. Our hotel was in a more modern area. Streets were lined with concrete towers from the 1960s and '70s. Hotels in the charming historic district had been a lot more expensive, so we'd opted for frugality. The added expense of a cab annoyed me.

"We can try walking tomorrow," Adam offered. "Once we know our way around a bit."

FIFTEEN

I wait until Freya falls asleep on the couch before I call Adam. I bring the phone with me into the bedroom and close the door so I won't wake her.

"So, how come you didn't pick up last night?" he asks right away.

I push down the wave of irritation. "I just didn't, Adam. But I wanted to know if you could come for supper tonight."

"Both of us?" he asks. He sounds suspicious.

"Yes, both of you. I'm just going to order in, but I thought she'd like to see you."

"Yeah, okay," he says. Then, "Hang on." He puts me on hold. I know I should be impressed that he agreed to come over before they even had a chance to talk it over. He picks the call back up and says, "We'll bring food. Anything in particular?"

"You know what she likes."

"Okay. See you later. Say around..." he trailed off, waiting.

"Say around five? Later, if that's no good."

"No," he said quickly. "Five is good. See you then."

I crack my bedroom door to check on Freya. She's fast asleep, her leg propped up on a couch cushion. I brush a strand of hair out of her face and she swats my hand away without waking, the way she always does. Ever since she was little, if I went in to kiss her goodnight after she'd already fallen asleep, she'd bat at me with her sleepy little hands.

WE HAD FOUR FULL DAYS IN KYIV BEFORE OUR FLIGHT LEFT, and after the first day, we crossed the bridges to see the tourist sights on the other side of the river. The summer heat had cooled away, but the skies remained clear and sunny.

I tried to produce a sense of belonging, of connection to the city—especially the Pecherskyi and Shevchenkivskyi districts with their stately architecture. Surely my ancestors must have come to Kyiv and seen these buildings, these statues and parks and monuments? But try as I might, I couldn't reconcile the image of my Gido and Baba, or their sisters, Mom's ancient aunties—with their flower-patterned furniture from the '60s, with their multitude of doilies and fussy china figurines—with the ornate beauty of the old city, much less with the stark lines of the newer buildings.

We took selfies at the Maidan Nezalezhnosti, and a tide of embarrassment washed over me—we looked like every other tourist taking the same pictures, trying to capture the Independence Monument towering high above us in the background. We marvelled at the golden spires atop the Holy Dormition Cathedral and followed a hushed crowd through the caves under the monastery; we marvelled at the miniatures in the Mykola Syadristy micro art museum. All around us, an array of languages—some Slavic, some European, some from farther away. I was seldom able to pick out any words in Ukrainian.

The food in Ukraine was different than I expected. We seldom saw the Prairie Ukrainian staples I'd grown up with. Here, the *pyrohy* were called *varenyky*. They often showed up at dessert, filled with cherries. There was borscht, or course, and a lot of chicken in rich sauce, and more fish dishes than I could have imagined. I realized that in Alberta, even Ukrainian immigrants tended to stick to the same handful of dishes you could pick up on at least three tables from any farmers' market, no matter how small.

Our third day in Kyiv, I went to see Pripyat. It was like an anchor in the middle of our trip. Each day before, I had felt myself dragged toward it, even as we marvelled at our day trip destinations. I set the alarm to wake me early. I hadn't been dreaming since we'd been on vacation—or at least, I hadn't been remembering my dreams, waking each morning after a sound, uninterrupted sleep. I swatted the alarm as it beeped in the weak dawn, and next to me Adam rolled over, burying himself in the soft hotel pillows.

I dressed quickly, light layers, then dropped a kiss on his exposed shoulder before slipping out of the room. He didn't stir again.

Outside the hotel, I turned my phone to the cab driver, showing him the address of the tour pickup. He nodded and drove me to a bland neighbourhood of boxy commercial buildings, gas stations, and fenced-in parking lots. He stopped in front of one-story cinder-block cube painted a dull, buttery yellow. Two white vans were parked out front. I could see two more behind the chain-link fence between that building and the next.

A man and a woman wearing black hoodies with the tour company logo stood at the centre of a small crowd. The woman, blond, with a squarish face and pale blue eyes that reminded me somehow of watered-down milk, held a clipboard. I edged past a middle-aged British couple and gave her my name. She checked her list and gave me a curt nod.

"Okay," the tour guide began, "I am Olena, this is Bodhan. We leave in ten minutes. WC is inside." She gestured at the glass doorway in the centre of the butter-coloured building.

I made a quick trip to the washroom, trying hard not to touch the dingy toilet or chipped Formica counter before returning to wait by the bus. We did not leave in ten minutes. It was closer to half an hour. Finally, a family of four loped their way around the corner. Olena shot them a question in Ukrainian—their names, probably—and they answered, chatting a moment before climbing into the van. She then gestured at us to follow.

I managed to squeeze into a window seat next to a bearded Scottish kid of maybe eighteen. His friends sat across the aisle and they chattered easily, leaving me in peace.

Without a word of announcement, Olena and Bodhan, who turned out to be the driver, climbed into the front seats and we rumbled away, through the outskirts of Kyiv and then out of the city. We passed unremarkable farms and towns. I'd studied the map on my phone earlier and knew that one of them, a suburb of Kyiv, was Dymer, the town where Vira and Petro had lived. I was surprised I still remembered their names. I wondered whether they still lived there, or whether they'd moved on. It was unlikely, I realized, that they'd been anywhere near Chernobyl the day of the accident. Still, I wondered what had become of them.

Finally, in one of these towns, we rolled up to the gate. Dytyatky, I realized. Bodhan exchanged a few words with a uniformed man before the gate opened, and we rolled through. We were in the exclusion zone, the (mostly) unpopulated area surrounding Chernobyl. It was first evacuated on April 27, 1986, a day after the disaster, and officially, people are still prohibited from living there because of the high radiation levels. Of course, not everyone has accepted that prohibition.

Once we'd past the second checkpoint—Lelev—the tour guide turned around in her seat. The Ukrainian couple shushed their children, who were arguing, and next to me, the Scottish kid reached across the aisle to nudge his friend playfully.

"Okay," Olena called back from her spot at the front of the bus. "You stay with us today. If you have questions, you ask. We will tell you a little bit about the history of these places." She turned back around in her seat. We all waited, expecting her to start explaining the landscape we were passing through, but she didn't.

We drove past abandoned buildings and farmhouses. I remembered hearing about old people, mostly women, who had returned to their homes in the exclusion zone. I kept peering at the tiny, flat buildings, looking for the shapeless flowered skirts and bright headscarves I'd come to associate with little old Ukrainian woman. At home, in Alberta, we called the headscarves themselves "babushkas," but here, I learned, the term—*grandmother*—was applied to the women themselves.

The forest started to crowd the pitted road. I noticed more of the yellow-and-black radioactive signs dotting the landscape. Olena twisted around in her seat again.

"We are in the Red Forest," she announced. "You see it's not red anymore. But after the disaster, April 1986, this area was badly affected by the radiation. The forest died; the trees all turned red colour. They had to be cut down and buried. But then the trees came back, and the animals came back. Today, it's a very healthy forest. Lots of wildlife, even endangered animals. But it is still very radioactive." As if to punctuate her point, we passed a small clearing, a yellow sign in its centre, the spokes of its symbol red. Grass grew up around the rusting signpost, tangling its way up to the pitted yellow sign. "We don't stop here."

Soon, the forest on the right side of the road began to thin. Pathways appeared, rough roadways veering of the main road, and here and there, patches of bare, cracked cement.

Ahead, a crossroads. Bodhan slowed and turned right, raising his fingers in muted greeting to a van coming from the opposite direction.

On our left, more bare patches of cracked, decaying concrete. Small, crumbling buildings. A wide grassy ditch with tangles of wildflowers blooming. Behind a screen of trees, a tower rose, white, ringed with discs, the whole webbed with a metal lattice.

I felt a kind of thump high up in my chest. The backs of my hands prickled as a nervous flush spread through me.

Bodhan stopped.

Olena undid her seat belt and turned to face us. "Okay," she said, "we are near the power plant. You see the chimney there, that is part of the reactor number 4. Today, the reactor is covered in a sarcophagus that was built to contain the radiation."

Panic enveloped me, pinning me in place. I could feel the green radioactive sludge pooling around my feet.

"Can we go closer?" the middle-aged English woman called from near the back. Her voice pulled me back to myself, back to this prosaic van of tourists. I shuffled my feet, making sure they weren't mired in sludge.

"No, we don't go closer," Olena replied. "You can take a picture from here."

Bodhan opened the doors and we milled out onto the cracked asphalt. The British couple and the Scottish kids waded into the ditch, trying to get a closer view of the chimney, but they soon realized the roadway offered the best vantage point.

I didn't take out my camera. I just stared at the weathered tower. It seemed so unassuming from here, screened as it was by the tender young trees that lined the ditch. I felt a wave of disappointment, suddenly, the way you feel when you pass an accident on a highway, expecting to see something horrifying and exciting, but as you roll past, it's only a couple of weary drivers exchanging insurance information. The day was warming up. Birds chirped. The two Ukrainian kids were laughing, chasing and swatting each other as they ran around the van. And there it was, right there, just on the other side of a flimsy green partition.

Of course, guides would later routinely take tourists right up to the power plant. In 2016, The New Safe Confinement structure would be built to cover the decaying sarcophagus like a giant Quonset hut, the kind they used in Grand Centre to build the pool hall and the curling club.

After about five minutes, Bodhan held the van door open for us and we filed back inside. He turned us around and aimed us back at the main road.

The Scottish guy next to me was quiet now, and I was grateful. I felt somehow jumpy and sombre at the same time. I remembered once, a few years back, Esmé had talked me into going to see a play with her. It was in a slightly rundown theatre on the fringes of downtown Halifax. There was no curtain, and as we filed into the audience the actors were already onstage, frozen in position. As we waited for the performance to begin, I imagined how awful it would be if I suddenly stood up and walked on stage and shoved one of the actors—maybe the one who was perched on the edge of a chair. The idea filled me with a sense of humiliation and excitement. Somehow, I felt the same way now.

Pripyat looks almost normal from a distance, I realized. There are long blocks of apartment buildings—a bit grim, the Soviet architecture, but not unusual. You can find buildings a lot like those in almost every city. And there are houses and shops and offices. But there are so many missing windows. Trees too close. Too much greenery poking through the cracked cement. From a distance, it looks just barely off.

In what seemed like the middle of the city, Bodhan parked the bus and Olena led us toward the Ferris wheel I'd seen so many pictures of, each of its yellow cars reminding me of a set of cupcake wrappers: one upside down, the other right side up. We saw the bumper cars, moored in grass and moss, and hedged in by trees that grew through the rusting metal cage that surrounded them.

The English couple took pictures of everything. The Scottish girl walked with her camera held out in front of her, filming in short bursts. The little Ukrainian boy, the younger of the two siblings, it seemed, started crying—I think he wanted to climb into one of the bumper cars, but his father held his hand tightly.

Then Olena waved us onward. We followed the crumbling pavement to a school. She led us down the hallway to the gym. The high windows were shattered, and it smelled like something between a basement and a forest. The parquet flooring had become unmoored from the concrete below, lying like so many matchsticks ejected from their boxes, many still in rough alignment. Olena waved us down the hallway. As we followed, another one of the Scottish guys mimed shooting a ball into the basketball hoop that still hung by the opposite door.

The desks were still there, in the classrooms. Some even held books, the Cyrillic script marching inscrutably across their faded, curling covers.

At the end of the hallway, a painted mural pointed its finger commandingly at us. I'd seen a handful of these old Soviet images painted on walls across the city. Most were peeling and chipped, but this one, shielded from the worst of the weather, stared at us, stony-eyed. A pile of gas masks, the grey-green colour that made me think of movie aliens, lay in the middle of the hall between him and us, half-buried in leaves and other detritus.

I felt it then, the first loss of the year. My baby, our baby. Our embryo, I reminded myself. Our blastocyst. Dead only a few weeks after conception, it had never been a baby. It had probably not yet reached the fetal stage of development. Still, I felt a hollow longing now, as I stood in the abandoned school.

With a wave, Olena herded us out the door.

We walked all afternoon. To the pool, its deep end dropping down toward the broken tiles and garbage, the leaves and stems that had blown through its wall of gaping windows. We went into an apartment building, climbing the two-storey cement staircase, broken glass from windows and bottles crunching under our shoes. We stopped in an apartment with a rusting bed—no mattress, though a rotting blanket was tangled in its rusted coils—and a chipped table, a chair with a smashed and gaping pleather cover, a headless doll. A cup sitting on the table, faded and stained. I wondered suddenly if someone—Olena, perhaps, or another of the tour guides—had placed the cup and the doll there for effect.

The Prometheus Cinema was eerily beautiful. The green growth between its paving stones, the way the trees caressed the shapely pastel relief murals on its outer walls. I hadn't been able to bring myself to take any pictures, but here, I almost wanted to.

The Scottish girl and the middle-aged Englishwoman were still taking pictures and videos. A couple of times, the Ukrainian mother tried to wrangle her family into frame, but they twisted away, each wandering off to look at something different.

We passed a handful of other groups—some walking, like we were, following their guides; others rumbling past in buses and vans. I felt like the groups were either picture-takers or not—either they all had cameras, or none of them did. Or perhaps some were boldly curious, and others were ashamed. It seemed as though we were the only mixed group visiting that day.

As she led us toward the stark Polissya Hotel, Olena was telling us something about the city of Pripyat and its relationship to Prometheus. I tried to listen, but it was the other sounds that held my attention. The family's voices, the children chattering to their parents in Ukrainian, the occasional recognized words—*dobre, mama, papa, lyublyu, ya znayu*—tickling my consciousness. The little girl's name seemed to be Oksana. The boy's, I didn't know. And the voices of other groups as we passed them, or the rumble of the vans and buses, near and distant. The bird-song. Somewhere, a dog barked. So many sounds.

There were a handful of other places Olena pointed out, but my mind had started to feel like it was shrinking inward. Later, I was unable to tell Adam where else we'd gone.

Finally, tired and hungry, we were herded back into the van. We rumbled out of the city, turning deep into the forest. The road cut through the thick trees.

Olena turned around in her seat again. "Watch through the front window," she said. "We will go past Duga-2. It was a Soviet radar array. They called it 'woodpecker,' for its clicking sound it made on the radio. It stopped the day of the accident."

It loomed ahead of us, a massive cage in the sky. Bodhan stopped on the road, not bothering to pull over. "You can take pictures," Olena said, opening the door.

The huge, climbing structure was fitted with what looked like bullets, white metal cages piled all the way up, all the way across. This was where I finally pulled out my camera, showing how they netted the blue sky beyond.

Then we clambered back into the van. The kids and the Scottish tourists fell asleep before we even made it back to the checkpoint and out of the exclusion zone.

As we pulled into Kyiv, I had to fight back tears. There was a deep, quaking feeling in my chest. I took a slow breath and dialled the number for the cab company I'd saved in my phone.

Adam was watching a movie on the British channel when I got back. "How was it?" he asked.

"Yeah," I said, pulling off my hoodie. That quaking feeling hadn't left. I'd managed not to cry so far, and I didn't want to start now.

"Take any pictures?"

"No," I said. "Not in town. Too weird."

I sat on the bed next to him. I wanted to curl into him, wanted him to put his arm around me, but I felt him stiffen. "Don't worry," I said. "We did a radiation check on the way out."

"Yeah?" His voice was wary. I still felt him holding himself away from me.

I told him about the checkpoint and its little booths. You stepped in, you put your hands on the panels on either side, you waited for the second light to tell give you the all-clear. Then back in the van. Safe, good to go. Thanks for the visit! See you next time!

"I'll go have a shower," I said.

I wondered what he'd done all day on his own. He'd clung to my side for most of the trip, his thin body buzzing with nervousness. He let me order for him at restaurants and buy the museum tickets, even though the only Ukrainian I managed was a self-consciously mumbled *dyakuyu* at the end of each transaction.

He'd done the same across Europe. In Paris, I thought it was because he trusted my French more than his own, but he'd been virtually silent, except directly to me, in Brussels and Berlin.

He'd been different in Great Britain. Even in Glasgow, which was bigger and sometimes rougher than he was used to, he seemed at ease. In London, he held his body a little tighter, his arms close to his sides as though he were afraid that a Victorian Cockney pickpocket might catch him out at any moment, but he rode the underground willingly. He ordered pints and chips at the bars, and nodded *hello* to strangers.

It was in the villages of Scotland and the North of England that he really was himself, though. Perhaps more himself than I'd sometimes seen him at home. We'd go walking and he'd wave to people as we passed them, an easy gesture I'd never seen him make in Halifax. He seemed to seek out strangers in the pubs, falling into friendly chit-chat as though they were old friends. And he hooked his arm around me loosely, none of the nervous fidgeting that sometimes characterized his embraces at home.

"I love you like this," I told him as we strolled through the alley-ways in York.

"Like what?" he asked, dropping a kiss on my cheek, low, near my jaw.

"Relaxed, I guess," I said. "I like Vacation Adam."

"I like Vacation Jess," he said.

But Vacation Adam had disappeared as soon as we reached the continent. I could see his tension ease now as we boarded our flight home from Kyiv. I'd seen that look before. He used to look the same way in university once finals were over.

As our flight took off, leaving Kyiv and our vacation behind, I felt a little bereft, as though I had gone to collect something, to retrieve an object of great value, only I was never able to find it, and now I had to leave it behind all over again.

I looked over at Adam, and he was smiling with relief.

After Chernobyl, the demand for abortions increased across Europe. Doctors and pregnant women were consumed by the idea that the radiation from the nuclear accident might harm their fetuses. Fear of deformities, stillbirths, babies born riddled with cancer or other terminal illnesses crept across Europe. Birth rates dropped across Ukraine and Poland, Belarus, and Yugoslavia, even Hungary and Italy, upwards of two hundred thousand women chose to terminate their pregnancies rather than incubate an irradiated baby. Almost a quarter of early-stage pregnancies in Greece were terminated immediately following the accident.

The cause was radiophobia. Fear of radiation.

Did they imagine trying to love babies made unrecognizable by mutation, these women? Did they doubt their capacity to care for children whose faces and limbs were distorted, unrecognizable? Were they afraid of the toll that a child who would not care for itself would take on them—their souls, their marriages, their finances? Were they trying to prevent the sorrow of giving birth to a dead baby, or of giving birth to a baby who would soon die? Were they pinning their hopes on future children, children free from the blight of illness and disability, or curtailed little lives?

They could not have known that in the months and years after the nuclear disaster, there would be no reported increases in birth defects or infant mortality, in Ukraine or beyond.

SIXTEEN

The phone rings. I leap for it, feeling a rush of irritation. Why would Adam be calling again? He should know Freya might be sleeping.

It's not Adam, though. It's Laura. My annoyance melts into a rush of gratitude.

"You hanging in there?" she asks.

"I'm okay," I reply, almost honestly.

"And Freya's good?"

I try to smile so she can hear it in my voice. "She's doing fine."

I want to say more. I search for the words, but when I open my mouth, I feel a catch in my throat.

"Tell her that her aunties love her," Laura says.

"I will."

Laura was never a big fan of Adam's. It's funny—she's the only one who never really liked him. Our friendship had waned when we went our separate ways after high school, and it wasn't until Adam left that it really picked up again.

She met Adam during our first trip together to Cold Lake. It was summertime, and we'd decided to spend a few days at my mom's place, then go camping together at the provincial park. I hadn't been camping since I was a kid. In the summer, Mom used to drive Kyle and me out to the campground. She'd drop us off with our tent, our backpacks and sleeping bags, and a cooler full of food. There was a pay phone in the parking lot, and we had instructions to call her if we needed anything.

We'd spend two or three days out there, eating cereal and hot dogs, swimming in the lake, and sitting around the campfire.

The last time we went, though, Kyle's friends Matt and Devon had come, too. They set up camp at the next spot over, and the three boys spent all their time together. In the evening, I'd light a fire for our dinner, and Matt and Devon would pull out the beer that Devon's older sister Kimberly had bought them. They'd guffaw and shoot friendly insults at each other. I'm not sure they even noticed I was there.

By the second night, I wanted to call Mom and ask her to come and get me, but I knew there was no way I could go home without getting Kyle into trouble. So I stayed, keeping an eye on them all night so they didn't get drunk and fall into the fire. In the daytime, I'd go swimming alone or go hiking the trails while they slumbered on the beach or in their tents.

Fortunately, the camping gear was still in good shape when Adam and I took it out to inspect it. The tent didn't need patching, and Mom had carefully washed the sleeping bags before putting them away in the big Rubbermaid bin. They smelled a little stale, so I aired them out on the clothesline.

"You're sure you want to go camping?" Mom asked the day before we were heading out. We were all sitting on the deck, where she was barbecuing hamburgers for supper. It was a nice evening—warm and sunny, but not too hot. "The bed here is more comfortable, and we can always light the fire in the evening." She gestured to our backyard firepit. I doubted it had been lit at all since I'd moved out but, like the camping gear, it was still in good shape.

"That's okay, Mom. We've been looking forward to it," I said.

Mom looked at Adam. "Are you sure? She's not bullying you into this, is she?"

Adam chuckled awkwardly. "No, I want to."

"I don't bully him, Mom," I said. I took a swig of beer and tried to swallow the flush of annoyance.

"Oh, come on," she laughed, taking a sip of white wine. "You've always been bossy."

"*Mom*," I said.

"And a bit of a know-it-all." She laughed, winking at Adam. "You know what I mean."

"Stop it," I said.

Adam just forced another chuckle.

"When she was little, her only friend, Nicole, told me she didn't like playing with her. 'Jessica is too bossy,' she said. Nicole's dad used to *make her* come over and play." She laughed, turning the burgers. "Can you believe it?"

My throat got tight as I fought away the angry tears that stung beneath my eyelids. "Stop it," I said again, my fists curling around the beer bottle.

"Lucky that other girl, Laura, was such a pushover—she always did whatever you wanted to do. Otherwise, you'd never have had any friends!" She turned to Adam again. "Tell me, why do you put up with her? What's in it for you?" She laughed loudly, inviting him to join in.

I looked at Adam, willing him to stand up for me. Of course, he didn't. I stood up, knocking over my beer. Adam jumped to pick it up. I didn't bother.

"Oh, don't get bent out of shape," Mom said, still smiling. "I'm just teasing you. Sit down and have some supper."

"I'm not hungry." I couldn't fight the tears that spilled over my cheeks. The tightness in my throat made my voice quake—why was I letting her make me cry?

"You're too sensitive," Mom said. "You're going to need to grow a thicker skin. Don't you think?" she asked Adam.

He didn't answer, fixing his gaze on the deck railing next to him.

I walked into the house and shut myself inside my bedroom. I sat on my bed, tracing the flower pattern of the comforter with my finger. When I heard them come into the house after supper, I took out my laptop and pretended to work.

Adam knocked softly on the bedroom door as he opened it. "You all right?" he asked, giving me the same nervous little smile he'd given my mom.

"I'm fine."

"Are you hungry? We kept you a burger."

"Nope."

"Are you working?" He gestured awkwardly at my laptop.

"Yup."

"Okay. I'll leave you alone." And he went to watch TV with my mom in the living room.

I pretended to be asleep when he came back into the bedroom later. He squeezed into the double-bed with me, dropping a quick peck on my shoulder before he rolled over to sleep.

THE NEXT MORNING, WE LEFT BEFORE MY MOTHER WAS AWAKE.

We didn't say much on the first day of our camping trip. He shuffled around nervously as I set up the tent.

"Hand me the pegs," I said.

I watched as he turned nervously from place to place, until finally I grabbed them myself.

"Can you start a fire?" I asked when I'd finished setting up the tent.

"Sure," he said eagerly. He wadded up two sheets of newspaper, then grabbed three split lots and set them overtop.

I didn't even wait for the paper to burn out before I went off to collect some twigs, moss, and dry sticks for kindling.

"Thanks," he said awkwardly as I blew the flames to life.

I pulled the hot dogs from the cooler and speared a couple onto the roasting skewers. I roasted them myself, turning them carefully over the flames so they wouldn't burn.

"These are good," he said appreciatively. I tried to push the memory of his nervous laughter at my mom's needling jokes out of my mind.

The second day was better. I awoke to the chorus of birdsong and the lapping of the waves on the shore outside our tent. The sounds had washed my hurt and anger away. I imagined that the air in my lungs was staled by her spite, and I blew it out in long, slow breaths, refilling myself with the sharp, fresh smell of fir, poplar, and fresh water. I leaned up against him as we ate bowls of cereal for breakfast. We talked about going for a hike, but we just lounged in our camp chairs until the air was warm enough to go for a swim.

I laughed as Adam yelped and jabbed his fists into the air, shocked at the frosty bite of the lake water. His strangled shout echoed back at us, bouncing off the low, forested rise that sloped up from the beach. A breeze rustled the poplars, and their leathery leaves rattled together in applause.

"There's a reason it's called *Cold* Lake," I called as I launched forward, diving under the sparking surface—no point trying to ease your way in. The icy water stung my eyes. When I bobbed back up again, my skin was tingling pleasantly from the shock. I bounced a bit in the chest-deep water, letting my gaze span the lake. It was huge, much bigger than the lakes we knew in Nova Scotia. From here, you couldn't see the opposite shore. It could be the ocean, except that the fresh water was glass-smooth and clear.

Adam groaned, then grabbed his nose with his hand and plunged straight down, sitting on the bottom of the lake for a split second before he bobbed back up, gasping and spluttering. I swam over to him, pressing my lake-cooled skin to his. Overhead, a fighter jet roared past on its way back to the base. For just the tiniest moment as the roar split the still air, my breath caught and the urge to run seized my legs. Then, just as quickly, the urge was gone. We watched it slice its path through the cloudless blue sky.

We said a stiff goodbye to my mom when we returned the camping gear a few days later. If she noticed that my anger hadn't fully dissipated, she didn't say anything. She hugged us tightly, first me, then Adam, then me again as we loaded our suitcases into the rental car.

"It was so good having you guys," she said. "I love you so much. You know that, right?"

"I love you, too," I replied, still trying to swallow my bitterness.

She stood, waving from the front step, as we drove down the street.

"I need a coffee," I said, steering the car toward main street and the town's only non–Tim Horton's coffee shop. I parked on the street, and Adam followed me inside.

There was a line at the counter. The woman ahead of us had short hair twisted into little knots, the tips dyed a bright magenta. She turned as we came in and I gasped: "Laura!"

She looked great. The short hairstyle made her dark eyes look enormous. Her lipstick matched the magenta shade of her hair. Her face broke into a wide grin as she saw me, and she threw her arms around my neck for a hug. "Jessie!"

Behind me, Adam shuffled awkwardly.

"Laura, this is my boyfriend, Adam."

He stuck out his hand to shake hers.

"Cute!" Laura said, winking at me. "Come, come, come!" She ushered us out of the line-up and to a table. She and I sat down, and Adam glanced at the counter.

"Do you want me to get us coffee?" he asked.

"I can't stay long," Laura said. "My parents are expecting me. But sit down, we have to catch up first!"

Laura, it seemed, had moved to Victoria a few years back. She'd been working as a salesperson for a big box store. "Electronics." She laughed. "Can you believe it? I've been dying to tell you." Computers had never been her thing. When we were in high school, I used to help her with her word processor and printer.

"Adam," she said, her voice light and teasing. "Tell me the truth. Are you good enough for my Jess?"

He blushed and laughed. "I hope so."

"My mom thinks so," I said with a grin.

Laura rolled her eyes. "Mm." She knew how my mom could be. Not that she'd really witnessed Mom's rages, not directly—Mom had always been on her best behaviour around guests, hers or mine. But Laura knew.

She glanced at her watch. "I have to go," she said. "I hate this, but Mom and Dad are waiting." She hugged me one more time. She smelled like sandalwood and vanilla. "Call me, okay?"

"I will," I promised, and I meant it.

She blew a kiss toward Adam. "Good to meet you!"

"Bye," he said. He watched her go, a kind of bewildered look on his face.

We got back into the lineup and picked up our coffees and some snacks for the road.

"She seems fun," Adam said as we got back into the car.

"She's the best," I replied. It was funny—I never would have called her "fun" growing up. "Sweet," yes, and "nice." But now, it was as though a light inside her had been turned on, illuminating something bright and vibrant and *fun* that had always been there, though I'd never noticed it before. I started up the car and turned toward the highway.

OF COURSE WE HADN'T TOLD MOM, BUT WE WERE STAYING overnight with Kyle, Juliet, and little Maddie in Edmonton before our flight home. Juliet was pregnant with their second, and I hadn't met my eldest niece yet.

Kyle and Juliet had a townhouse in Leduc, near the airport. When we got there, Kyle wanted to show off his new truck and his snow-mobiles in the garage. Juliet wouldn't let him until we'd had some sand-wiches and iced tea.

Maddie was a shy toddler. She was wearing a little tutu, and all she wanted to do was twirl the skirt around by herself in the living room. Juliet kept calling her back into the dining room, but Maddie would duck in, bury her face against Juliet's round belly, then squirm off away again as soon as she could. She sang a tuneless, wordless song to herself as she twirled.

Juliet was due in October. "I'm showing so much more than I did with Maddie," she complained, rubbing the even roundness of her belly. I wondered if I was supposed to ask her to touch it, to feel the baby kick and move. I didn't really know Juliet, so I didn't ask.

"How's the job in Halifax?" Kyle asked, grabbing a beer for Adam and one for himself out of the fridge.

"Good," I said. "We're both working in our field now. I'm electrical, and Adam's civil."

Kyle nodded, not asking for further explanation. "You buy yourself a place yet?"

"We're still renting."

"Why?" Kyle directed the question to Adam.

"Oh," Adam replied, glancing at me, "we don't really know what we want yet. Like, a house or a condo, or whatever."

"You gotta buy," Kyle said. "Renting is basically just flushing your money."

"For sure," Adam replied, nodding.

"You don't even know what our rent is," I said.

"Doesn't matter," Kyle said. "It's all going into your landlord's pocket."

"I'm not going to buy up the first money pit I can get my hands on just to stop paying rent." I looked pointedly at Adam's beer. Neither he nor Kyle seemed to notice. "Think I can get one of those?"

Kyle shrugged, ambling back to the fridge. "Suit yourself," he said. I wasn't sure if he meant the beer or the apartment.

In the living room, we heard a thump as Maddie spun herself into the coffee table and fell to the floor with a wail. Juliet stood with difficulty and made her way to the living room to comfort her daughter.

"What do you drive?" Kyle asked Adam.

"We've still got Jess's Taurus," Adam said. He looked a little sheepish.

Kyle snorted. "Isn't that thing like twenty years old? Why don't you get yourself something new?"

"I'm not stopping him," I snapped. Adam had never expressed interest in buying a car. He took the bus and the ferry to work, and I drove us to the grocery store. I knew he'd gotten his license at sixteen, but I'd never seen him drive. But he was nodding thoughtfully now, as though the idea of buying a car of his own was only just occurring to him.

Fortunately, the subject didn't come up again. I helped Juliet make supper, roast beef and potatoes, and over dinner we made idle chit-chat and then listened as Kyle told us about his new job as a journeyman operating engineer.

"Both of us, engineers," Kyle said, chuckling. "Tell that to Mom."

"Hmm," I said with a little smile. Of course, he knew that an operating engineer was not an engineer. He drove the big equipment. He'd never finished high school, much less university. It was an entirely different class of job.

"Do you work?" Adam asked Juliet. Then he caught himself and blushed. "I mean, other than…" he gestured at Maddie, who was eating peas, one by one, with her fingers.

"I was a medical receptionist before Maddie," Juliet replied. "I might go back once the kids are in school."

I looked around their neat, bland, newly built condo and shuddered inwardly. I couldn't imagine spending all day every day here, with no one but a toddler to talk to. Suddenly, I couldn't wait to get back to work.

Our flight was early the next morning. We left before Juliet or Maddie woke up, but Kyle got up to say goodbye. He and I had coffee together while Adam showered.

"You and Mom still talk?" he asked. He was leaning back in his chair, smirking a little bit, as though the idea of keeping in touch with our mother was silly. Like sleeping with a night light or taking a superhero lunch box to work.

"Sometimes."

He was quiet for a minute. His smile faded. "I felt pretty bad, leaving you there."

I cleared my throat. "It was okay," I said. "She wasn't as bad with me as she was with you." It was true, but I felt guilty for admitting it—as though I had somehow stolen his share of goodwill from our mother, leaving him with my share of the acrimony.

"Yeah. Still." He laughed a little. Flat, humourless. "I almost left lots of times before."

"You did?"

"Yeah. This one time, I was in grade nine. She and I had a fight the morning before school. I had a rip in the sleeve of my coat, couldn't remember how it happened, and she went ballistic. Then she got all quiet like she did." His eyes were fixed on the faded company logo on his coffee cup. "I kept waiting for her to really let me have it, days it felt like, but she never did. Just froze me out, you know?"

I swallowed. There were tears prickling behind my eyes suddenly and I couldn't answer, so I gave him a quick nod to say, yeah, I did know. I knew that perilous quiet so well.

"So I got to school and Mr. Banerjee, he starts in on me about my homework, and I just lost it. I threw my math book at the window. I thought I was in shit for sure, but he didn't send me to the principal, he sent me to see Mr. Desjarlais instead."

"Oh." The guidance counsellor. The one who had asked me if I wanted to be a nurse or a teacher.

"And when Mr. Banerjee started walking me down the hall, that's when I realized I was crying. Like, full-on bawling. I couldn't believe I was crying in class, in front of everyone, like a baby. So anyway, Banerjee leaves me in Desjarlais's office, and I finally stop bawling, and Desjarlais asks me if there's anything I need to tell him, and I say no, it doesn't matter anyway because I'm leaving, I'm going to live with my dad since my mom doesn't want me around."

"Shit. What did he do?"

Kyle laughed again, that same mirthless sound. He ran his finger slowly along the edge of the counter. "He told Mom."

I felt my stomach drop. It was as though I were a kid again, knowing Kyle and I were going to catch it. "What?"

"Yeah. I knew as soon as she got home from school that day. I think she said something like, *I had a very interesting talk in the teacher's lounge today.* And that was it. I don't think she said a word to me for like a week. I thought I was going to catch frostbite off her. Honest, it scared me shitless."

I didn't know what to say. I tried to remember a prolonged coldness between Kyle and Mom around that time. I couldn't think of any. I felt a slow, sinking guilt. It had been that bad, and I hadn't noticed.

Adam came downstairs then, carrying both of our bags.

Kyle and I stood. Time to go. He reached an arm out for a hug. It was quick, self-conscious.

"Well, take care," he said. Then to Adam, "Let me know what you decide to get for a car, eh?"

"Yeah, for sure!" Adam replied. He gave Kyle a kind of salute-wave as he climbed into the rental car.

Kyle stood out in front of his house watching us drive away, until we turned the corner and out of sight.

WHEN WE GOT HOME, ADAM WENT INTO RESEARCH MODE. He brought home brochures from dealerships, bought automotive magazines, and spent hours almost every night reading product reviews online. Finally, after a month or so, he'd made his choice: a compact hybrid sedan.

"It's got more leg room than the previous model, and it gets close to twenty kilometres per litre," he gushed. "It's more expensive than some of the other hybrids, but they've got a good track record, and lower emissions."

"That's interesting," I lied, not looking up from my phone. I still wasn't convinced he was going to commit. But the following day, as soon as he got home from work, he asked me to drive him to the dealership in the North End. He drove himself home in his hybrid sedan.

The next day, he insisted on driving me to work. He dropped me off in front of the office just as Yash was arriving.

"Sweet car," Yash said, placing his palm against the fender the way you might touch the flank of a horse.

"Thanks!" Adam said through my open door. "It's new."

"I've been thinking about a new car, myself."

"Yeah?" Adam asked. "Want to give this one a drive?"

"Sure," said Yash. "You free after work today?"

"Absolutely!" Adam was virtually beaming.

"Okay, I've got to get in," I said. "See you at five?"

"You got it!"

Yash held the office door open for me as Adam pulled away. "You been behind the wheel yet?"

"Nope." I'd dropped him off at the dealership and let him do his thing the night before.

"Hope you're not jealous," he teased.

I shook my head. "All yours."

That evening, Adam was already waiting as Yash and I emerged from work. He handed the keys to Yash and climbed into the back, leaving me the passenger seat. I gave Yash directions to our apartment and he drove cautiously, like someone who's not comfortable behind the wheel.

"What do you drive now?" I asked. I'd never seen him in the small company parking lot behind our office.

"My bike," he replied with a smile.

"That's a lot safer, actually," I said. "You have a one in three hundred chance of dying in a car accident, and only a one in forty-five-hundred chance of dying in a cycling accident."

Yash chuckled. "Good to know."

Adam launched into the technical details of the car—engine size, gas mileage, emissions. Yash listened patiently. The two of them stayed outside as I went into the apartment. They stood on either side of the vehicle, talking over the hood. It was nice, I thought. Adam hadn't really had a lot of friends since university. And Yash was a good guy.

SEVENTEEN

In the last few years, the best times I've had with Freya have mostly come out of nowhere. There was the trip to Montreal, of course—that was special, for both of us. But often, when I plan something for the two of us together, we both end up grumpy, sniping at each other. We probably expect too much.

One day, after a doctor's appointment, she and I were walking back to the car when we passed a little cart advertising horchata.

"What's hor-cha-ta?" Freya asked, pointing with her chin.

"I don't know," I muttered, barely glancing at the street vendor. The doctor had gone over post-operative routines, and I was trying to work out a schedule in my head—when she'd eat and sleep, when I'd have to change her dressings and give her medication, when we'd have to return for a follow-up. I dug through my purse with one hand, feeling for my keys.

Freya stopped. "Let's find out," she said.

I opened my mouth, ready to tell her no, that we had to get going, I needed to stop for groceries on the way home, and we'd need to call her dad and let him know what the doctor said. But then I looked at her, my beautiful, stubborn, brilliant, irreverent daughter. Her expression was so wide open, so expectant, it dissolved all my mundane concerns.

"That's a good idea," I said. "Why don't you order for us."

She nodded and turned to the vendor. "Two horchatas, please," she said, her voice lowering ever so slightly in timbre—her grown-up voice.

We walked slowly back to the car, sipping our drinks. "It's like an iced latte, but without the coffee," she observed.

"Since when do you know so much about coffee?" I asked. I felt like I should scold her, lecture her on the dangers of caffeine. Did it really stunt your growth? I'd need to look that up. But I didn't want to let this easiness between us slip away.

She shrugged. "Dad gets lattes sometimes, and he lets me try his."

"Do you like it?" I asked.

"Not really. Unless there's a lot of sugar in it." She stopped then, prodding the bottom of her cup with her straw. "Mom, are you afraid about my surgery?"

My words caught in my throat. I forced a cough to give myself a second to answer. "Yeah. I am," I said at last. "I know Dr. Huang says not to worry, but I do."

She nodded. "Me too."

We walked on, then. I glanced at her, but her attention was on her drink. "Does it make you more worried, that I worry about it?"

She looked up at me then with a scared little smile. "No, it kind of makes me feel better. Is that weird?"

"Yep, you're weird," I said, wrapping my arm around her shoulder. "Like mother, like daughter," I added, pulling her tightly to me as we walked, horchatas in hand.

WHEN PEOPLE ASKED ME WHY ADAM AND I DECIDED TO HAVE KIDS after so many years together, I'd say it was because we got bored. I said it as a joke, but it wasn't completely untrue. Once Adam got his first engineering job, our lives flattened out. We both worked, and we both liked our jobs. Everything just…was.

I spent a few months of the year travelling. I'd been promoted a couple of times, first to professional engineer on the Risk & Compliance group, signing off on my own work instead of doing the routine technical stuff for more senior team members. Then Sam left Maritime Energy to work at a plant somewhere out West, and I applied to be the senior engineer, Process Safety, the position he had just vacated.

I didn't get it. Yash did—he had a Master's degree; I didn't.

I tried to remind myself that it was only fair—Yash had been on the job longer, and he had more education. Still, the form letter thanking me for my interest and informing me that, *with regret,* they were *unable to offer me the position at this time,* stung. The senior engineer title stoked my ambition, certainly. It was the process safety part that I truly craved, though. Taking charge of the entire system of safety, from machinery to processes, product to personnel—the ability to visualize and direct an entire safety network, to ensure that part of that system worked together seamlessly under every imaginable circumstance. I wanted that. I wanted it to be me.

But instead, the following year, I was promoted to senior engineer: project leader for Risk & Compliance. Douglas's old job—he had moved up to a senior managing engineer position. I chose the team members, met with clients, set up the schedules and the work projects.

"I told you, you were meant to be running these things," Douglas chortled.

I refrained from pointing out that I'd gotten there without an MBA.

In truth, I hated turning over so much of the technical side of the job to a junior team member. I didn't like meeting with executives and government types to translate the complexities of our work into business-speak. I resented that my purview had largely shifted from the technical to the interpersonal. I was spending most of my time in Halifax now. I missed the control rooms, with their intricate orderliness. And I hated interviewing for engineers and technicians.

"What's the point?" I asked Douglas. "Who cares whether they're good at answering questions? Let's have them submit samples of their work—that's the only way we're going to see whether they know what they're doing."

"There's more to the job than just the technical competencies, Jessica," he replied. "You need to get a feel for your team members."

I remembered Sam at the party, years ago now, and cringed. I was thankful he hadn't been the one to interview me for the job.

"Fine," I said, looking over a stack of résumés. We were getting ready to start an expansion project on a hydroelectric plant in western New Brunswick.

After that first project, I started calling interviews the Asshole Filtration System. I made sure applicants had the technical ability to get the job done, then I asked a few questions to make sure they wouldn't be too unpleasant on the job site.

I soon learned that it did me no good to have Douglas or any of my other male colleagues in the interview room. On my first job, I hired a junior engineer named Lance. He'd just earned his degree from a university out west. In the interview, he was eager to tell Douglas about his scholarships and awards, and about his time as vice president of the university's Engineering Students' Society. I noticed that he only spoke directly to Douglas during the interview, but I didn't think about it until we were in rural New Brunswick, and Lance would abruptly walk away from me during meetings.

The first time it happened, it was during a start-up meeting at the plant.

"We're not done here," I called after him as he strode toward his workspace.

"Whatever, I've got it," he replied without looking back. It became a kind of refrain for him whenever we spoke. He'd listen for a moment or two, then abruptly tune out. "I've *got* it."

When I pointed out errors in his work, he'd cross his arms and glared at me. "I'm supposed to be getting guidance," he'd snap. "You're supposed to be *mentoring* me."

One afternoon, when Lance and the team were back in Halifax for a few days, I overheard him grumbling to an engineer from another division. I only caught the words "affirmative action" and "feminazi," but when the other engineer caught sight of me, he coughed and dropped his gaze to the ground.

I got pretty good at filtering out the assholes after that. I'd recognize something Lance-like in their gaze or their tone, and I'd ask the kind of question that was really an accusation—a skill I'd learned from my mom: "I see it took you almost six years to finish your degree. Why is that?" or "Can you tell me about this gap in your employment?"

The Lances would always get hostile. They'd usually imply I didn't know what I was talking about: "Well, my specialization is actually pretty complicated. You can't just breeze through it like in other fields."

Sometimes, it hurt not to hire them, especially when I could tell they were good at what they did. But considering the amount of time I'd wasted in New Brunswick, redoing Lance's work, or re-explaining things he couldn't be bothered to listen to the first time, I knew it wouldn't be worth having them around.

So, over the next few years, I'd work in Halifax to put the projects together and wrap them up, spending days, rather than weeks or months, at various power plants across Atlantic Canada, designing and upgrading control systems—or rather, supervising the staff who did the hands-on designing and upgrading. Adam, meanwhile, had trouble settling at work as an engineer, moving from position to position in his first few years. He started off working mainly on roadways, eventually specializing in bridge construction. He persuaded me to buy a recently refurbished bungalow in Dartmouth, but I drew the line when he suggested we get a dog.

"I'm always travelling," I said, even though that wasn't strictly true anymore. "Are you going to take care of it all by yourself?"

"I had dogs when I was a kid," he replied.

"I don't want our yard to be full of dog shit."

We settled on a cat, an affectionate calico named Gemini.

Adam had joined a rec floor hockey league with Yash—they played once a week, going out with the rest of the team for beers afterwards, but I was never much for sports. Adam and I mostly watched TV together in the evening. It was the monotony of those nights that made me wish for something different. It made me remember Kyle and Juliet's bland condo. There were moments when the pity I'd felt during that visit rushed back at me, and I felt the way I had then: pressed in, restricted.

There was an elementary school down the block from us. I'd always thought there was something charming about the seasonal parade of schoolchildren—their excitement for a new school year each September, their funny cartoon-character Halloween costumes, the snowsuits, the reappearance of bare knees and arms in the spring, their giddy excitement at the end of the school year in June. It was the same pattern repeated over and over, but always with the same joy, the same excitement.

"We should have a kid," I said to Adam one night. We'd just finished watching a movie. I expected to have to talk him into it, but he got this big, goofy grin on his face.

"Hell, yeah," he said.

He kissed me, his tongue flitting against mine, his hands grasping my hips. I shifted over on the couch, pressing my body the length of his. The sex we had there in the living room was passionate, urgent, our bodies moving together in the perfect synchronicity of our desire. Since we'd been young—studying, then fucking, then studying again—I had often thought of our attraction in atomic terms, an attractive electromagnetic pull between his body and mine. There was no thought, no calculation, only the force of my want, and his. Afterwards, we kissed lazily until we were hot again, and then we moved to the bedroom, teasing, playing, laughing. Making love.

Three months later, I knew before my period was even due. My breasts felt suddenly tender and full. I felt a momentary clutch of regret. Good god, there was so much we hadn't talked about. I wasn't ready. And we only had nine months—fewer in fact. How could we get ready to become parents in under nine months?

But it didn't take. Four weeks later, I felt a familiar ache deep in my groin as I drove home from work. I already knew what I'd find when I got to the bathroom at home: a smear of blood in my underwear.

I called my doctor's office, asking if I could come in for an appointment that evening.

"We can get you in next week," the receptionist said.

"No. It can't wait," I replied, feeling the panic mount. Next week would be too late.

"Is this an emergency?" the receptionist asked.

"I think so," I said. "I'm six weeks, but I think I'm having—I think I might be losing it."

"Oh, honey, I'm sorry," the receptionist said. I knew from her tone that the doctor wouldn't be able to stop what was happening.

As I hung up the phone, I thought about that feeling of regret. The guilt washed over me. Then, with the guilt, a feeling of emptiness. There had been something alive inside me. And now—nothing.

Maybe it was because of my panic. Maybe my body could sense my unreadiness. I pressed my hands into the flat flesh of my lower belly, imagining my organs shifting inside me, yielding to the invading fingers pressing inward through skin and muscle. It felt alien, this flesh under my fingers. My body an adversary to me, rebelling against my panic and my uncertainty.

Maybe it was my fault.

I got in to see my doctor the following week. She told me we should wait three months before trying again. "If you get pregnant too quickly," she said, "you increase your odds of miscarrying again."

By how much? I wanted to ask. *What are the odds?* But I didn't. I'd just look it up when I got home. That, and the degree to which taking the prenatal vitamins she'd suggested would mitigate the risk of birth defects. We were already looking forward to our trip to Europe, only a few months away by then, and I realized it was probably better that I wouldn't be pregnant while we were travelling abroad.

But we didn't wait three months to start trying. Because just a couple of months later, I got a phone call from the Cold Lake Regional Hospital. Suddenly, I had other plans to make, problems to sort, and even though the idea of waiting and trying again fell away from my thoughts, my body, it turned out, would soon make plans of its own.

EIGHTEEN

It's hard to find specific data on your individual odds of having a heart attack. Your odds go up if you're a man; if you smoke, drink, and eat red meat; if you have high blood pressure or high cholesterol. The odds go up as you age.

Women are much less likely to have a heart attack than men are, but they're much more likely to die if they do. Part of the reason for this discrepancy is that the women who have a heart attack, the people around them, and even medical staff are less likely to recognize the symptoms. Women receive treatment later, or not at all.

The last time I spoke to my mom on the phone, she told me she'd been having trouble sleeping. She was tired all the time. And she was anxious and grouchy. Privately, I thought that pretty well described her most of the time. I asked her whether she'd been drinking more than usual. She didn't answer. Instead, she asked about work, and we talked about that for a while before I told her I had to go, that Adam was waiting for me to have supper. Adam was out playing floor hockey. My dinner, takeout from the Punjabi place near the office, was getting cold.

Later, Janet would tell me that Mom thought maybe she had a stomach bug. She'd stopped by Janet's for a visit, but she left abruptly, feeling sweaty and sick to her stomach. Janet had made a joke about menopause and hot flashes.

My mom had been less than a block away from the house. Instead of following the road as it turned, however, she'd gone straight, smashing into her neighbour's parked car in their driveway. Another few minutes and she'd have made it all the way home.

She was in hospital. She was not yet conscious. She'd had an ST segment elevation myocardial infarction. A STEMI, they called it.

I don't remember hanging up the phone with the hospital. I just remember the strange buzzing sensation in my ears, my jaws, my arms and legs as I planned and prepared. I found a flight to Edmonton that left in just a few hours. I booked it, then I threw a mix of work clothes and sweats into a bag. Then I called Kyle.

"What's going on?" It was how he always answered the phone. Easygoing, not urgent.

"You in Edmonton?" I knew he was. I'd called his landline. It was hard to reach him up at the camps—cell service was spotty, and he kept his phone off during the long shifts.

"Yeah, 'til Monday. Why?"

"Mom's in the hospital." When I said it, I noticed how clear my voice was. I wasn't crying. I should be crying, I thought. "My flight lands at 11:20. Can I stay with you tonight?"

"What happened?" he asked. His voice was clear, too.

"Heart attack. She was driving, and she crashed the car. I don't think the crash was bad, though." In fact, I hadn't asked. But then, the woman who had called from the hospital—was she a doctor? I wasn't sure. I couldn't remember what she'd said. But the woman, she had talked mostly about the heart attack. She'd only really mentioned the car accident in passing.

"Shit," he said. "Yeah, of course. I'll pick you up at the airport."

"You don't have to," I said.

"Come on."

"Okay. See you soon."

"Yeah. Take care."

I glanced at the clock. By the time Adam got home, I'd be flying over the prairies. I called him next.

I got his voicemail. "Hey," I started, but I didn't know what I should say. I hung up and called again.

He picked up this time, out of breath. "Everything okay?"

"Yeah." I said it automatically. "Um, no, actually. I have to go home. Mom's in the hospital."

"Is she okay?"

Irritation and laughter bubbled up at the same time. "Of course not," I said. Only when I said it, I didn't laugh, I cried.

"I'll be right home."

"Don't," I said, hiccoughing. "I have to leave. I booked a flight. I have to get to the airport."

There was a pause. "I'll be right home."

I was waiting out front with my suitcase when Adam pulled up, still sweaty in his gym shorts.

"You didn't book a flight for me?" he asked quietly as we drove.

"You weren't here," I said.

We were quiet the rest of the way.

As we pulled up to the airport, I realized I'd need to tell someone at work I wasn't coming in. I fumbled for my phone.

"Just send them an email when you get there," Adam said.

"Right." I felt dumb for not thinking of that.

Adam put his hand on the back of my neck and pressed his forehead to mine. "Do you want me to come?"

I pulled away and unbuckled my suitcase. "You don't have to."

"I can get a flight tomorrow?"

Something pulled in my chest, wanting me to say, "Come with me now. We'll book your flight at the ticketing desk." But I couldn't do it. "Whatever you want," I said, and got out of the car.

He lowered my window. "I'll be there tomorrow."

I nodded and pulled my suitcase into the airport. I didn't want to look back at him. I was afraid that if I did, I might start to cry again.

Turning my phone off for the flight was torture. Every minute, I imagined that the hospital might be trying to call me. Or Kyle. Or Adam. Or even Mom herself, to say that she was fine, she was already back at home, it wasn't that serious. But when I turned my phone back on in Edmonton, there was nothing—no voicemail, no texts, no missed calls. Not a word.

Kyle was waiting for me just outside baggage claim. He put one arm around me as we walked toward the parking garage. It was unseasonably cold, but he didn't bother to zip up his jacket as we walked to the truck. I hadn't packed a jacket. It was summer-warm in Halifax.

His place was dark. He and Juliet had split up a couple of years earlier. They had joint custody of the girls, Maddie and Kayleigh, but with Kyle still working on the rigs, I doubted they were with him more than a couple of days a month. If I happened to catch them at his place when I called, he'd put them on the phone. Maddie was still shy, but Kayleigh was a talker. She was full of stories—a strange collage of things she and her sister had done and stories she had seen in cartoons. There were no boundaries between reality and fiction for her. She made me laugh.

He stumbled a bit on some shoes in the porch as he let us in, fumbling to find the light switch. When the hall light blazed on, I realized how tired I was. It was three in the morning in Halifax.

"I made up the bed in Maddie's room for you," he said.

"Thanks." I started making my way there.

"What's the plan?"

"I was gonna rent a car and drive up first thing," I said, turning around. "Unless you want to come with."

He rolled his head back and forth as though he had a crick in his neck. "I don't think so," he said at last, rubbing his hand over the back of his neck.

"Okay." My legs felt heavy as I walked up the stairs to my niece's bedroom. "Goodnight."

"Night," he called.

HE DID DRIVE UP WITH ME, THOUGH. WE DIDN'T EVEN TALK ABOUT it. We had a quiet breakfast together in the kitchen, then Kyle got up and said, "I'll be ready in half an hour." Then we were on the road, him behind the wheel of his pickup, and me in the passenger seat with a sweatshirt rolled behind my lower back to ease the ache brought on by the airplane seat.

We didn't talk much at first. I dozed a bit, jerking awake every time my head lolled too far forward. I hadn't slept much the night before, in Maddie's twin bed.

"So, uh, Zoë and I are getting married," he said at last.

I looked over at him. He was staring at the road ahead, but I thought he might be smiling a bit. "Holy shit, Kyle, that's awesome. Congratulations."

"Yeah, thanks." He did smile now, glancing over at me. He looked almost sheepish, like a teenager talking about his first girlfriend. Except I couldn't remember Kyle smiling like that when he was a teenager. Or talking about any girlfriends. "We thought we might do a destination thing, like to Mexico, maybe in April or May because it's cheaper. You think you and Adam might come?"

"Yeah, of course," I said. "Absolutely."

"Cool."

We were quiet again. Then I had to ask. "You think you'll tell Mom?"

Kyle made a *pshhh* sound that was half-laughter, half-exasperation. "If she'll let me," he said.

I had been the one to tell her about Maddie and Kayleigh. Of course, she'd asked both times whether Kyle and Juliet were married and I'd told her no. Both times, she'd just shaken her head, as though it were dark news that she'd expected all along. I don't know whether she'd ever spoken to her granddaughters, or seen pictures. I was sure she'd never met them.

"I tried to go see her," he said. "Couple of years back."

I looked over at him, surprised. "Yeah?"

He shook his head. "She wouldn't even let me in the house. Said something like, 'If you really wanted to have a relationship with me, you'd put in some effort.'" He slammed his hands on the wheel. "And I got mad. I said, 'What the fuck you think *this* is,' then she got mad and shut the door, and that was it."

"Shit," I said. "I'm sorry."

He changed lanes. "I don't know how you put up with her."

I tossed up my hands. What choice do I have? Of course, I had a choice. Kyle's choice.

Kyle drove fast. We were set to make the three-hour drive in under two and a half. But with less than an hour of road ahead of us, my phone rang. I'd just been dozing off and it startled me awake, making me jerk my head up. A buzzing feeling spread through my jaw, my face as I talked. I don't think the conversation took long. But that buzzing felt so huge by the time I hung up, I thought Kyle must be able to hear it.

"Well?" he asked.

"She's gone," I said. As the words came out my throat tightened up, and I started to sob. Kyle reached over and squeezed my shoulder, and that made it worse. Soon, I was crying so hard I was hiccoughing.

I was thinking about how the frustration would bubble up in me every time Mom and I talked. I was thinking about how I used to *hope* she knew how much she was pissing me off. I'd hope that if she knew how mad she was making me, she'd realize what she was like, how other people saw the things she said and the way she acted. I hoped she'd notice how mad I was, and when she did, she'd just try hard to be better.

But now the idea that she *had* noticed was unbearable. I thought about every time I'd cut off our conversations, every time I'd lied and told her I had something else to do, every time I'd responded to her questions with a tight *Okay, Mom*. Each one tortured me. The idea that she'd known how much she annoyed me, angered me, was unbearable.

Finally, I got my sobs under control. Kyle found a squished box of Kleenex behind his seat and wiped all the snot and tears from my face and calmed the hiccoughing brought on by the sobbing.

"Should we go straight to the hospital?" he asked when I was under control again.

I shook my head. "They said we don't have to. We can just make arrangements—" The tears were welling up again, so I shook my head.

So we went home, instead. To Mom's house.

My bedroom was still *my* bedroom, though it didn't have much of my stuff in it. Between Mom and I, we'd cleaned most of my old toys and books and clothes out years earlier. Kyle's bedroom was a guestroom. It wasn't Kyle's anymore, and it hadn't been in years. His old bed was in there, and his old dresser. The same wallpaper he'd chosen as a kid still hung on the walls—light blue with criss-crossed yellow and red lines. But there was nothing of his left. Not a thing.

The summer after Kyle had left, when it was clear he wasn't coming back, Mom had gone in there with a garbage bag and stuffed anything he'd left behind—clothes, toys, pictures and yearbooks, old schoolwork—inside. Everything had gone into the plastic bag. I didn't ask where it had gone. Maybe she threw it out. But as my brother walked in and set his duffel bag on the bed that used to be his, I suddenly wondered whether we'd find it tucked away in the house somewhere.

ADAM ARRIVED THAT EVENING. HE'D SENT ME AN EMAIL WHILE I WAS flying in to Edmonton to let me know he'd be flying right in to Cold Lake. I'd never been to the Cold Lake airport. It had been there all my life, just at the edge of the military base, but until just a couple of years ago, no commercial flights had come through. I'd looked at flying right into town myself, but the earliest I could have gotten there would have been the middle of the day. I couldn't stand the thought of waiting around Edmonton for a connecting flight. Plus, this way I'd been able to bring Kyle up with me. I was glad he was there.

Kyle offered to pick Adam up at the airport. I was on the phone with the funeral home, and I still had to call the newspaper and the caterers, so I agreed. Kyle was pleasant enough, and helpful enough in his way, but I was taking on all the planning myself. It didn't feel right to ask him for help with the service.

Service. Funeral. Because she was gone. Dead. Passed. So many words. They all felt strange in my mouth when I tried to say them— to Kyle, to the funeral home, to Janet when she called. None of them seemed right. After all, we were talking about my mom. How could any of those words fit my mom?

I was talking to the newspaper about Mom's obituary when Adam walked in. He came up behind me and gave me a hug, his arm crossing my body from one shoulder to another. I wanted to lean back, to melt into him, but I couldn't. I had too much to do. I couldn't let go yet.

The service would be held at the funeral home on Friday afternoon. She would be cremated. I remembered my grandparents' service, with the urns and the flowers and the big, blown-up photos. I pulled out our photo albums. What to use? A picture of Mom, Kyle, and me? There was a good one from our family vacation to Banff, the summer before Kyle left. Our last family vacation. We'd taken a drive to Lake Louise, and the teal lake gleamed behind us. I remembered Mom had cornered a hotel employee into taking the photo, even though we weren't staying at the hotel. It was out of our price range, she'd told us. We'd just come to look.

But a photo like that said too much, and not enough. What would Mom say about a photo of a happy family, the three of us together, when she and Kyle had scarcely spoken in years? Everyone there would know. She'd made no secret of her estrangement from her son, though of course, she'd told her own version of the story. I wondered what everyone thought of that version. How much they believed.

I wondered what they all thought of Mom. How much they'd seen of her icy temper, of the barbs and stings she called "teasing." Did her students get to see that side of her? Her colleagues, her neighbours? Did Janet? Or the handful of men she'd dated over the past few years?

Those relationships never lasted long. Mom would tell me she'd met someone, usually from a nearby town, Bonnyville or Ardmore, Cherry Grove or Pierceland. She'd gush about how sweet they were, how they always sent her a *Good morning* email. Then a week or so later, there'd be a series of bitter complaints. They were uneducated or inconsiderate, they didn't appreciate her cooking, they didn't put any efforts into their appearance. I knew she was meeting them online, using a dating site, though she never said so and I never asked. I wondered how many of them she actually met in person before the attraction soured.

What did they think of her, though? Did they see the anger that was always there, simmering, waiting to erupt? Or did she just break things off suddenly, leaving them perplexed?

Would any of them come to the service?

What would they think of Kyle, when they saw him at the funeral? Would he be the son who broke her heart, who disappeared without a word? Or would he be the son whose mother shut him out, left him adrift in the world at seventeen? Had Kyle wondered the same thing? I couldn't ask him—if he hadn't, I didn't want to seed those questions in him. I wasn't even sure he'd come to the service. We hadn't talked about it.

He did come, in the end. Friday afternoon, while I showered upstairs, Kyle retreated to the half-bathroom in the basement to shave and comb his hair. Adam and I shared the main bathroom, he at the sink and me at the mirror. I smoothed my hair into a bun and stared at the dark circles under my eyes. Should I put on makeup? If I cried, I'd make a mess of it, but was it disrespectful not to put in an effort for your own mother's funeral? In the end, I touched my lips with a tinted gloss and left it at that. But I put on earrings, and I chose my navy skirt to go with the grey blouse instead of the black slacks.

The funeral director had asked if I wanted to give the eulogy. I did not. Instead, I gave him a list of her biographical details. I didn't mention she'd never met her granddaughters. When he gave the eulogy, he called her a "valued member of the community." I looked around the room as he said it. Kyle, Adam, and I were sitting at the front. Janet was next to us. The room was mostly full of teachers and their spouses. Her colleagues. A couple of neighbours. The only other people I recognized were Laura and her parents, sitting across the aisle, a couple of rows back. The tips of her hair were blue now, but otherwise she looked the same as she had last time I'd seen her. She gave me a smile with a long blink when our eyes met. It felt good. I raised my fingers in a little wave back.

I had ordered sandwiches and squares for the reception. The wake, I suppose. But I also ordered a tray of Ukrainian food. *Holubtsi, pyrohy, nalysnyki, kovbasa.* Mom's favourites. No one was eating them—maybe it was the smell of the cabbage, maybe it was because you needed a plate to eat them, unlike the sandwiches and sweets. I filled a plate. I felt like I was doing it for Mom, somehow. Plus, it gave me something to put between myself and everyone else. I couldn't shake their hands or accept their hugs. My hands were full.

Adam followed me, filling a plate for himself. I touched my forehead to his shoulder, a thank you. Adam was a picky eater. He didn't like pork or cabbage. He'd never had *nalysnyki* before. He didn't like to try new things. He'd much prefer the chicken salad sandwiches, I knew. But he took the Ukrainian food instead.

Kyle filled a plate, too. I noticed that he managed to get a huge forkful into his mouth every time someone came to give us their condolences.

Laura and her family waited until almost everyone else had come to talk to us before they made their way over. I set down my plate. Nadine folded me into a big hug. Her hair, short and grey, her bangs left longer and tapering off to the side in a fashionable cut, smelled like lavender. I hugged her back, letting myself appreciate the warmth for just a moment. When she pulled away, I noticed that Mr. Clayton—he was still Mr. Clayton to me—had his hand on Kyle's shoulder. And Kyle didn't seem to mind. I wondered when they'd spoken last. Had it been that dinner at our house? The one and only time we all spent time together, both of our families.

Laura took my hand in hers. "Hey," she said. That was it. She just held my hand for a moment and looked at me, her big, dark eyes steady and searching. It was a balm.

AFTER THE FUNERAL, KYLE DROVE US HOME. ADAM SAT IN THE BACK, on the plush bench seat of Kyle's massive truck. I sat up front, holding the urn in my lap. All that was left of our mother. I carried it into the house and set it on the dining room table. It looked like a decoration—a vase, maybe. We all just stood there and looked at it for a long minute.

"All right," Kyle said at last. He opened up the cupboard above the fridge. The liquor cabinet. He pulled out a bottle of whiskey, almost full. He tilted it toward me, a question.

I nodded.

Kyle looked at Adam.

"Um, okay," Adam said. "Thanks."

Kyle poured three drinks over ice, then opened the fridge. There was a bottle of flat Coke.

"Gross," I said, "I'll drink it straight."

He poured some Coke into his glass, and Adam held out his own.

We all stood for a moment, as though waiting for someone to propose a toast.

I wasn't going to do it. Instead, I took my glass into the living room and sank down on the couch. Adam followed me, and Kyle took the armchair in the corner.

"Well, that sucked," Kyle said, taking a gulp.

"It was a nice service," Adam replied.

"It still sucked," I said, taking a sip, enjoying the warming flush that rolled across my tongue and down my throat.

Kyle laughed, a slow, tired sound. "What do you think Mom would have hated most?"

"Oh, the eulogy," I said. "For sure, the eulogy."

"Or my outfit," Kyle said. He was wearing dark pants that were not quite jeans, not quite dress pants, and a plain black dress shirt.

"Yeah," I said. "You're right."

Kyle thinned out his lips and narrowed his eyes. "'You don't have one nice suit? Not a single tie to wear? Do I mean that little to you?'" It was uncanny.

I laughed, the sound bubbling up out of me like a cork had been popped. Kyle joined in. Adam chuckled nervously and sipped his drink.

"When are you going home?" Kyle asked.

I closed my eyes. Right. That. "I don't know," I said. "I guess after I take care of this." I gestured around us. To the house. To her car, which had been towed somewhere after the accident—I'd have to figure out where. To the furniture and the bank accounts, the utilities bills, her clothes in the closet, her retirement savings, her credit cards, the jars of pickles and jams on the shelves under the stairs, the photo albums lined up on the lower shelf of the dining room hutch. All of it.

Kyle nodded. "I could stay for a while, if you need some help."

I shrugged and took another sip. "If you want."

NINETEEN

In the end, it took a week to take care of my mother's estate. Adam called his parents to ask for their advice—Adam's grandfather, Gayle's dad, had died a couple of years earlier. They'd just been through all of this. Normally, I would have hated the suggestion. I'd always felt that Gayle didn't like me, and that Gary tried too hard to be nice to make up for it. But it all seemed so mountainous, I was glad for the guidance.

"So, Dad says to hire a lawyer," Adam said, hanging up. "He'll take a percentage of the estate, the inheritance, or whatever, but he'll pretty much take care of everything."

"Okay," I said, pulling a stack of bath towels out of the linen closet and handing it to Kyle. "Sounds good."

"Did Mom have a will?" Kyle asked. He stuffed the towels into a plastic bin we'd found in the hall closet. It was at the head of what looked like a queue of boxes lined up down the hallway. Everywhere we went in the house, we had to weave our footsteps around boxes and bins, some empty, some full and taped shut, some yawning open, waiting to be filled the rest of the way.

"I have no idea." I hoped not. I was pretty sure that if she did, Kyle wouldn't be in it.

I was right. He wasn't. I called all the lawyers in town until I found Mom's. His name was André Dumont. He sounded young on the phone. A dude-bro. But he had a copy of my mom's will, and he worked in estate law, so I hired him.

Mom had left half of everything to me, and half to Kyle's daughters. I was relieved. That was something. That was better than I'd expected.

André took over all the paperwork, all the financials. He even hired a real estate agent to list the house. He tracked down Mom's car and handled the insurance on the accident. All we had to do was go through her stuff. All of it. A house and a lifetime full of *stuff*.

Kyle found the bag of his old things from his bedroom. It was under the stairs, stuffed into a suitcase. He pulled out a shirt and a teddy bear wearing a hockey jersey. He looked at them for a tiny moment, then jammed them back in and put the whole suitcase and its contents in the *Donate* bin.

The next morning, Kyle came into the kitchen as I was having breakfast. He leaned on the counter in front of the coffee pot, his hands stuffed deep into his pockets. "I gotta get back to work," he said.

"Okay," I said, taking a sip of coffee.

"I'm driving back tonight."

A wave of irritation rose up inside me. Of *course* he was leaving me with all the work to do. I pushed the feeling down. After all, why should he go through all of Mom's shit? This wasn't his home. It hadn't been in a while. I swallowed. "Okay," I said again.

"How're you guys gonna get back?"

"We'll book our flights out of the airport here," I said.

"All right, then." He turned and poured himself a cup of coffee.

That day, Kyle hardly took a break as he sorted through the storage room under the stairs. He drove three truckloads of donations to the only thrift shop in town, and arranged for them to come and pick up the rest of the furniture.

Before he left, we packed up a bunch of boxes Kyle had agreed to store in his garage—old photo albums, some of the stuff I wanted to keep from my bedroom, some dishes and linens that had belonged to our grandparents. He gave me a one-armed hug and clapped Adam on the shoulder before he got in and drove back to Edmonton.

It was just me and Adam now.

"So," Adam said once Kyle's truck had disappeared around the corner.

"So?"

"So, when do you think we'll be going home?" He hands were stuffed into his pockets, and I realized he was mirroring Kyle's posture. Probably unconsciously, but still.

"You don't have to be here," I snapped. I went back into the house, leaving Adam standing alone in the driveway.

I only had two rooms left: the kitchen, which we were still using, and Mom's room. Even my old bedroom had been stripped back to the bare furniture, the clothes we'd brought with us, and the bedding.

I went into Mom's room. It was faultlessly tidy, of course. It always had been. I pulled open the closet doors. There it was—the scent of Bounce laundry detergent. She'd never worn perfume, so this was her scent. I'd smell it every time she pressed me into one of her brittle hugs.

I piled the clothes on the bed without looking at them. No point in trying to sort through it; it was all going to the thrift store. Adam stood in the doorway for a moment, then disappeared. Fine, I thought. But he reappeared a few moments later with clear plastic bags. He half-folded, half-stuffed the clothes inside and then carried them, two by two, down to the rental car parked in the driveway. Mom's car would be repaired, then sent to the used car lot off the highway.

I stripped her bed and carried the bedding down to the laundry room. That's when the tears started to well up. When Adam came back inside, I was on the floor against the washing machine. I felt like I couldn't get enough air into my lungs, so my breathing was jagged. He just sat down on the floor next to me and put his arm over my shoulders. I leaned into him, pressing my face into the thin material of his T-shirt over his shoulder as I sobbed.

I cried until I felt like I was empty, like I'd let everything drain out of me. Adam stood up and put his hand under my elbows to pull me from my feet. My back and legs were stiff from sitting on the cold concrete for so long. "I want to go to bed," I said. My voice sounded plaintive and childish to my ears. I wiped the snot and tears onto the sleeve of my shirt.

Adam helped me pull off my jeans and shirt, then tucked me into bed. He moved to go, but I grabbed his hand. I couldn't be there, alone, in my mother's house. Not even for a few hours, not even if he was just in the living room at the end of the hall. So he pulled off his jeans and slid into bed next to me. I turned so my back was against him, and I pulled his arms around me. I pressed up against him. I wanted to feel him against every part of me. I wanted to feel enveloped by him.

I felt him grow hard. He shifted away, mumbling an apology, but I didn't let him go. I pressed against him harder, moving my hips slowly. Hesitantly, he moved his hand up over my breasts. I turned and kissed him, deep and hard. I opened my legs and guided him into me. I gave myself over to the thrusting and the needing that was the core of me.

WEEKS LATER, I COULDN'T BE ENTIRELY SURE IF I'D BECOME PREGNANT then, or later, in Europe. I'd had a period in between, but it was light, just spattering the panty liners I affixed to my underwear, waiting for the regular flood that never arrived that month. I told myself it was because of the grief, the trip, because I hadn't been eating or sleeping properly. And it might have been true. Then again, it might have happened later. In Europe. In Kyiv, perhaps.

Which would be worse—to carry a barely formed embryo into the Chernobyl Exclusion Zone, or to conceive while you're visiting Ukraine, to form a zygote from an egg that had been exposed to a dozen or so microsieverts of ionizing radiation?

When we told Adam's parents and Gayle said, "So, you're getting married, then?" I thought of my mom. I wondered, would she and Gayle have gotten along? Or would they have eyed each other with a territorial mistrust, each angling for the superior position?

After we'd told Adam's family, after I'd told Kyle, I called Laura.

We'd always kept in touch over the years. Or at least, we could if we needed to. I knew I'd be able to reach her through her parents, that it wouldn't be weird to call her mom and dad and ask for her number, and I assume she felt the same way about reaching out to my mom. If she needed to.

After we ran into each other in the coffee shop in Cold Lake, she'd found me on social media. The remote contact gave us the illusion of friendship. I knew that she'd moved to Toronto, and that her partner's name was Violet. I saw photos of their vacation to Costa Rica, and from their apartment in Cabbagetown. It was like being in touch. But after we'd told our families about my pregnancy, I wanted to tell someone who would be excited for *me*. So I sent Laura a message: "Can I call? I have news." She sent me her number right away.

She reacted exactly the way I hoped she would. She squealed with sincere excitement and said, "Oh my god, Jess. Oh my *god!*" She asked about the due date, and whether we knew the baby's sex. She asked whether we were setting up a nursery. "And Adam?" she asked. "Is he... happy?"

"Yeah," I said, feeling suddenly protective of him. "He's gonna be a great dad."

"Good," she said. "I'm really glad."

Right away, Laura sent a gift—a tiny newborn sleeper printed all over with little frogs. I remembered how she'd always come frog hunting whenever I asked her to, even though the frogs made her squirm away in nervous disgust, and she'd hated getting mud on her boots and pant legs. I hugged the sleeper to me and felt a glow of gratitude.

We started calling each other, once a week or so. We'd always start off talking about the baby, about the pregnancy. She was patient, listening me to complain about the feeling that my body was being taken over. We talked about our jobs. She was still working in electronics sales, and sometimes she'd ask me to explain the technical specifications of the products she was selling. She was the only woman in her department, and the only Black person. Asking her supervisor or her colleagues wasn't an option.

She was quiet when I mentioned Adam. She never said anything bad about him, but whenever I brought him up, she'd retreat into politeness.

"Adam's making a list of names," I said. "He actually got a library card to sign out baby name books. I thought he was done with libraries for good, after university."

"Oh," she said. "That's good of him."

I wanted to defend him, to gush about him, but after all, she wasn't trashing him. He didn't need a defence.

During our weekly calls, Laura told me about Violet, who did layout and design for a Toronto fashion magazine. They'd met through mutual friends, and Laura confided that they were getting serious. I'd seen pictures of them together on social media, so I wasn't surprised when Laura finally mentioned Violet's transition. Vi was strikingly beautiful. She'd once been a model.

For most of our relationship, Adam and I hadn't had a lot of other friends. We had our coworkers, we had our families, we had each other. We certainly never had any couple friends. But when I got pregnant, our lives seemed to open up. We spent more time with Yash. He and Adam were still playing sports together, but with me pregnant, he'd sometimes pop by for supper, a big takeout order in hand. He brought a gift, too—a little white stuffed bear that had a blanket for a body.

"He looks like a ghost bear," I said, looking at the trailing fabric of his lower half.

"It's safer for babies," Yash explained. "My sisters bought them for all their kids. Plus, you can wear it under your shirt so that it smells like you and comforts the baby at night."

"Ah," I said, knowing I wouldn't be wearing a ghost bear under my shirt.

"Thanks," Adam said. He gave Yash a goofy, excited smile.

THAT SPRING, WHEN EYJAFJALLAJÖKULL SPEWED ITS ASH INTO THE air, Laura called. She and Violet had made plans to come out and meet the baby. But they felt nervous flying with the ash clogging up the airways.

"You can still come," I said. "It's safe. And anyway, the ash will settle. Eventually."

"God, I hope so," Laura replied.

The ash did settle, of course. And Freya was born. Laura and Vi came. They stayed in a little bed and breakfast on our street. They snuggled Freya, they brought me croissants and sandwiches and smoothies, they teased Adam about being such a cute dad.

And when they left, I felt full and happy. I looked into Freya's sleeping face and felt like I had all I'd ever need.

FREYA WAS MAD AT ME. I'D TOLD HER SHE COULDN'T HAVE HER BEST friend Charlotte sleep over that weekend. I had to travel to New Brunswick on Monday—Jordan was wrapping up his cybersecurity enhancements to Mispec, and I had to go up to review the plant's control system functions. He and his team had caught a hacking attempt. His emailed report had included laughing emojis—apparently, it wasn't a very sophisticated attempt. "Even before the new security, no way they'd have gotten through," he said.

"Who was it?" I asked. The possibilities spun through my head— North Korea, maybe, or even Russia. They couldn't do any real damage to the plant, but who knew what kind of information employees shared in their emails. Classified files, confidential documents—even maintenance schedules and equipment specifications that a malicious agent could leverage to do real damage. You couldn't cause a meltdown by hacking a server, but you might be able to find out how.

Or maybe it was just some assholes trying to ransom the system. What might go wrong while we were locked out as the Maritime Energy executives negotiated and dickered over a fair price to regain control? All the possibilities made my chest tighten. Safety and control systems are not internet-connected, I reminded myself. At worst, a hacker would be able to get into staff email and file sharing. Not exactly a comforting thought, but they could do minimal damage from there. Jordan had installed failure modes and effects analysis tech. A cyber breach would be almost impossible.

Almost.

"Who knows," Jordan said. "It was weak, but still not traceable."

That didn't make me feel better. So, with the trip coming up, I wasn't much feeling like hosting a sleepover. The trip and, of course, today's appointment.

We sat in the chairs facing a living wall at Freya's doctor's office. Spider plants and philodendrons poked out of brown cups all up and down the wall. The staff had nestled little plastic dragons, elves, and fairies into the greenery.

Freya was swinging her foot, poking at a gnome near the bottom of the wall.

"Stop it," I said, putting my hand on her knee. She shifted away from my touch, glowering at me. I opened a social media app on my phone, scrolling absently to distract myself.

"Can I dye my hair like that?" she asked as a news story about a pop star with acid green hair rolled down the screen. It wasn't a real question. She already knew the answer. She was just looking for more ammunition for her anger.

"No." I put my phone away.

She puffed out her breath, a show of restrained defiance.

Dr. Huang called us in then. I followed my daughter into the small exam room. Dr. Huang patted the exam table and Freya hopped up.

"How are things today?" Dr. Huang asked.

Freya shrugged. I gestured at her to talk. "My leg hurts when I play soccer," she said. "Here." She pointed to the spot near her hip.

I had prodded it when Freya had come back from her Dad's house. I'd felt it. The soft swelling.

"Dad says it's probably nothing," Freya had said. "Just swollen because it hurts."

"Could be," I'd said, trying to force down the worry that bubbled up in my chest.

Dr. Huang prodded it now, murmuring questions to Freya about the pain. "Is it a sharp pain, or more of a dull ache?"

"It just hurts," Freya said, shrugging.

"Okay." Dr. Huang gestured for Freya to hop down off the table. She made some notes on a pad. "I'm going to order an MRI." She looked at Freya. "It won't hurt. You'll just lie down in a big machine that will take a picture of the inside of your leg and hip to let me know what's going on in there."

I watched the colour drain from Freya's face, but she nodded and flicked the hair off her forehead, an *I don't care* gesture. I wanted to hug her tight, but I knew she'd squirm away.

Or she might not. Judging from the pinched look on her face, she might lean into me and cry. And I might cry, too.

I didn't hug her. Instead, I asked Dr. Huang, "What do you think it is?"

"It could be a number of things," she replied. "We'll know better after the MRI." She gave us a quick little smile. For a half second, my heart leapt. I thought the smile was meant to tell us that it wasn't serious, that Freya was fine. But of course it wasn't. Dr. Huang was polite. She was used to working with children and their parents. It was a reflex. I could see that in her mind, she was already preparing for the next patient.

Freya led the way to the parking lot. I could see by the looseness in her limbs that she'd already forgotten she was angry with me. She slipped her hand in mine, a long-forgotten gesture that my big girl had suddenly slipped back into. I could feel the tension running through her body. I would feel it in mine, too, fear-fed, and I gave her hand a squeeze that I hoped was reassuring. "It won't hurt, though, right?"

"Dr. Huang said it wouldn't." There. If it did hurt, at least I hadn't lied to her.

"Good." She slipped her hand loose of mine, but she stayed next to me, almost pressed up against my side all the way to the car.

TWENTY

At four months, Freya went through a particularly fussy period as her first tiny teeth erupted, piercing her tender gums. For a handful of weeks, the moments of bliss I'd come to rely on were upended by frazzled exhaustion as I struggled desperately for ways to stop my baby's wails. Her cries at night were no longer the gentle bleating I'd gotten used to—they were outraged shrieks that jolted me awake, as though I'd touched a live wire in my sleep. Adam would come home from work, and I'd hand our howling, drooling daughter to him and lock myself in the bathroom, sinking my ears below the surface of the bathwater to try to muffle the sound of her cries. The moments of pure joy weren't entirely eliminated, but for the first time since she'd been born, those moments were almost balanced out by feeling that I had become threadbare.

"My mom says to try a frozen teething ring," Adam said. He was bouncing gently on a yoga ball with Freya on his lap. It used to soothe her, the bouncing. Before she started teething. "Or teething gel, or whatever."

"Were you even listening at her last appointment?" I snapped. "All of that is bad for her."

"Mom said it worked for us when we were little."

"No." I took Freya from him and rubbed her back. Her cries waned, just for a moment, before starting up again.

There were hard days, but most of the time, I loved being with her. I loved taking her for long walks, looking into her face as she gazed up at the trees, the houses, as she watched cars and people pass by us on the sidewalk. In the evenings, we'd sit together on the couch or the yoga ball, and I'd binge TV shows that had passed me by before Freya was born.

"That's way too violent for her," Adam said, coming home one evening. I was catching up on a cable cop show everyone had been gushing about the year before.

"She doesn't know what's going on," I replied.

Adam sighed and retreated to our bedroom.

I don't know that I would have gone back to work, if it had not been for the Fukushima Daiichi nuclear disaster.

IT WAS MARCH, AND I WAS WATCHING THE END OF MY LEAVE DRAW ever closer, when an earthquake and tsunami knocked out Fukushima Daiichi's electrical systems, causing three meltdowns, three reactor building explosions, and a massive containment leak at the Japanese nuclear power plant.

Meanwhile, Fukushima Daini, Daiichi's sister plant to the south, survived the natural disaster without any serious incident. Both Daiichi and Daini had been built to a design basis that prepared the plants to survive the massive earthquake. The design basis of a system is the set of requirements that had to be met for it to function safely and adequately within a defined set of conditions. The design basis of a nuclear power plant has to consider all of the foreseeable factors that might reasonably threaten its function and stability, and it is established by imagining the maximum credible accident: the most terrible thing that designers can reasonably imagine going wrong. The problem, of course, is that sometimes, engineers don't imagine an accident bad enough.

The 2011 tsunami off the coast of Honshu exceeded Daiichi's design basis—the plant simply wasn't built to withstand the impact of the massive undersea earthquake itself, or the surging seawater that engulfed the plant's inadequate seawall. Neither was Daini, but the engineers and technicians there managed to cobble together a backup power supply and avert the disaster. In the wake of the earthquake and tsunami, which knocked out three of the four reactors and all but one of the backup generators, the reactors' core temperatures climbed critically. Each of the redundant cooling systems was reliant on electricity, but the plant had been launched into station blackout condition. The operators and technicians at Daini struggled through the darkness and the seawater to connect the unaffected reactors to the surviving power systems. They used the bits and bobs they found on site to restore the cooling systems and avert disaster.

Most people think of nuclear power plants as secretive entities, highly classified sites that guard their information from outsiders. In fact, the global nuclear power industry may be one of the most collaborative organizations anywhere. When an accident—or even a close call—happens in a nuclear power plant, a network of information-sharing jumps to life, as risk engineers work together to avert any similar accidents at other plants.

After Fukushima Daiichi, I knew that an Operating Experience Forum would be called. Engineers from around the globe would be looking for ways to plan for backup processes in case another beyond-design-basis event, like the Tōhoku earthquake and tsunami, were to happen again. The goal would be to significantly reduce and mitigate the risk of the unimaginable. We had to imagine the worst possible thing, the kind of disaster no one could ever anticipate, and then prepare for it.

I knew that the Maritime Energy Nuclear Risk & Compliance Group would be planning a new risk assessment for the region's three nuclear plants. I wanted to be there. I wanted to help plan for an event *beyond* any that we'd already experienced or even imagined.

I wasn't part of the nuclear group, though. I was a project leader for the utility's general Risk & Compliance Group. My team's job was to mitigate risk at all non-nuclear plants, and my own area of specialization was coal-fire plants.

I called Douglas. "I want in on Nuclear Risk & Compliance," I said.

"Hey, congrats, there, Mama!" Douglas said. Right after I'd had Freya, he and a few other senior engineers had sent over a gift basket full of baby supplies—powders, oils, ointments, and lotions, mostly. I hadn't found a use for most of them. This was the first time we'd spoken since my leave had started almost eleven months earlier.

"Thanks," I said. "I want to switch to nuclear process safety."

"Well, Jessica, you don't have any background in nuclear."

I guess I shouldn't have expected him to remember our interview over a decade ago, but a part of me did. "I didn't have any background in coal-fired before I started there," I pointed out.

"We can't just start you at senior engineer. Like I said, you don't have the background, and anyway, there aren't any positions open."

"Professional engineer, then."

"Hey, listen, Jess," he said. "Think this through. That's a demotion. Don't be too rash here. Talk it over with your husband."

"He's not my husband."

"Right, okay, but you'd be looking at a pay reduction. Don't you think that's the kind of thing you should loop him in on?"

I took a slow breath. There was nothing to be gained in snapping at my boss. "Is there a professional engineering position open in the NR&C group?"

Douglas cleared his throat. "Well, just between you and me, they're opening up hiring. We're looking at two, maybe three new positions."

"I want in."

"Well, the thing is," he said, "we love having you as a team leader. You're great with people and all."

"Douglas," I said, "I'm really not. What I am *great* with is control systems design and retrofit. I'm a great engineer, not a great manager."

There was a pause. I could hear him sigh. It was a long, sigh that was meant to show how patient he thought he was being. "Well, okay, then. I'll put your paperwork in tomorrow."

"Great."

"If you're sure."

"I am."

"All right, then." He made it sound like a warning.

And so, May first, I joined the Nuclear Risk & Compliance group as a process safety engineer.

"So, you're getting paid less?" Adam asked as I got ready for work. He'd taken the week off to help transition Freya to daycare.

"Yeah."

"Is that because you took a mat leave, or whatever?"

"God, no," I said. "It was my choice."

His eyebrows shot up. "It was?"

I slipped on my shoes. Were they always this tight, I wondered. Adam was holding Freya, and I leaned in to kiss her cheek. She put her little hand on my chest. Damn. This was harder than I thought. In a flash, I fantasized putting up a tall fence around the house and just barricading ourselves in, me and her. Instead, I stayed there a moment, breathing in her sweet baby smell. Adam put his free arm around me and rubbed my back. I straightened up and grabbed my purse.

"Why didn't we talk about this before?" Adam asked.

"We're talking about it now," I said, looking him in the eye.

Adam sighed, deflated, holding Freya up to me. "Have a good first day back."

"I will," I said, giving my daughter a kiss on her cheek.

I heard Freya squeal in protest as I closed the door. It felt like a fish hook in my heart, pulling me back toward her. I needed her—we needed each other—but I needed more than just her. I set my jaw and got in my car. To work.

NEAR THE END OF MY SECOND DAY BACK, YASH CAME TO SEE ME. We didn't share a cubicle any more. In fact, when we were both senior engineers, we'd had offices. Now that I'd let my rank slip, I was moving to a cubicle of my own. It was next to a window, though, and it had space for a full desk and a couple of filing cabinets.

Yash tapped his knuckle softly on the edge of the cubicle divider. "Welcome back," he said. He gestured to an empty chair in the next cubicle. "May I?"

I waved him into my workspace, and he sat down across from me.

"Big change," he said.

"My choice," I replied shortly. He put his hands up in the air, a gesture of surrender, and I relented with a muttered "Sorry." I knew a lot of people assumed the demotion was a punishment of sorts— perhaps for having dared to take a maternity leave. There were other female employees at Maritime Energy, of course, even a handful of female engineers, but in my time there I'd been the only engineer to take the full year. Already, I was aware of the grumblings. They came from two factions—one (mostly women, mostly non-engineers) was angry because they thought I'd been demoted for having a kid, and one (mostly men, mostly engineers) felt I'd received special privileges for being a woman. I wasn't interested in correcting anyone. Let them have their drama. I just wanted to do my job.

Yash wasn't part of either faction, I knew. I realized that he'd become our closest friend, Adam's and mine, over the past year. It wasn't his fault I was on my guard now that I was back in the office.

"I know," he said. "Pretty gutsy." He smiled, his bright, shiny, magazine-cover smile. "You miss being home?"

"I'm fine," I said, forcing a smile. The truth was, there were moments I ached to be with Freya, to kiss her soft cheeks, but most of the time I was immersed in my work, and she was far from my thoughts. I didn't want to admit either of those things to him, or to anyone else at work, though.

"You're a good mom," he said. "You and Adam, you're both really good at this."

I had nothing prepared for that. I only had a store of defences I'd packed for work that day, and here he was, being kind, just as he always was. "Thanks," I said at last. I picked up a pen and turned it over slowly in my hand.

"Welcome back," Yash said, standing and returning the chair to its spot.

FREYA'S DAYCARE HAD A FIRM FIVE O'CLOCK PICKUP TIME. MY WORK-day, and Adam's, officially ended at four thirty. If we got into our cars and drove straight to the daycare in the North End of Halifax, we could both be there with a few minutes to spare.

Of course, getting out of the office right at four thirty was a near impossibility. At least for me. There was always a phone call I couldn't wrap up, or an email that had to go out before tomorrow, a junior engineer whose work needed to be reviewed before I could sign off on it. Soon, I took on the job of dropping Freya off in the morning, and Adam picked her up after work. Often, by the time I got home, Yash would be there. Freya loved Yash. He'd bounce her on his knee and sing her little songs. When he came in the door, she'd hold her arms out to him and squeal.

"You work together," Adam said one evening after Yash had left and we'd put Freya to bed. "How come he can get home before you?"

"We don't work in the same group," I replied. "Yash's job has nothing to do with mine."

"Still."

"Don't start," I snapped. "I don't know your job, and you don't know mine."

He raised his hands in the air and backed out of the room.

Ever since Freya was born, Adam had been intensely interested in schedules. He installed an app on his phone, and he predicted when she'd have cranky weeks and sunny weeks. At six months, he pressed me to start her on solid foods. He kept an eye on the clock for bedtimes and mealtimes. He'd never been much of a schedules guy before, but with Freya, he was firm. Rigid, I thought. But when my work pushed into the evenings, I didn't want to put Freya to bed right away.

"I just want to read a book with her and have a snuggle," I said when Adam came into Freya's room to get her ready for bed.

"She's gonna be tired and cranky tomorrow," he replied.

"So, she'll have a longer nap."

He crossed his arms. He was standing in the doorway. It looked like he was blocking the exit. I knew that wasn't what he was doing, but the thought irritated me anyway. "That's not how it works."

"Adam, I just want to spend a little time with my daughter."

"So come home earlier."

"It doesn't always work like that." I was trying to keep my voice low, even, but Freya squirmed in my arms. She was almost two, then, and she'd been walking for almost a year. She wanted down, but I held onto her. She gave an angry little wail.

"You can't just come home whenever you want, and keep her up all night because you're always working late."

I felt the anger flare up in me. Freya was now struggling to get down and crying in earnest. "I don't *always* keep her up late." I could hear the venom in my voice. I sounded like my mom. The realization flooded me with shame, but still, my anger kept aflame.

"That's not what I said," Adam replied. Adam, who almost never got angry, was having trouble keeping from shouting, too.

"It's what you meant."

Freya slid off my knee with a shriek. She ran toward the doorway but Adam intercepted her, scooped her up. Her wails rose. She kicked and flailed, wanting to be let down. He carried her over to the change table to get her ready for bed. "Don't tell me what I mean, Jess," Adam said. His voice was flat. Deflated.

I went out to sit on the front step, letting the spring air cool my cheeks.

He was just tucking Freya in when I came back inside. I waited until he left her room, then I went over to kiss her forehead. Her eyes were already closed, and her breath even and deep.

The next day, he sent me a text message near the end of the day. *I can't pick Freya up today.*

Fine, I replied. *I'll get her.* I made sure to be out of the office right at four thirty. No way I'd let the daycare call him to ask why we were late. I'd be there. I'd be on time.

There are no lessons to be learned from Chernobyl—not from a risk management standpoint. When other incidents have happened— accidents and close calls—nuclear engineers, risk management lawyers, and process safety specialists call an Operating Experience Forum to discuss ways to reduce and mitigate future risk. We never say *prevent*.

After Three Mile Island, we applied new monitoring protocols to mitigate the risk of human error.

After Fukushima, we learned to plan for beyond-design-basis events.

Nuclear engineering is all about planning. We study ways to implement new safety protocols and government regulations. Our application and implementation plans are exhaustive. We look at every imaginable outcome, and as many unimaginable ones that we can conceive of, and we plan for it.

Most transfers from other sectors don't stay long in nuclear. They don't like to spend so much time on the process, so much time planning and studying and testing. They're interested in design and implementation. Skip the planning, get 'er done. We call them Cowboy Engineers. But Cowboy Engineering doesn't come close to explaining the catastrophic convergence of sub-par materials, sloppy design, poor engineering, bad processes, and half-assed monitoring that went on at Chernobyl. No sensible outfit would ever make any of their mistakes again—it beggars belief that anyone would have fucked up so badly in the first place.

That's why there are no lessons to be learned from Chernobyl. It's simply inconceivable to us that anyone, let alone a massive team of engineers, operators, and technicians, could be so stupid or so reckless. There are no lessons, no warnings. Nothing to take away from an event like that, except horror and incredulity.

TWENTY-ONE

I drove Freya to her MRI appointment at the children's hospital. Adam was waiting for us in the parking lot. He raised his hand in greeting as we pulled in. Freya waved back excitedly, forgetting, for a moment, her fear. I wished I could forget mine—or, at the very least, that I could prevent it from leaching into her.

He looked good, I noticed. Healthy and relaxed, even today. Lately, whenever I caught my reflection unexpectedly, slack and un-self-conscious, I cringed. When I was expecting a mirror or a camera, I looked all right, I thought. I kept my hair short these days, and the cut made my cheekbones sharp and my eyes big and bright. But unexpected glimpses of my face showed my softening jaw, my sagging eyelids, the creeping little lines around my mouth. And today, I knew I was looking extra worn. I hadn't slept the night before. I'd fallen asleep just before eleven, but I woke up every hour or so, anxiety whooshing through my chest, feeling like a many-footed creature trampling its way around my heart and lungs.

It wasn't always about Freya. Some of it was about work. At night, I couldn't keep my thoughts from drifting to the hacker attempt at Mispec. Someone had tried to get into the system. Jordan had said they didn't get in, but was he sure? What if they didn't give up? What if they sent someone to the plant to compromise the safety or control software? Would Jordan have detected the bad code? He wasn't my hire. I hadn't interviewed him, reviewed his work. Once I'd finally convinced my bosses they *needed* to create his position, I'd been shut out of the process. I was still only a professional engineer, after all. I wasn't involved in hiring anymore. I didn't really know him, or his team. I was trusting someone else with *my plant* and I couldn't be sure, not completely sure, that the software hadn't been compromised. There were vulnerabilities. Someone could get past security at the plant. Or in software development. We were relying on their security, but what did we really know about them? Someone could have tampered with the program in transit. Who had delivered the software? How was it sent? I didn't know. Jordan had received it. He and his team had installed it.

I'd gone to review the installation, of course. I'd reviewed his plans, gone over the safety and control systems when he was finished. But I hadn't really checked over his work. I hadn't asked him what he'd done to look for bad code in the software. Had he looked for a logic time bomb? Is that something he might miss?

But it wasn't my job to ask him to check. I wasn't his boss. Still.

Checking over his work would introduce some complications to the workplace dynamic, sure, but what was a little social awkwardness when the security of a nuclear power plant was at stake? I should have done it. I should have checked it over. As I lay there thinking about it, I tasted blood. I was doing that thing again—worrying that rough spot on the back of my tooth with the tip of the tongue. My tongue was raw now. So raw it was bleeding.

The taste of blood shifted my thoughts to Freya. Freya and her appointment tomorrow. We'd know. One way or the other, we'd know. I had to get some sleep. I had to be rested so I'd be alert when we spoke to the doctor. I forced myself to breathe slowly, pushing the thoughts of both Freya and Mispec out of my head. I focused on the softness of my pillow, the weight of the comforter on my body. I'd always liked a cool bedroom and a heavy blanket. Finally, I drifted asleep. But an hour or so later, my worries woke me again. And again and again, all night long. And this morning, I looked tired and haggard and old. But there was Adam, looking fresh, as though he'd slept a solid eight hours. He seemed to get *more* handsome as he got older; Yash, too.

So? I thought. Why did that even matter? I snapped my mind back to where we were, at the hospital, waiting to find out what was causing that painful swelling—that lump—on Freya's leg, and I was ashamed of letting my thoughts drift in such a shallow direction.

Freya shot a panicked look at me as the technician left the room. I was standing on the other side of a wall of glass, and my daughter was alone with the massive, humming tube. I forced a smile, and she closed her eyes. I could see her willing herself to lay still. I could feel her tamping down the panic.

But soon it was all over, and we were on our way out of the hospital once again. Freya wasn't even limping.

"We're going for horchata," she announced. She was using the bossy, brassy tone that usually grated on me.

Normally, I'd snap, "Manners," or tell her to ask, not tell. But not today. I pretended to hesitate. If I seemed too easy, she'd know how worried I was. "All right," I said at last.

"*All* of us," she added, emboldened by her success. She swung her dad's hand back and forth. "Call Yash."

"Bossy," he replied. But his phone was already out. We were all going for horchata together. A happy, blended, extended family.

I DIDN'T NOTICE ANYTHING WAS OFF AT FIRST WHEN I GOT HOME from picking Freya up at daycare. I set her down as soon as she got in the door, and she toddled straight over to the TV, tapping it with her little hands and squealing for my attention. "Mummy," she said, "shows! Shows!"

I found one of the shows Adam and I had agreed on for her. Little animated letters that went on adventures together, spelling out words. Educational. Adam had pressed for no screen time before she turned two, but once I went back to work, we compromised on one educational show each evening while we made supper.

I went to the kitchen and took a tray of lasagne out of the fridge. I preheated the oven, wondering what was keeping Adam at work tonight. He wasn't usually one for overtime.

While the oven heated, I went to change out of my work clothes. I was in my underwear, searching for a T-shirt, when I noticed something was off.

Adam's night table was empty. And his side of the dresser. A pricking sensation washed over my arms, down my hands. I reached for the top drawer, his sock drawer, and yanked it open.

Empty.

His underwear drawer, his T-shirt drawer. Empty, empty.

His side of the closet. Empty.

I glanced into the living room. Freya was sitting on the couch, entranced by the dancing letters. I pulled the bedroom door closed and dialled Adam's number. He didn't answer.

"Call me," I said to his voicemail. "I need to know what's going on."

His text landed before I'd even hung up. *I'm at Yash's,* it said. *We'll talk tomorrow. I'll call you when I'm ready.*

Yash.

Traitor, I thought. I had waved goodbye to him as I dashed out of the office today. He'd barely waved back—he'd been on a call. But he'd known. He'd known, and he hadn't warned me.

Of course, I didn't sleep that night. I kept Freya up late with me. I tried to cuddle her on the couch, but she was too squirmy. She hadn't really cuddled, not much, anyway, since she'd learned to walk. I wanted to press her to me, for us to comfort each other, but she squirmed away, toddling about the living room, picking up her toys and dropping them, becoming cranky and demanding as her bedtime came and went.

I went to bed soon after she did. I didn't sleep, but I did piece it together as I lay alone in the darkness.

Adam and Yash.

I hadn't seen it. *How* had I not seen it?

TWENTY-TWO

I f Yash had been a woman, I would have railed against her, would have spat hateful words at Adam, words I hated. *Bitch* and *whore* and *cunt* and *slut*. If Yash had been a woman who worked with me, a woman I'd known for years, a woman I'd introduced to Adam, I would have been cold and hostile to her in the office. I would have quietly belittled her work and raised my eyebrow in sly judgment whenever her name came up. I would have chipped away at her from every side.

I know, because that's what I wanted to do. That's how I wanted to act. I wanted to make Adam feel like shit for loving Yash, and I wanted to shake our office's faith in his work, his integrity, his professionalism.

But Yash wasn't a woman. He was a man. A gay man. A gay person of colour, a second-generation Canadian. If I railed against him, it wouldn't be righteous hurt and anger. It would be an attack. I'd be the hateful cunt who made life even harder for him.

I couldn't even bring myself to hate him. It's not fair, I thought. It's not fucking fair.

I DIDN'T SEE MUCH OF ADAM THE FIRST YEAR AFTER HE LEFT. AT FIRST, he didn't call much, he didn't text or email. He left the fucking cat, Gemini. He never even asked about her. "I *knew* she'd end up being my responsibility," I wanted to hiss at him nearly every time we talked. I didn't.

I arranged to buy him out of his share of the house. I hired a lawyer to make the financial arrangements, and she asked me if I wanted to start shared custody proceedings.

"No," I said. Let him start the process if he wanted to. If he did, I'd get a lawyer, but as far as I was concerned, I wasn't going to make it easy on him. After all, he'd left me and Freya. I *had* custody.

"That's a very naïve view," my lawyer warned.

"Maybe so," I replied. But she didn't know Adam. So.

A couple of weeks after he left, I had to schedule a trip to New Brunswick for a site visit of the plant near Bathurst. I'd be there three days, maybe four. At first, I toyed with the idea of hiring a nanny to come with me and look after Freya, but I dismissed it almost immediately. Freya was shy with strangers. She hated when the daycare hired new staff, and when we were together, Adam and I had seldom gone on dates because she kicked up such a fuss when we left her with a babysitter.

I texted him: *Going to NB next week. You'll need to take Freya.*

It took him nearly a whole day to get back to me. *We're not set up for her.*

Of course they weren't. They were living the life of newlyweds. *Then stay here,* I replied.

When the day arrived, Adam came alone.

"So, you're back Wednesday?" he asked. He was standing in the front hall, shifting from foot to foot. Freya was in her high chair, eating breakfast. It annoyed me that he hadn't gone to her, hadn't picked her up or kissed her. Of course, if he'd interrupted her breakfast that would have annoyed me too.

"Probably," I said. "It could be Thursday."

"And you'll let me know?"

"Of course," I snapped.

I went to the kitchen to kiss Freya goodbye. The tug in my chest was like the first time I'd left her with her father. I must have had a dozen work trips since then, and none of them had felt like this. Of course, things had been different before.

I didn't tell Adam where to sleep. Let him decide between my bed— our old bed—and the couch. I considered telling him to take the couch. The thought that he and Yash might share my bed was like a blow to the ribs. But I wasn't going to help him navigate the situation. After all, no one was helping me through it. Let him figure it out on his own.

I texted Wednesday night to let him know I was staying until Friday, even though I knew I could wrap things up by Thursday afternoon. I was disappointed in his reply.

OK. Freya's fine. We're great.

I didn't see him when I got back. I picked Freya up from daycare on Friday afternoon. She squealed when she saw me, and I peppered her face in kisses.

I couldn't tell whether my bed had been slept in or not. I stripped it down anyway and washed all the bedding, even the duvet.

After that, he'd text me once a week or so. *How's she doing?* or *What's new with Freya?*

She's fine, I'd text back, or *She's got a cold.*

He didn't ask to see her, and I didn't suggest it.

I hardly saw Yash at the office. I suspected he was working hard to make sure we didn't cross paths. Fine by me. Of course, everyone in the office knew what had happened. They all avoided mentioning Yash when I was in the room. They asked me how I was doing. They asked it a lot.

Laura called often. "How's my sweet niece?" she always asked. She was an only child; Freya was the closest thing Laura had to a niece or nephew. I'd tell her what new words Freya had learned, what songs she'd pretend to trill along to on the radio, what gifts from Auntie Laura had held her attention the longest.

I also talked to her about work, about the flatness that seemed to have descended onto my tasks. About Adam's slow trickle approach to getting his space set up for Freya, his and Yash's, which meant that every visit I had to pack a duffel bag full of clothes and toys, diapers and linens.

I usually remembered to ask her how she was before the end of the call, trying to recall details of her job and her life that I could ask her about next time we talked. I usually failed. I'd remember later, the shame at being such a shitty friend burning through me.

We were chatting one evening a couple of months after Adam left and she suddenly said, "I'm worried about you, Jess."

The sound of my laughter surprised me. It was brittle, bitter. "Nothing to worry about," I said.

"You're miserable."

"I'm not." But when I said it, I realized I was. I was constantly either tired or bored. Work would overwhelm me in a rush. I struggled to keep up with the paperwork in a way I never had before, not even as a team leader with interminable, tedious hiring and performance review tasks. The senior engineer on our team, Dylan, was constantly sending me emails that started with the phrase "Just following up on..."

At home, I struggled to keep a cheery facade with Freya, but more and more, I was setting her in front of the TV. We used to read books, play games, go for walks. But all of it, our life together, the things we used to do, felt insurmountably dull. I couldn't bring myself to put on her jacket, to take her out, to pull a book down from the shelf. I had shrunk, our life had shrunk, collapsing into itself. All I could manage was the play-acting routine of being a functional adult in a family of two: Get up. Feed child. Get dressed. Dress child. Take child to daycare. Go to work. Don't forget to eat. Don't forget to shower. Don't forget to smile sometimes so the child knows it's loved. All the air had been let out of me, of us, and I didn't have the breath to blow it back up. So I'd do my best to ignore the guilt that bubbled up in me and set her down in front of programs about counting or the alphabet. At least they're teaching her something, I told myself. I, who used to keep her up late for extra snuggles and stories, was staring longingly at the clock every night, aching for seven thirty so I could put her to bed.

And when I did, I'd pour myself a glass of wine and sit on the couch, and then I'd search through TV shows or scroll through my phone, bored and unsatisfied, until bed.

Miserable. I was miserable.

"I mean, lately, things have been—" I couldn't finish. My throat tightened up. I felt as if I said anything more, I'd break open. I *was* breaking open. I was crying, not quietly, but snuffling and gulping, my nose running wet snot onto the mouthpiece of my phone.

I tried to laugh. "Fuck, I'm a mess."

Laura didn't laugh back. "Leave," she said earnestly. "Quit your job, sell your house, and leave."

"And go where?" I imagined myself moving back to Cold Lake to work for an oil company, or to Edmonton, become neighbours with Kyle and work for a coal-fired power plant.

"Anywhere," Laura said. "Here."

"Toronto?" I'd never considered actually living in Toronto. Or anywhere else, for that matter. I managed to get my breath and the tears under control as I pondered it.

"Sure," she said. And she hummed a bit. "Actually, Vi and I have a bit of an idea. But I don't think this is the time to talk about it."

"About what? Tell me."

"Just a sec." There was a muffled sound. I knew she was quickly conferring with Violet. But she came back almost immediately, and she offered me a job.

Laura and Violet were starting a company. They'd be selling and installing residential solar- and wind-power systems. Middle-class Torontonians were eager to generate their own clean energy, and Laura and Violet were poised to offer them the means. It'd been in the works for some time, but they'd avoided telling me about it because Adam's departure and my sudden single-motherhood had consumed all of our conversations.

They needed an engineer to design the systems. They wanted me.

I felt unbalanced. I'd never been *offered* a job before. It wasn't even related to control systems. It seemed so rash, so impractical—I couldn't just pack up and follow a job I'd never even asked for to another city, could I?

"Can I think about it?" I asked.

"Of course," Laura said. "Take your time." I could hear Violet mumbling her dissent in the background. Violet, I knew, did not approve of Laura's impulsivity.

After we hung up, I realized I hadn't taken a sip of my wine. I set it down on the coffee table and looked around the room.

I loved that room.

Our house—mine and Freya's now—was a mid-century bunga-low. It had big windows that looked out over a curving, treed street. I loved the view from the living room. We had a Japanese maple in the front yard, and I loved its lacy leaves. I loved the neighbours' garden across the way—they were retired and tended it like a beloved child. I loved the breakfast bar in the kitchen. The counter was just the right height to lean on while you chatted with someone.

I was miserable. But how could I leave?

What about my job? I was finally working in nuclear. I'd always wanted that. Now that I had it, I should step up, shouldn't I? Why was I letting my work drag the way I was?

Because I was miserable. I couldn't go on being miserable. I couldn't.

So I asked for a leave of absence. Six months. They granted it to me immediately, no questions.

I rented my house to a couple of grad students. They seemed nice. Not the types to wreck the place. And they agreed to look after the cat. I didn't want to haul her with me to Toronto, but I couldn't bring myself to dump her at a shelter either. It was a relief to leave her with the renters.

Laura and Violet helped me find a place in Cabbagetown. It was the upper floor of a converted Victorian, a month-by-month sublet from a couple who were teaching English overseas. It was only affordable because they insisted on no lease, no official documentation of our tenancy. It was a risk, for sure. We could be evicted at a moment's notice. Part of me couldn't believe I'd go in for it. But then, part of me couldn't believe I was here at all. There were two bedrooms, a big kitchen, and a fireplace with a gas insert in the living room. The hardwood was charm-ingly crooked, and the upper part of the windows in the living room had squares of stained glass.

When I told Adam about the move, he insisted on coming over.

"Why didn't you tell me about this?" he asked. He was standing between the kitchen and the living room, leaning his shoulder against the wall. Freya had hold of his hand, and was swinging it back and forth, singing to herself.

"I just did," I said.

"I mean, why didn't we talk about it before you decided?"

I took a measured breath in though my nose. "Because you don't get a say in my decisions anymore," I said. "That was *your* choice."

"I get a say in what happens with Freya," he replied. "I'm her dad."

"Really?" I scoffed. "I thought you were done with that, too."

"Well, I'm not," he said.

"Fine," I replied. "You can come to Toronto and see her as much as you want."

"That's not fair, Jess."

I laughed, the bitterness bubbling up in me. "Tell me about it."

He held Freya for a long time before he left, hugging her tightly until she squirmed free. I thought he might talk to a lawyer after that, maybe seek joint custody, but he never did.

On my last day of work, Yash came to talk to me. I was packing up my desk.

"Hey," he said, "can I sit down?"

I gestured to the empty chair. *Be my guest.*

"I hate that you're taking Freya away from her father," he said. He was looking right at me, his eyes frank and soft. He looked hurt.

It was that hurt, more than anything, that made me angry. I stood up, knocking over the box of office supplies I'd been sorting. "*I'm* taking *her* away from *him?*" My voice rose. I knew it was carrying across the floor. I knew everyone could hear. I didn't care. "That's rich, Yash. That's fucking rich."

"Jessica, please," he said, standing up slowly, his hands out in surrender. "Calm down."

It was so fucking ridiculous, I laughed. "Fuck off, Yash."

He shook his head, sorrowful. I wanted to kick him. "You take care, Jess," he said as he backed away from my desk.

"Fuck *off*, Yash," I repeated.

I stood there for a moment, looking at the paper clips, post-it flags, and strips of staples that were all over the floor. I paused, then reached for my purse and my coat. Fuck, this, I thought. Let someone else clean up the mess.

TWENTY-THREE

An uncertain shadow. A dark spot. An image of indeterminate nature. That's what showed up on Freya's MRI.

"We don't know what it is yet, but we need to find out," Dr. Huang explained. She was talking to Freya. When the receptionist had called to schedule our follow-up, she'd encouraged us to bring Freya along.

"That has to be good, right?" Adam had asked when I'd called him. "She wouldn't want Freya there if it was…bad."

"Maybe," I'd replied. I felt bile rising in my throat. "Or maybe she figures she's just better at explaining it to kids than their parents are." God. How could you possibly tell your own child they had cancer? The thought made me want to cry and scream and throw up all at once. But finding out at the same time as your kid? Hearing the words and forcing yourself not to react so you don't scare them? Would that be worse?

"What do you think it is?" Freya asked. She was still holding my hand, her fingers squeezing tight. I don't think she even noticed.

"Well," said Dr. Huang, "it could be a lot of things. We're going to do a special surgery to find out for sure. But—"

Freya drew in a sharp breath at the word *surgery*. "An operation?" She looked up at me, then her dad. Tears had sprung to the corners of her eyes. "Do we have to?" she asked.

"Yes, I think it's important to find out what we're dealing with so we know how to treat it," the doctor replied. "One of the things we'll be looking for is something called chronic recurrent multifocal osteo-myelitis, CRMO. It causes inflammation, swelling, around the bones,

224

so that would explain the pain in your hip." She gave my daughter a comforting smile.

Freya nodded. The tears spilled out over her cheeks. Adam put his arm around her and hugged her tight. I squeezed her hand in mine.

The doctor glanced at me and Adam before returning her gaze to Freya. "We're going to give you special medicine to fall asleep so that you don't feel the surgery, then we're going to take a tiny sample of the affected bone so we can test it to find out what is causing you all this pain."

"Could it be—" I couldn't finish the sentence. Couldn't say the word. When the swelling on Freya's upper leg had turned out to be just that, swelling caused by irritation, I had felt an easing in my chest. It was just swelling. Not a lump, not a bump. But now there was a shadow.

"It could be any number of things," Dr. Huang replied. "And we just need to rule them out. CRMO is a diagnosis of exclusion. Once we know what it's not, we'll know what it is."

"So how do we make it go away?" Freya asked. "Is there a medicine?"

I felt a surge of pride in her for asking the questions herself. I glanced over at Adam. He gave me a small, weak smile, the corners of his lips twitching up and down, not quite trusting the relief at the good news.

"It depends," said Dr. Huang. "If it is CRMO, we'll get you some medicine to manage it."

To manage it. To mitigate. Not to cure it.

"And if it's not?" Adam asked. "If it's something else?"

"We'll talk treatment plans when we know for sure," Dr. Huang said. She gave me a smile. A bland smile to let me know the conversation was over. Her hand was already resting on the doorknob.

Yash was in the waiting room. Freya ran to him for a hug, letting her tears loose. His eyes widened in alarm, but Adam quickly shook his head and said, "We don't know yet." Yash wrapped his arms around Freya's shoulders and squeezed her tight as she wept into his chest.

As we walked back to our cars, I wondered again when, exactly, I'd gotten pregnant. It was probably in the last week or so of our trip to Europe. I thought back to my day in Pripyat. Could she have already been germinating inside me then? And if she was, what had I subjected her to? They said the tour was safe. What did that even mean?

That night, I dreamed I was back in Pripyat, only this time, Freya was with me. She had run off, demanding to see the Ferris wheel and swim in the pool. I kept running through the abandoned city, tripping on weeds that grew up through the sidewalks, pulling futilely on stuck doors, trying to get to her, to tell her we couldn't stay here any longer, we had to go. It wasn't safe. But I couldn't catch up to her to tell her so.

ADAM AND YASH COME BY JUST BEFORE FIVE. FREYA IS AWAKE WHEN they knock on the front door. She makes an excited move to get up, then leans back, wincing.

"I've got it," I say, stroking her fine hair back from her forehead as I pass.

"Hey," Adam greets us both, holding up two big bags of takeout.

"Hi, Daddy," Freya says. "Hi, Yash."

Yash gives me a half-hug, then sits gingerly on the couch with Freya as Adam and I bring the takeout to the kitchen. There's a bit of everything—fish and chips, butter chicken, sushi, shawarma.

"We went to the food court on Spring Garden," Adam explains. "What do you feel like eating?" he calls to Freya.

"Um...ice cream?" she says, testing the waters.

"Dinner first," I reply before Adam has a chance to cave.

"Is there sushi?" she asks.

"Is there sushi?!" Yash teases. "You think we'd show up without sushi? Come on, now."

We eat in the living room, Yash stays on the couch, next to Freya, and Adam takes the armchair on her other side. I pull a chair away from the dining table and balance a plate of butter chicken on my lap.

"You're looking better already," Adam says to Freya. He'd helped me load her in the car yesterday, after she woke up from the surgery.

The anaesthetic had made her nauseated and weepy. She'd clung to him as he tried to buckle her seat belt.

"My leg still hurts," she says.

"It probably will for a while," Adam replies.

"I know."

My phone blips, and Laura's photo pops up on the screen. "It's the aunties," I say to Freya. "Okay if I tell them you'll chat later?"

Freya nods, picking up a volcano roll with her chopsticks.

I send Laura a message: *The dudes have all her attention. Call you later.*

The reply comes back right away. *Fine. Remind her we're still her favourite grownups.*

Always, I message back.

WHEN WE GOT TO TORONTO, LAURA AND VIOLET FOLDED US INTO our lives, making us a family immediately. I was carrying Freya on my hip, waiting for our luggage, her diaper bag slung over my other shoulder. When Laura saw us, she reached out both arms to Freya, calling, "There's my girl!"

Freya grinned and reached for Laura, almost lunging into her arms. "More!" she laughed as Laura covered her face in kisses. It was the first time they'd ever met in person.

"Besties night," Laura announced, looking at me. "You and me."

I glanced at Freya, who was trying to put her fingers in Laura's mouth and giggling when Laura pretended to bite her. "Oh, Vi's on little goblin duty."

I glanced at Violet, who gave me a tight smile. Forced, polite. I recognized that smile. I'd smiled that smile.

Still, after I put Freya to bed in the fold-up crib in the corner of Violet and Laura's tiny spare bedroom, I let Laura drag me out for drinks at a quiet café in the neighbourhood.

Laura didn't say much at first. She bought us a couple of beers and a piece of pie to share, and toyed with the whipped cream. I watched her for a minute before I spoke.

"You don't like Adam," I said.

"Hell, no," she scoffed. "Do you?!"

"I mean, you didn't like him before."

She shrugged, taking a bite of pie.

"Why not?" I asked. "Could you tell he was…" I couldn't say it.

"Gay?" She looked up at me, her big dark eyes fixed on mine.

"Yeah," I said, the word sounding like a sigh. It somehow felt heavier and lighter all at once, hearing her say the word.

"What makes you think he is? It's not that simple."

"Gay, bi, pan. Whatever." Right then, the distinction hardly mattered. "Could you tell?"

"Could you?" she asked.

I didn't answer right away. Since he'd left, I kept thinking about it. The sex. It was usually pretty good—not that I had a lot of experience to compare it to. But we both always enjoyed ourselves. And maybe I initiated it more often than he did. Had that been a warning? A red flag?

I remembered our early days together. I kept thinking about that very first kiss. The way he'd tightened his mouth and pulled away. At the time, I'd thought he was just shy, caught off guard. Or loyal. *I have a girlfriend*, he'd said. I'd thought it was sweet, endearing. I'd seen his resistance as a challenge. But now, I felt stupid when I remembered it. Surely it was an indication of how he felt about me. Of his attraction. Wasn't it?

But then, when we did have sex, there was no resistance. No feint. The way he'd trail his mouth over my breasts, tease my nipples with his tongue. The way he'd grab my hips with his hands, pull me down onto him. Thinking about it then, I felt myself getting wet.

But there was more. His clumsy adoration. I remembered the multicoloured daisies and the inept little lunch he'd made the day of my interview with Maritime Energy. I remembered how, before Freya, he used to rub my feet when we sat together on the couch, making a big show of buying expensive, peppermint-scented lotions for me. The way he used to slip my socks back on so tenderly when he was done.

He adored me. I knew he did.

At least, he had.

"No," I said.

Laura nodded slowly.

"You didn't answer my question," I said. "Why didn't you like him?"

She sighed. "I didn't *not* like him," she said. "He's just the kind of guy who's always looking for the emergency exit, you know?"

I laughed. It sounded like a cough, dry and humourless. "No, that's me."

She smiled and shook her head. "No. You're the one looking for the fire extinguisher."

I laughed again. This time, it sounded real.

She pushed the pie toward me. "Do you like Violet?" she asked.

"I do," I said honestly. I liked her bluntness, the way she wasn't afraid to show her disapproval. I liked that I knew where I stood with her. "But I'm not sure she likes me."

Laura smiled. A tender smile. Protective. "Vi's just crusty," she said.

I watched Laura's face. I liked seeing her like that. Twitterpated. Moony-eyed. It suited her.

WITHIN A WEEK, WE WERE SETTLED INTO OUR LIVES IN TORONTO. Violet and I did most of the legwork to get the company off the ground. Every day, Freya and I would head over to their apartment, which was only a few blocks from ours. Like us, they had a two-bedroom, but they'd converted the smaller room into an office. Violet was using her marketing skills to build us a website and some online advertising, and I was researching materials and equipment, regulations, and the grid infrastructure.

Laura, meanwhile, would entertain Freya, playing games with her, reading her books, and walking her to nearby parks.

"Make sure to cut up her grapes and her hot dogs," I said. "And no hard candies. They're a choking hazard."

"I will take good care of my girl," Laura promised, dropping a kiss on Freya's head. And she did.

Soon, Violet had snagged us some leads on potential clients. Laura met with them to figure out what kind of system they wanted. She was good. I could see that they were drawn in by her mildness, the soft tone of her voice, the way she listened intently to what they had to say. She barely had to suggest upgrades and they were clamouring for more, bigger, pricier.

"Wow," I heard her telling one couple from Oakville. "That sounds like a great system for you. Have you ever considered adding a second array on the garage?"

She had a talent for making them think it was their idea. She was born for sales.

Soon, I was busy designing the systems, calculating the loads, and applying for permits. Within a couple of months, we were running at capacity, the three of us sharing a desk and a side table in the small home office. I enrolled Freya in a daycare in the neighbourhood. We talked about renting an office and hiring an assistant and a second sales person.

We didn't hear much from Adam in those first few months. He'd call once a week or so, and he and Freya would video chat for a few moments until she got too bored to focus. "We'll be out soon for a visit," he promised her at the end of each call, but he never came.

Laura and Violet were the centre of our lives in Toronto. Sometimes, I felt bad about infiltrating their lives so completely. Besides them, I had no friends, no family in this city.

Of course, I reflected, my social circle in Halifax hadn't been much bigger. I was just not a social person. But now, I felt like an imposition, an intruder on Laura and Violet's life. They always invited me along with them when they went out with their friends, or had plans together. I usually said no, staying home with Freya, half-wishing I were with them, half-fearing what their friends would think of me, a single mom, a nerd who worked in a boring technical occupation, a prude who'd just ended the only serious relationship of her life.

Sometimes, when I saw them together, I felt a wave of jealousy overwhelm me. When Vi was working at the computer, Laura would often come up behind her and slide her hands down Vi's arms, holding her in an embrace. Vi would look up, and they'd kiss. I could see their tongues caressing each other, their kisses always deep and tender. And it seemed that they were always touching. Even if they were just standing in the kitchen as we took a break to eat a quick snack before returning to work, their bodies naturally curved into each other. I wanted that.

THE BUSINESS PICKED UP AND TOOK OFF. LAURA AND VIOLET HAD mastered the alchemy of reading the demand for individual renewable power sources just at the right moment and finding the customers willing to pay for them. Me, I was just doing the simple, rather repetitive work of producing the designs that would safely and efficiently generate the most power and pass the scrutiny of the provincial regulatory board.

Five months after I moved to Toronto, Adam texted me to say that he was coming to visit Freya.

A mutinous feeling surged in my heart. *You can't*, I wanted to say. *Stay away*. Instead, I tucked my phone away. I'd answer him later.

Violet was in the office with me when I got the text. We'd decided against individual offices in our new space, setting up a small room in the corner with couches and coffee tables for client meetings, and putting our work desks together in the main office area. "Whoa," she said. "We should hook *you* up to an inverter."

"What do you mean?" I grumbled, even though I knew. I could feel the waves of angry energy emanating from me, too.

She shrugged. "I mean, you don't have to talk about it."

"It's nothing. Just Adam. He wants to come for a visit."

She spun her chair around so she was facing me. She nodded, as though she were choosing her words carefully. But all she said was, "Good."

I turned my chair back around, but I couldn't see what was on my computer screen. I couldn't focus. My hands itched to pull my phone out of my purse.

I turned my chair around again. Violet was still facing me, her head leaning on her hand. Waiting. She smiled, and I couldn't help laughing.

"Exes," she said.

"Exes." I drew a slow breath in through my nose. "He wants to see Freya."

"Good," she said again.

"I know, but…"

Vi spread out her hands, a *But what?* gesture.

"But I'm mad." It sounded so petulant when I said it, the words unable to contain the aching bitterness I felt.

"Fair enough," she said, the ghost of a smile on her lips.

"You're close with your parents, aren't you?" I asked.

She nodded. "My mom's a bit much sometimes. Like, she *lives* for trans activism, it's crazy. But they love me."

Violet's parents had divorced when she was little, I remembered. She called her stepmother That Snooty Bitch, but I don't think there was any real animosity there. In fact, they often went shopping together. I'd hear Vi bickering with her stepmother on the phone sometimes, and she always ended the calls with "Love you, bye." Or sometimes, "fuck off, love you, bye." Three parents who loved her. I couldn't imagine it.

Last Christmas, Kyle had told me he'd been in touch with our father. Louis—Dad—was living in Winnipeg. I knew he'd remarried and had a couple kids after he and Mom had split up. I'd never met them.

When we were little, really little, Dad used to call every now and then. Mostly, he'd talk to Kyle. Kyle remembered when he was around. "Not when he and Mom were together," Kyle had said at Christmas. "I don't remember that far back, but before he moved away. He had a place over by the arena. We used to go visit him."

"We did?" To me, our father was nothing more than a faint voice on the phone, a name scrawled on a Christmas present under a tree. He used to buy me a lot of dolls, I remembered, Barbies and whatnot. I remember putting them away in their boxes so they wouldn't get wrecked. I wondered what had happened to them. Mom had probably gotten rid of them.

"Yeah," Kyle said. "Anyway, our youngest sister, Kristin, she's in high school. Dad's talking about bringing her out next summer to meet my girls."

"Cool," I'd said. But somehow I felt he was being traitorous just by talking to Dad, let alone meeting his other kids.

I remembered that feeling now. Who was I being loyal to, I wondered. Mom? She was dead. She'd never know if Kyle spoke to our dad, or if I did, or if we met his other kids, or introduced him to his grandkids. There was no sense in it, but I couldn't bring myself to even entertain the idea, and I couldn't help but feel bitter toward Kyle.

And I certainly couldn't help my bitterness toward Adam. For what? For leaving me? Certainly. For cheating on me? Yes, that, too. But also for waiting so long to see Freya. For wanting to see her now. I was angry with him for wanting to be her dad. I knew, though, that it didn't even matter when he'd let her slip out of his life—either before we moved to Toronto, or after—I would have been just as mad if he'd insisted on seeing her the week after, the day after he'd left.

I leaned back in my chair and closed my eyes. "Okay," I said. "I'll text him. Let him know it's fine."

"Good girl," Violet said, turning her chair back around.

"Thank you."

"I didn't do anything," she said. "Don't thank me."

Make sure you get a room with a crib, I texted Adam. I watched the little bubbles bounce on my screen for several minutes as he typed his reply. Finally, it came through: *Yeah, I will. Thanks.*

Later that day, he sent me his flight details: he'd arrive in town Thursday night and leave Monday morning. His flight landed after Freya's bedtime, so we agreed he'd pick her up Friday morning and drop her off after dinner on Sunday. I briefly considered suggesting we all have dinner together Sunday evening, but I quickly rejected the idea. I wasn't ready to eat a meal with him. Also, I didn't know whether he was bringing Yash. I hadn't asked. I certainly wasn't ready to have dinner with the two of them together. A couple. With me on the outside.

I watched his car pull into the driveway Friday morning, but I didn't go to the door right away. He got out, alone, and checked the address on the front of the building. I took a last gulp of my coffee, put the empty cup in the dishwasher, and then plucked Freya from her high chair. "No, no—toast!" she complained, reaching for her unfinished breakfast. I handed it to her. She was munching on it as I opened the door.

Adam gave us a nervous smile, the corners of his lips flickering up and down. "Hey."

"Come in," I said, nodding my chin toward her bedroom. I handed her over to him. "Mummy!" she cried, reaching for me. "Mummy, up!" Adam tried to give her a kiss, but she was too intent on getting back to me. I felt a mean little bubble of satisfaction in my chest.

I picked up the duffel bag I'd packed for her in one hand and her diaper bag in the other. But she was still reaching for me, so I asked Adam, "Switch?" He hesitated. "Just to get her into the car."

As we walked I asked, "You rented a car seat, right?"

"Yup." He didn't look at me, adjusting the bag on his shoulder.

I pushed down the urge to question him further, to ask about the weight restriction and the expiry date. Instead, I wrinkled my nose at Freya to make her smile.

When we got to the car, I gave Freya a squeeze and a kiss on the cheek. When I went to put her in the car seat, she started to fuss. I kissed her again and whispered, "I love you." To Adam, I said, "Call me if you need anything."

"We'll be fine," he said, putting the bags on the other seat. "See you on Sunday."

I forced a big smile for Freya. "Have fun, Sweet Pea!"

She started crying in earnest. I pretended not to notice, smiling, waving, blowing kisses at her as they drove away down the street.

I let out a slow breath and went back inside to finish getting ready for work.

It was a strange weekend. Friday night, I felt untethered. I picked up some takeout on my way home from the office and ate it standing at the kitchen counter. Afterwards, I took my phone to the living room and scrolled through my social media feeds without really registering anything. I started half a dozen shows and turned them off again. Finally, I ran myself a hot bath. I soaked until the water turned lukewarm, then I went to bed.

Of course, Laura had suggested I spend the evening with her and Violet, but I didn't want to. I couldn't remember the last time I'd had a night to myself. I wanted the quiet. And I couldn't tell whether I was imagining it or not, but I thought I saw Violet gritting her teeth every time Laura suggested we all hang out after work. It was a lot of hours to spend with someone.

Saturday was better. I slept in. I hadn't done that since I was pregnant. I lingered over my toast and coffee, listening to an entire Beastie Boys album I tried not to play when Freya was listening. Then I went grocery shopping. It was gloriously efficient all on my own. I tidied up the apartment, revelling in the knowledge that it would stay tidy until Freya came home. I had a nap. I woke late in the evening and picked up my phone to order takeout, then I thought, *fuck it*. I grabbed a book from my dresser, a memoir I'd been meaning to read since before we left Halifax, and read it over a beer and a poutine at a pub I'd been meaning to try.

I walked home late, slightly tipsy after a few beers. I fell asleep with the TV on. I woke up late and made myself eggs at eleven. It was like living a different life, I realized. Like being a different me.

Adam and Freya came back late Sunday afternoon, a couple of hours earlier than I expected. As I stood at the door, considering reaching my arms out for her and dismissing him, I felt a twinge of guilt. She was perched on his hip, gazing intently at his jaw. I realized I'd forgotten how much they loved each other, how good he always had been with her. I moved aside, inviting him in.

I decided that cooking supper for him would make me seem like too much of a doormat, and Freya got bored and noisy in restaurants, so we'd order in.

"It's a little early to eat," I said as he pulled off his shoes, still holding our daughter.

"I thought we could maybe talk a bit."

I gestured my assent. He set Freya down, but she held on to his hand, guiding him into the living room. I wondered how long it had taken for her to get that comfortable with him again.

He pulled a wooden puzzle out of his bag and handed it to her. She happily dumped all the pieces out on the living room floor, while

Adam and I sat at the kitchen table. I had a cup of tea, but I didn't offer him anything. Let him ask.

"So," he said. I almost laughed. *So.* "So your leave of absence is almost up."

"I know." Michael, Douglas's replacement, had called last week. "Just to see how I was." I'd told him I was fine. He'd trickled through some small talk, waiting for me to bring up the leave. I hadn't. He'd finally told me to take care and ended the call, his disappointment palpable.

"What do you think you're going to do?" Adam asked.

"I don't know." It was true—I didn't. In some ways, I loved our life in Toronto. Laura, Violet, and I were a family. But once the initial excitement over launching the company had levelled out, I'd realized that the work was rather monotonous—versions of the same designs, the same paperwork, over and over. And, truthfully, I knew that eventually, Laura, Violet, and I would need a break from each other.

I remembered the film of dullness that had settled over my life in Halifax, the way our home and my job had become an unbearable, endless slurry of time. But what if all of that had simply been the result of Adam's leaving? Perhaps my anger and sadness had infected the rest of my life. After all, I'd worked so long to get a job in nuclear risk process safety. I wasn't sure I could give that up. And if I didn't go back now, I might never find my way back in.

"I know I didn't do so great with Freya after you and I split," Adam continued. I subdued the urge to snort. "But it's time for me to be her dad again. And I think having me in her life, me and Yash, well, I think Freya needs it, maybe." He trailed off.

I took a long sip of my tea. The urge to fight him, to punish him, was almost overwhelming. I knew if I gave in to the impulse, he'd probably back down, fade away, give Freya up, just like my own dad had done. But maybe not. He might keep at me. He might keep showing up, insisting. He might even get a lawyer. I thought about the order he'd imposed on our lives after our daughter was born, his uncharacteristic insistence on regular bedtimes and meal schedules. He'd found a firmness of character when it came to Freya that I'd never seen before.

It suddenly occurred to me that without Freya in his life, Adam might never have found the conviction to leave me for Yash. There was an irony.

"If you're not coming back," Adam said, "I'm moving to Toronto."

My breath caught. "What?"

"I need to be with her," Adam said. "She's my everything."

"What about Yash?"

He looked down and shrugged. "We'll figure something out." His finger traced a scratch in the wooden tabletop. I wanted so badly to touch him in that moment.

Instead, I looked over at Freya. She was stacking the puzzle pieces on top of each other, building a tower. "Fall down!" she cried as she knocked them over. The pieces clattered across the living room floor.

I sighed. "You don't have to," I told Adam. "We're coming back."

TWENTY-FOUR

The morning of the surgery, Adam met us at the house. We drove downtown to the children's hospital together. Adam tried to chatter about normal things, school and the snow that had covered the city over the last few days. Freya didn't say much in response. I watched her in the rear-view mirror, the hollow look in her eyes tearing at my chest.

We checked in on the main floor then headed up to a small pre-op room upstairs. Adam and I waited while Freya changed into a hospital gown in the adjoining washroom. She refused my offer of help quickly—"I can get changed myself"—but she sounded nervous, not annoyed.

The walls of the room were lined with a handful of curtained alcoves. A teenaged boy, a cast covering his leg from hip to ankle, played a gaming system opposite us while his mom perched on the side of the chair, staring at the window. In the next alcove, a man and a woman took turns bouncing a toddler on their knees while he gurgled in delight, trying to grab fistfuls of the light blue curtains.

Finally, Freya emerged, arms crossed protectively across her chest, holding the flimsy cotton in place. She sat on the chair, pulling the striped hospital blanket over her knees. Without a word, she reached down to grab each of our hands, Adam's and mine. She held them in her lap. She was shivering, either from cold or from fear. I didn't ask.

Finally, a nurse emerged. She looked at us with a kind smile. "Okay, Freya," she said.

Freya stood up, still clutching our hands. I wanted to say something encouraging, but I didn't trust my voice not to waver. It took everything in me to let go of her hand, to give her a little nod to encourage her to follow the nurse. She held on to my fingers a second or two after I released my grip, then I watched her square her shoulders, steeling herself. We watched as our daughter disappeared through the door with the nurse. She cast one desperate little look back at us before she disappeared.

I could feel Adam's anguish vibrating in tune with my own.

We waited.

WHEN FREYA TURNED FOUR, I GAVE HER A KITE FOR HER BIRTHDAY. It wasn't the cheap paper kind Kyle and I flew when we were kids. It was huge, a butterfly whose wingspan was almost five feet across. Its fabric wings were patterned like stained glass, greens and purples, blues and pinks.

"So pretty," Freya breathed as she ran her fingers over the light fabric.

The first time we took it out, the wind wasn't strong enough to lift it. Freya stood, holding the spool of string as I ran back and forth across the empty soccer field with the kite held above my head, trying to force it aloft. Every time, it soared for a second before it spun and crashed its wings into the dry, scrubby grass.

"I want a different present," Freya grumbled as we headed home, defeated. "I hate this." Tears rimmed her lower lids, and I felt them as though they were blows from her little fists pounding on my chest.

The next week, a big wind picked suddenly up one afternoon, buffeting the trees outside my office. I scrambled to leave work a few minutes early, delighted at the prospect of getting Freya to the park, of lifting her reproach.

I felt the kite tugging in my hand as we walked to the field, its painted wings already begging to fly aloft. When we got to the park I handed her the spool, lifting the kite above my head. She started running, shrieking with joy as the kite soared, its bright colours darting and weaving above us.

It took me a moment to realize that her shrieks had turned from joy to terror.

The wind was stronger than I'd realized, and it was snatching at the kite. With one fierce tug, it stole the kite from my daughter. She sobbed as we watched it sail up over the thick forest of spruce and red maple.

I caught up with her. I bent down to hug her, but she twisted away from me, shrieking, reaching.

"Get it, Mommy!" she howled. "There!" She pointed. The kite had stopped, bobbing slightly over the thick stand of spruce that had snagged its string. "Get it!" Freya begged again.

I hesitated. It didn't look far. We might be able to reach it, to retrieve it.

She wrapped her arms around my waist. "Please, Mommy!" her tears dampened the front of my shift.

"Okay," I said, taking her hand. "Let's go."

I closed my eyes for a moment, relishing the wind's power. Some years back, a hurricane had swept into Nova Scotia, flattening trees in areas too close to the shore. Adam and I had gone to bed feeling that peculiar kind of excitement you experience when you hear about a crime in your neighbourhood—the closeness of something so shocking and dangerous. Our excitement felt shameful and delicious. Throughout the night, the wind had rattled the walls, and we'd woken up to find our windows plastered with pulp. Some of the trees had lost branches, limbs littering the streets and yards of our neighbourhood.

This forest, where Freya and I were now, had been one of the hardest hit. Thick logs still littered the ground, treacherous barriers that kept us from walking in a straight line. Freya's little legs wouldn't get her across the criss-crossing branches, so I carried her.

As I stepped over a jagged stump, my foot slipped on a patch of moss, sliding into a hole in the uneven forest floor. I held Freya close to me as I went down, the sharp pain jolting through my ankle. Freya, who had stopped crying at the prospect of reaching her fugitive kite, whimpered and tightened her arms around my neck.

"We're okay," I said, trying to stand. But I couldn't—the weight of her, as well as me on my ankle, shot another jolt of pain up toward my knee in protest.

I set her down and tested my weight. It wasn't that bad, I realized. I might be able to get back on my own. "You're going to have to walk," I said.

"My kite," she protested.

"I'm sorry, baby. I think we have to let it go."

Her face crumpled back into tears. She clung to me, her arms tight around my waist.

"Come on," I said. "We have to walk."

"I can't," she wailed, and I realized she was right. There was no way she'd be able to pick her way through the maze of fallen logs and moss-covered granite boulders.

I took a deep breath to quell the rising panic in my core. I pulled my phone out of my pocked. I dialled Adam.

Voicemail. I was relieved. I wouldn't have to tell him how foolish I'd been.

But I'd have to call for help. Shame replaced relief as I called 9-1-1. What kind of mother was I, trailing my kid behind me into the woods, getting stuck, and for what? A lost kite? What had I been thinking?

Freya and I sat on the mossy boulder. At first, she clung to me and sobbed, mourning the loss of her kite that bobbed a few more minutes, tantalizingly close, before ducking and weaving, and finally disappearing behind the clump of trees. Then she busied herself with peeling back strips of moss, examining the dirt and bugs beneath.

The police called my cellphone when they reached the parking lot about a half hour later. "I'm going to turn on my siren," the officer explained. "It'll give you an idea of what direction we'll be coming from."

"I know what direction you're coming from," I replied, trying to keep the annoyance out of my voice. "I'm not lost, I'm just stuck."

"All right, ma'am," he replied, his voice a practiced calm. And he did blip his siren once. "I'm on my way."

"Hullo!" he called out a moment later, his voice piercing the forest.

"Hello!" Freya called back. She stood up on the boulder and waved her arms above her head theatrically.

He was sweating when he reached us, his think, dark hair plastered on his forehead. "Pretty rough terrain in here," he observed.

"I know," I replied. "I can't carry my daughter back out."

"Can you walk?" he asked.

"Yes," I said firmly, even though I could feel a swelling and a dull ache building in my ankle.

"All right, he said, reaching a hand out to Freya. "Come to me?"

I thought she wouldn't go, that I'd have to persuade her. But she reached out to the officer, cheerfully taking his hand. He hoisted her up and lifted her over the stump that had foiled me. I followed, leaning heavily on tree branches as we made our way back out.

We emerged from the forest, Freya clinging happily to the officer's neck as he negotiated the same tricky path that I had with her in my arms, just a little while ago. I limped a few more steps, my ankle throbbing. He set my daughter down and looked at me. She looked too, still holding his hand.

"Do you need an ambulance?" he asked.

"No!" I said quickly. "But can you get us home?"

He nodded and offered me his free arm. I hesitated before I took it. He guided us to the police car parked at the edge of the field, me leaning on one side of him, Freya clinging easily to his other hand. Another wave of shame washed over me. *Idiot*, I chastised myself. *What kind of mother are you?*

Adam called me back just as I was getting Freya out of the bath that evening. I'd wrapped my swollen ankle in a Tensor bandage. Freya joyfully told her father the story of the lost kite, the forest, the police officer, and my injured ankle as I dried her hair and wrestled her into pyjamas. She'd already turned it into an adventure.

"Why didn't you call me?" Adam demanded once Freya had handed the phone back to me.

"I did," I replied. My pride was smarting. I wished there had been a way to conceal the whole story from him, to swear Freya to secrecy.

"You could have left a message," he said. "Next time, leave a message. Tell me it's an emergency."

"There won't be a next time," I snapped. "Goodnight, Adam."

Freya fell asleep as soon as I put her to bed that night. A tiny miracle. She usually begged for one more book, a snack, a glass of water. She would often lie in her bed, singing and talking to herself, long after I'd turned out the light and closed her door. Not tonight.

I looked down at her sweet, sleeping face. Why had I *done* that? Why had I just forged into a forest with my four-year-old daughter? What a stupid thing to do. My ankle ached, but the pain seemed insufficient. A reproach. It wasn't that bad. It could have been worse. It could have been so much worse.

I limped to the couch and propped my ankle up on a pillow. It still throbbed, but only faintly. Already, the swelling was easing. I remembered the police officer calling to us, and Freya answering back, her buoyant *Hello* bouncing back to him. Here he was to rescue us. What fun! Me, I hadn't been able to bring myself to call back to him. Remembering it now, I felt the same flush rise in me again, up my chest and neck into my cheeks. I had wanted to tell him to go back, we'd figure it out on our own. We didn't really need to be rescued.

I remembered Mr. Clayton suddenly. Splayed as I was across my couch, I remembered how he never looked at ease on his own couch. Whenever he'd lean back, he always looked as though he were poised to leap forward, as though he were afraid someone would catch him relaxing, off-guard and informal in his own home.

Sometimes, when Laura's parents watched movies with us during our sleepovers, Laura would curl up against him. He always kept his arm draped lightly over the back of the couch, leaving a hollow for her to cuddle up against his ribcage. When she settled in, his hand would come down and give her an absent little squeeze, but he never kept it there, draped over his daughter. It would always drift back up along the top of the couch, poised to help him lever himself up and away from the soft comfort there.

TWENTY-FIVE

Ewing's sarcoma, osteosarcoma, CRMO, and subacute osteomyelitis can all appear as uncertain shadows on an MRI. Subacute osteomyelitis is an infection of the bone that is usually treated surgically. CRMO is an auto-inflammatory disorder typically treated with non-steroidal anti-inflammatory medications or immunosuppressant medications. Ewing's sarcoma and osteosarcoma are cancers.

How can a parent reduce and mitigate the risk of their child getting cancer? Or infection? Or auto-inflammatory disorders? What about a disorder like CRMO, which is sometimes passed genetically from parent to child, a generational blemish of the bones? What is the risk assessment procedure? What are the process safety procedures when it comes to your child's heath? What can you do to keep the most precious person on the planet safe, when their own body might be producing the aggressive cells that could make them sick—or worse?

It was August when Dr. Huang first ordered the MRI, and it was late September when she told us we'd hear from the children's hospital about a surgery date. As October approached, I called her office to make sure that the referral had gone through.

"It can take a while," the receptionist reassured us. "If you don't hear from them by the end of October, get in touch."

The end of October. It could take that long just to get an appointment.

"Think of it this way," Laura said. "If it was serious, she'd get in right away. It's kind of a good thing she's not a priority."

244

It was a Saturday afternoon and we were having one of our regular video chats. I'd never mastered the art of making friends as an adult. My personal life consisted of Freya, Laura and Violet, Adam and Yash, and the occasional phone call with Kyle and his girls. Sometimes, Laura would encourage me to "get out there."

"Out where? Most people are horrible," I'd reply, just to end the conversation.

Laura looked off screen, sending an excited little smile to Violet. "Hey, listen," she said. "We have news."

Violet appeared onscreen. Laura tilted the camera so that it was pointing at her own belly. She was sitting on a stool, so there was nothing remarkable about the curve of her middle, but still, I gasped and said, "You're not!"

Laura tilted the camera back up to their faces. They were grinning like fools. "Seventeen weeks!" Laura squealed.

"Holy shit," I said. "That's amazing!"

Violet squeezed Laura tight, pressing a kiss into her hair.

I felt a flutter of excitement and nervousness for them. I hadn't considered that they'd ever want a baby. Laura had never mentioned it to me. And she was over forty. She was healthy, certainly, and lots of women were having children at that age nowadays. But I had to repress the urge to calculate the risks on their behalf, to ask about ultrasounds and nuchal measurements. They were happy.

WHILE WE WAITED FOR FREYA'S SURGERY APPOINTMENT, I surreptitiously monitored her for more painful spots on her bones. More shadows. When she sat at the table doing her homework, I'd rub her shoulder blades, my fingers searching for anomalous swellings, probing her for a wince or any indication of pain. When she snuggled up with me to watch a movie, I'd put my arm around her, patting her hips and legs and shoulders. A hug was an opportunity to pat her down, search for evidence that her risk factor had leapt. The waiting was excruciating.

Work was my only escape. One morning in October, I opened my email. A senior engineer position in Nuclear Process Safety opened up at Maritime Energy. I sat at my desk, staring at the email from HR for a long time.

Senior engineer. Nuclear Process.

I couldn't apply for a new job. Not now. It would mean more hours, more pressures, more to think about. And I had Freya to think about, and her surgery. She had to be my priority right now. I deleted the email.

The next day, as I was reviewing a junior engineer's work, Yash came by my desk.

"I heard about the job," he said.

"What job?" I asked, keeping my eyes fixed on my work.

He smiled and sat down in the empty chair opposite mine. "'What job.' Come on, now."

I sighed and leaned back in my chair. "Bad timing, I guess."

"Maybe," he said. "But I don't think there's such thing as good timing."

Bitterness rose in my chest. "Well, you can tell Adam not to worry. Freya's my priority."

His smile disappeared. "I'm not here to spy for Adam."

"Okay."

"Jess. You want this. I know you do."

"Don't tell me what I want," I snapped.

He put his hands up in surrender. "I'd never," he said. He turned to go, and then he stopped, looked back at me. When he spoke, his words were measured, cautious. "Everyone knows you're a great mom," he said. "But Adam and I, we're pretty good parents, too."

He waited a moment. I knew I was supposed to say *I know,* or *Of course you are.* But I didn't trust myself not to say something awful instead. He left, and I couldn't fight the tears that welled up, falling onto my keyboard.

THE CHILDREN'S HOSPITAL CALLED AT THE END OF THAT WEEK. Our appointment for day surgery was January 8. It seemed an eternity. How many spots could grow in that time? How many infections could creep in, slowly killing my daughter from the inside out?

"You'll receive a letter with instructions on how to prepare for the procedure," they added. I sat in silence long after the dial tone ended.

Five months from the time we made our first appointment to see Dr. Huang until the surgery. I stood up, started pacing. I couldn't hold still.

Should we tell Freya? She sometimes got weepy when the subject of the surgery came up. Would she dread it more or less, knowing the date? I didn't know.

I pulled out my phone to send Adam a text. *Surgery date Jan 8th. Waiting for letter with more info.* I hesitated before I hit send, then I added Yash to the recipients. There.

Yash was the one who replied right away. *Good that we have a date. Apply for the job yet?*

The little icon told me Adam had seen Yash's message. I waited for him to text back *What job?* He didn't.

I imagined my mom looking at the messages and scoffing. *Well, that's a trap.* I could almost hear her voice, flat and cold, forming the words.

IT WAS AROUND THAT TIME MY NIGHTMARES INTENSIFIED. THE PLANT in Mispec was melting down. I was at home, digging through my kitchen cupboards to find something, anything, to cobble together a power supply to keep the cooling systems going, but there was nothing. Just pots and pans, measuring cups, and bags of rice. Freya was standing in the corner of the kitchen, screaming at me to hurry, and couldn't find anything to fix it. The world was going to end, and I couldn't find what I needed to stop it. I'd wake up, the many-footed anxiety creature trampling its way through my chest again.

A few days after we got her surgery date, I was watching Freya do her homework at the dining room table. She was in what I thought of as Concentration Mode. Her foot was swinging under her chair, rhythmically brushing the floor at each swing, and her tongue moved around her mouth, making it look like she was chewing gum.

I leaned over to see what she was working on. Math.

She noticed me looking. "It's hard," she said, "but I kind of like it. How weird is that?"

I shrugged. "Not that weird."

"Did you like math when you were my age?"

I remembered the look of triumph on Nicole's face as she held up yet another perfect mark. I remembered fighting back tears at my 8s and 9s.

"Not really," I said.

"What was your favourite subject?" Freya's foot was still swinging, but she was leaning back in her chair now, looking at me.

"Science, I think," I said.

She nodded. "Because you wanted to be an engineer when you grew up."

"I didn't, actually," I told her. "Not yet, anyway."

"Really? What did you want to be?"

"A hairdresser," I said.

"Oh." She tilted her head a moment, looking at me like I was a puzzle piece, dropped into a box where it didn't belong. Then she leaned forward again, her attention back on her work.

"What do you want to be when you grow up?" I asked. When she was littler, she used to say she wanted to be a veterinarian or a zookeeper. But now, I realized she hadn't said that in a while.

She shrugged. "I might be a businesswoman," she said. "Like the aunties. But a hairdresser would be cool, too."

"Yeah," I said. "It would."

The next day, I sent in my application for the senior engineer position. I was hired by the end of the next week.

MY FIRST DAY IN THE JOB, I SCANNED THE OUTGOING SENIOR engineer's files for any hint that Mispec or any of our other plants might be vulnerable. Dylan had been a delegator. I knew it when I was working for him. He'd barely glanced at my work, already mentally checking it off his own to-do list.

I found a notice from the CSIS Special Division on Cyber Warfare. It was marked confidential, and dated two years prior. It should have been destroyed, but he'd kept it, filing it away in his desk drawer. Sloppy.

The notice identified an attempt by a malicious state actor to compromise an American control systems software developer in America. The developer wasn't one of our suppliers, but the CSIS notice still advised us to validate the configuration of all our safety and control software. They wanted to make sure they hadn't missed something, that bad code hadn't been slipped into other developers' software without anyone noticing.

Had it been done? Who had Dylan delegated the task to? Certainly not me. And not Jordan, who was still working for a private engineering company in Montreal when this notice had gone out.

My chest tightened. I could feel a quaking begin in my thighs. I sent Jordan a meeting request. We'd need to check all of the maintenance records to confirm the last configuration validation. If necessary, we'd have to perform that work on all of our software now. Every last bit. Immediately.

He replied that he was in PEI until the end of the week. There was no way we were having this conversation over the phone. Fuck.

I thought then about the death tolls after Chernobyl—official and unofficial. The difference between the Soviet count of thirty-one casualties and the UN estimate that a total of four thousand people eventually died as a result of the disaster. Numbers. Digits in sequence. Did it matter? Thirty-one or four thousand or one. If any of those people belonged to you, even just one, then it would never matter how many more were bundled together in a statistic. One. It would only take one to make you feel as though the world had lurched to a halt. No more spinning, no more circling the sun, no more whirling through the galaxy. The mornings, the workdays, the weekends and holidays, the bedtimes and mealtimes would disintegrate in that second, incinerated as surely as a body tossed into the mouth of the reactor-core fire itself. Just one, and all the motion and all the meaning would end, halt, just stop. Forever.

All that week, I kept noticing the coppery blood taste fill my mouth. When I took a bite of pickle, the end of my tongue burned. I kept catching myself flicking my tongue against the sharp barb of my tooth.

Freya noticed my edginess. It made her grumpy and intractable.

"Have you done your homework?" I asked her after dinner one night.

"*Yes*," she hissed, rolling her eyes.

"You don't have to say it like that," I snapped.

She narrowed her eyes at me. "I can't even talk the way I want now?"

I drew in a slow breath. I was at the edge of my patience. "Fine."

"You can't control my voice," she pressed.

"Fine," I said again.

She stared at me through narrow eyes.

Don't push, I warned her silently. *Not today.*

She held my gaze for a long second before she turned and stalked off to her bedroom.

I pulled Jordan into my office on Friday afternoon. He looked tired from travel. His shirt was rumpled, and he sagged into the office chair across from me.

"I need to know what you've done," I said. "Upgrades and updates, reviews, site testing. Everything."

He gave a kind of halfhearted shrug, his palms turning upward. "Dylan had all my reports."

I shook my head. "You've updated all the plants. Any updates could include compromised software."

"Sure," he said. "But it's not likely."

I looked at him hard, willing him to sit up. Christ, he'd been to Charlottetown, not Johannesburg. *Get a grip.* "You do realize that we're just one minor change in operational state away from a meltdown," I said. "All of our plants. All the time."

"I know."

"So?"

He shook his head, uncomprehending. "So?"

He reminded me of Adam suddenly. I tried to suppress the flare of annoyance.

"So, I need full quality reviews, software site testing."

Now he sat up, eyebrows raised, wrinkling his forehead right up to his receding hairline. "Where?" he asked.

I waited a beat before answering. He wasn't going to like it. "Everywhere."

He groaned and slumped back in his seat. He was looking at three days on-site minimum per plant. Probably five. And they wouldn't be short days either. Maritime Energy ran four nuclear plants—two in New Brunswick, one in PEI, and the new one up in Cape Breton. He would have a tough fall, I knew. But it was necessary.

"Start next week," I said. *Start today*, I wanted to say.

He stood up slowly. "Anything else?"

"That's it," I said. He hesitated, and I held his gaze.

He left my office without saying anything else. I could see him shaking his head as he walked down the hall.

There, I thought, trying to ease the compressed feeling in my chest. It'll be fine. It will.

TWENTY-SIX

Three weeks before Freya's surgery, I booked a flight to Saint John. It had been weeks since Jordan had completed the quality reviews, the software site testing. He'd declared everything in good order, but I felt no relief. The CSIS memo, sitting in a drawer for two years, haunted me. What else had Dylan slacked on? What was he missing?

Soon, Christmas holidays would reduce staff in the plants to a skeleton. As the end of the year approached, worry flooded over me, constant waves. Worry for Freya. For Mispec. For Dylan, what he'd done and what he hadn't. Finally, right after New Years, I decided I couldn't stay still any longer. I had to see for myself that everything was safe. I called Adam to let him know he'd need to take Freya for a couple of days.

"Sure," he said, "no problem."

Still, I felt my temper rise. *None of your business*, I want to snap, even though he hadn't asked for an explanation.

A snowstorm had been forecasted, and I stayed up most of the night before my flight, checking and rechecking my phone, expecting it to be cancelled. It wasn't. The storm blew past, and when I got up that morning there was nothing but a sugar-dusting of snow on the ground. I sent Freya off to school, feeling a low murmuring of guilt.

Dr. Huang had decided an open biopsy was necessary. At first, she'd suggested a needle biopsy might be possible—a simple outpatient procedure performed under local anaesthetic. But in the end, she'd decided a more intrusive operation, cutting through the skin and muscle to the bone, laying it bare and cutting away, was necessary.

Freya cried when we told her. Adam and I sat in my living room—what had once been our living room. Freya gulped at the air, chewing at it almost, trying to be brave. At last, the corners of her mouth and her shoulders collapsed, her voice dwindling to a small thread. "Why can't it just be the needle, though?"

"It will be all right, love," Adam replied. He was rubbing her right shoulder and I had her left hand squeezed in mine. She leaned into him, and her fingers clutched mine. "Dr. Huang says this way is best."

She nodded, trying to be tough, but her chest shook with sobs. I felt each of them, tremors in my ribcage, quaking me to my core, threatening to crumble my resolution, my courage, my very foundation.

AFTER DISEMBARKING THE TINY PROPELLER CRAFT IN SAINT JOHN, I rented a car and drove straight to the power plant. Jordan was scheduled to meet me there that afternoon. I'd called him just a few days before, directing him to book a flight. I'd become used to the weary resignation in his voice when he spoke to me.

I went straight to the control room, tried to find comfort in the screens and stations. It wasn't exactly state-of-the-art, but it was in good shape. The technician on duty kept clearing his throat. I could tell I was making him nervous. I didn't care. I set up a station to go through Dylan's logs once again. There was nothing here that I couldn't look up from Halifax. But I felt my heart rate slow, just enough, being on site.

I heard a knock while I was eating my lunch in the small break room that I'd commandeered as an office. I assumed it was Jordan, arriving early for our meeting. It wasn't.

"What are you doing here?" I asked, nearly dropping my sandwich.

Yash opened his hands, a familiar gesture of surrender I'd come to think of as his *I come in peace* move. "I thought you could maybe use some support."

I felt a fire burning in me. "I don't need any help to do my job."

"I know," he said carefully. He closed the door, pausing to look askance at me. I didn't react, and he took a careful step towards me. "I'm here as a friend."

A guttural sound escaped me. "Are we *friends*?"

"I don't know if there's a word for us," he said. He smiled a little, and I felt the smallest erosion of irritation. He must have seen something in me ease, and he sat down.

"What are you doing here, Jess?" he asked.

"My job," I snapped. "I'm reviewing Jordan's quality reviews, doing on-site testing, assessing the threat levels."

"Why, though?"

"Because it's my fucking job, Yash." But as I said it, I saw myself the way he saw me. Irrational. Draconian. Hysterical. Oh, god. My throat tightened and my eyes stung. Oh, fuck. I could not cry at work. Not in the plant. Not in front of Yash.

"You know you're good at your job. And you know we all know it, too, right?"

A bitter laugh burst out of me, and with it, the tears I'd been trying to dam up. "Oh yeah? Because I think everyone sees a woman having a meltdown on the job. You don't know what it's like."

He leaned back in his chair and looked at me a long moment. "Know why I've always liked you, Jess?"

I bit back the urge to ask *Why should I care?* "Why?" I asked.

"Because you truly believe you can save the world."

I looked down at the table. There was a crack in the laminated surface that ran from one end to the other. I pressed my fingernail into the widest opening. I could feel Yash's gaze on me. I could feel the patience, the kindness radiating from him.

"But I can't." As I said it, I split open, the words a fissure in me that let all the doubt and shame I didn't even realize I'd been storing bubble up and spill over. I could see her in front of me, Freya, my beautiful daughter, and I imagined all of it surging at her, enveloping her, like the nuclear sludge from my nightmares. Everything I'd ever tried to do to keep her safe, it was all useless.

I heard the wail before I realized that it had come from me. A howl. I was one of the abandoned dogs of Pripyat, long past the days of trust, now slinking and skirting, feral and frightened. After Chernobyl, they sent soldiers to shoot the abandoned pets, to bury their radioactive bodies. Fear was survival.

I cried until my throat was raw. For Freya. For Laura and Violet and their sweet baby who would need to be guarded and taught wariness. For my mom and for Kyle. For Adam and Yash. And for myself. For everything I'd had and lost, everything I couldn't save.

I don't know when Yash held out his arm, or when I sunk into his shoulder. The awareness that his shirt was soaked with my tears and snot stole upon me, and I pulled back, ashamed, until I met his eyes. He was crying, too, and I reached out for the love that had always been there. I had so much love, I realized. For all of them. From all of them.

"It's not on you," he said. "It never was."

I leaned my head against the wall and closed my eyes. I took a deep, shuddering breath.

I CAN TELL FREYA'S SLEEPY BECAUSE SHE STARTS STARING INTO SPACE, still holding pieces of sushi with the chopsticks in her hands. I reach to take the half-full takeout container from her lap.

"Don't," she snaps, clutching at the tray. "I'm not done."

"You can finish later," I reply.

She glowers at me and stuffs a roll in her mouth, then picks up another. "Fine," she mutters around the food. When she's done the second bite, she holds the rest out to Adam.

I want to smile. The defiance seems a good sign, somehow.

Adam and Yash collect the leftovers and put them in the fridge.

"Can I carry you to bed?" Adam asks our daughter.

"I want to watch a movie," she says. "Don't go."

"We're not going anywhere," Yash says, but he casts a cautious look in my direction. I nod at him. *Stay.*

I take the easy chair, leaving the half of the couch Freya isn't occupying to Adam and Yash.

Freya picks a movie—a science fiction film she'd been talking about. Of course she falls asleep almost right away. It's a good movie, though. The futuristic technology isn't too far-fetched, and the main character is a woman, a physicist. I try not to reflect on the fact that her lab coat seems improbably snug and low-cut.

"Want popcorn?" I ask, pausing it halfway through.

"Sure," Adam replies. Yash has fallen asleep, too, and Adam takes another blanket from the ottoman in front of him to cover Yash's feet.

I make the popcorn, handing Adam a bowl. When the movie ends, he moves to wake Yash.

"Let him sleep," I say.

Adam stands up carefully, trying not to disturb either sleeper. He picks Freya up gently. She throws her arms around his neck without waking. He follows me to her bedroom, and we tuck her in together.

"So, she's okay," he whispers, staring at her. It's a question, not a statement.

"She's okay," I say, trying to sound more sure than I feel. I fight the urge to run my hands over her bones.

Maybe tomorrow I'll suggest we all play a board game together. Freya loves playing Risk. The irony isn't lost on me. She gets so competitive. If one of us attacks one of her territories, she'll come after us in her next turn, whether it helps her win or not. She gets this look in her eye. Bloodlust. Adam thinks it's hilarious—he'll attack her just to bring it on. Not me. I do my best to stay out of her way.

We head back into the living room and put the news on. There has been some sort of incident, a Ukrainian flight downed in Tehran. There is talk of an Iranian missile. Fifty-five Canadians on board. I think again of my mother's cousins in Ukraine, her panic when Auntie Maria had been unable to reach then, and her almost immediate silence ever after. Was it indifference? Or had she learned something that was too hard, too much to tell us? I'd never know. But I think I understood.

The news shifts to talk of American politics, the ongoing attempts to impeach the president. I start to say something to Adam, but I notice he's snoring. His head is resting on one of the couch armrests, and Yash's head is on the other. Their feet are pressed together on the centre cushion. I can't help but smile. The blanket Freya was using is on the floor. I pick it up and put it over Adam's legs. He doesn't wake.

Tomorrow, I will call Dr. Huang's office to ask whether the results of the biopsy are in. The receptionist will tell me to wait, will promise to call to arrange an appointment when Dr. Huang has something to tell us. I know this is what will happen, but I will call anyway.

I take our empty popcorn bowls into the kitchen. Adam's put away the leftover food, but the empty takeout containers are left on the counter. I dump them into the garbage and quickly wipe down the counters before turning out the lights.

On the coffee table, Yash's phone lights up with a notification. I turn it over so the blue light doesn't wake him or Adam.

It feels like an encroachment, an intimacy without consent, touching someone else's phone. Especially Yash's. It's funny. People are so possessive of their phones, of the universe of personal information they store on them. But the mere act of having a phone is a surrender of your privacy. Every app, every service is constantly gathering data on you. Owning a smart phone is consenting to allow dozens of corporations to penetrate every aspect of your life.

Cybersecurity has become a vital aspect of nuclear process safety. Our cybersecurity engineer's job is to make sure that our control and safety systems are secure. Compromised software could be our generation's Chernobyl. But not for Maritime Energy. We're getting out ahead of hostile foreign governments, terrorist organizations, mischief hackers—we're building a wall. Keeping them out.

The first thing I did when I got the senior engineer job in Nuclear Risk & Compliance was to review Jordan's work. He was good, I realized as I looked over his reports. They were solid. No, more than that. Elegant. Some engineers bash things together into something blunt and serviceable. A few see the beauty in design. They think past what will make a system work. They see how it will flow, the synchronicity. They see the future; they're already thinking about the next engineer, the next upgrade, the next modification. I'd always wanted to be that kind of engineer. Sometimes, I thought I was. But Jordan certainly knew what he was doing. He was thorough. No compromises.

I still have the dreams sometimes. Not nearly as often, but sometimes. The last time, just a couple of days ago, I found coils of cable, crates of electronics in the back of my cupboards. Freya was still calling at me to fix it, to make it stop, but I asked her to help me. Together we managed to get the jumble of equipment from my kitchen cupboards all the way to Mispec. In my dreams now, I still can't stop the meltdown or save the world, but I don't feel so helpless.

My thoughts drift to Laura and Violet. To their baby. To the things that would need to be done to safeguard them, the biracial child of two mothers. Freya and I will go to Toronto after the baby is born to see if we can help out for a few days. I think of Mr. Clayton, of that pleading look he gave me that day. I wish we lived closer, I wish Freya could look out for her little cousin, shield them from hard truths as long as she can. *Please.*

Before I go to bed, I crack Freya's bedroom door. She's snoring, and I realize that she and Adam sound exactly alike—a soft little snuffle in, a faint whistle out. I tiptoe over and kiss her forehead.

In my own room, I sit on the edge of the bed for a long minute before I get undressed. I can't hear Adam's or Freya's quiet snores from here, but it's as though I can feel them, all three of them, breathing in their sleep. It's as though the whole house is slumbering, breathing in and out deeply. A gentle rocking. I imagine that it's not a house, but a boat on calm waters, far, far from anything that can touch us. Safe.

ACKNOWLEDGEMENTS

M y deepest thanks to Whitney Moran, my editor, and to Vagrant Press and Nimbus Publishing for once again giving me a space to tell a story. I am immensely grateful to my brother, Philip Malanchuk, who taught me about nuclear power plants, control systems, and what an engineer does. Your patient explanations and gentle corrections have made my story real. Thank you also to Dr. Mélanie Benoit for helping me decide how to make a fictional child sick, and to Dr. Greg Christian for reviewing and correcting my descriptions of physics. And thank you, with all my love, to my family, and especially to my Trent, for your support, love, and encouragement.